With his fingertip, Sam traced the contour of her jaw.

"You can do anything, remember?"

Finn held her breath; the last time he'd looked at her this way, he had kissed her. Or had she kissed him? Not that it made any difference. Standing in the circle of his strong arms, she'd felt vulnerable and safe and more womanly than she ever had before...all at the same time.

And because it scared her, she'd tried putting some distance between them to figure out if she could trust him. Until this moment, looking into eyes lit with kindness and caring—for *her*—she hadn't considered the possibility that he might be battling the same fears.

"Thanks, Sam," she said, taking a half step closer.

"For what?"

Finn shrugged, wrapped her arms around him and rested her head on his chest, hoping the gesture would be answer enough. She wasn't ready to say the words out loud.

At least, not yet.

Dear Reader,

Close your eyes for a moment and picture your first crush. Call to mind the way it felt, knowing you were falling in love with him—and had no idea how to admit it. If you're like me, you were terrified. What if you put your heart out there and he rejected it! Far better to keep your feelings hidden.

Then one night, perhaps he tenderly tucked your hair behind your ears, or confessed that he couldn't talk to anyone the way he could talk to you, or kissed you as you'd never been kissed before, and you thought, *This, this is the time!* But when he looked surprised and uncomfortable instead of happy, you faced a whole new challenge: hiding your disappointment and heartache long enough to get home, where you could cry yourself to sleep.

Remarkably, your second crush came along, and yet again, your heart drummed with the sweet beats of new love. But this time, you were older and wiser: Why risk a repeat performance of that agonizing moment by blurting out "I love you"?

That's pretty much the dilemma faced by the main characters in *The Firefighter's Refrain*.

Finn Leary has learned the hard way that living by the saying "better to love and lose than never love at all" is dangerous and reckless. Sam Marshall, the product of a big, loving family, believes the exact opposite, and his impatience with her guarded behavior threatens to end them before they can begin.

Thankfully, we needn't remain prisoners of the past. My wish for you, dear reader, is that you'll open every dark corner of your heart to the possibility of love.

Hugs from me to you,

Loree

HEARTWARMING

The Firefighter's Refrain

—

Loree Lough

Recycling programs
for this product may
not exist in your area.

ISBN-13: 978-0-373-36789-4

The Firefighter's Refrain

Printed in U.S.A.

www.Harlequin.com

Loree Lough once sang for her supper. Traveling by way of bus and train, she entertained folks in pubs and lounges across the United States and Canada. Her favorite memories of days on the road are the hours spent singing to soldiers recovering from battle wounds in VA hospitals. Now and then she polishes up her Yamaha guitar to croon a tune or two, but mostly she writes. With over a hundred books in print (sixteen bearing the Harlequin logo), Loree's work has earned numerous industry accolades, movie options, and four- and five-star reviews, but what she treasures most are her Readers' Choice Awards.

Loree and her real-life hero split their time between Baltimore's suburbs and a cabin in the Allegheny Mountains, where she continues to perfect her "identify the critter tracks" skills. A writer who believes in giving back, Loree donates a generous portion of her annual income to charity (see the Giving Back page of her website, loreelough.com, for details). She loves hearing from her readers and answers every letter personally. You can connect with her on Facebook, Twitter and Pinterest.

Books by Loree Lough

Harlequin Heartwarming

Saving Alyssa
Devoted to Drew
Raising Connor
Once a Marine
Sweet Mountain Rancher

For more books by Loree Lough,
check out Harlequin.com.

This story is dedicated to firefighters everywhere, and to the committed instructors who prepare them for the dangers they'll face every day of their lives.

It's also dedicated to songwriters, singers and musicians whose tenacity makes the world a better place with every note they produce.

Last, but certainly not least, this novel is dedicated to Jesse Spencer, whose wholesome good looks and spot-on portrayal of a firefighter inspired the descriptions of Sam Marshall.

Acknowledgments

My thanks to Torry Martin, actor, author, comedian and all-around terrific guy, and Mark Ligon, singer and guitarist, who graciously consented to appear as themselves in this story.

A big thanks to all the friendly and knowledgeable people at the Nashville Chamber of Commerce. The list of individuals is too lengthy for the space allowed here, but you know who you are! Your input and guidance helped lend authenticity and realism to every street, shop and museum that makes Music City one of the world's most sought-after tourist attractions.

My heartfelt gratitude, too, to my friends and family, for tolerating my crazy-weird schedule *and* putting up with countless recitations of "the exciting, fascinating stuff I learned" while writing this book.

I love you all!

CHAPTER ONE

SAM WROTE HIS name on the whiteboard, wincing when the dry-erase pen squeaked across the polished surface.

He recapped the pen. "Sorry, and I hate to admit it, but that happens all the time."

"It's because you're left-handed," said the student sitting nearest the door. "Left-handers hold things... weird."

The female cadet beside him knocked on her desk. "It's *weirdly*," she said, "not weird."

For the moment, Sam was more interested in the left-hander than proper grammar.

"Yeah, yeah," the student said. "I was with the ditzy blonde on Monday."

Sam had lucked into a slot on Open Mic Night at the Bluebird Café, a lifetime dream made more fantastic when the crowd had stood to cheer the song he'd written and performed. Amid the applause and whistles, a cute woman had climbed onstage and wrapped him in a hug that belied her size...while her wide-eyed date had looked more stunned than Sam felt.

"When the lieutenant straps on a guitar, he turns

into a babe magnet." The student smirked. "My girl-friend says it's all *his* fault that she clung to him like a plastic wrap."

Laughter traveled through the room, and Sam felt the beginnings of a blush creeping into his cheeks.

The young woman piped up. "Wait. You got a standing O at the Bluebird?" She flipped a copper-red braid over her shoulder. "That's one tough crowd, so…" She frowned slightly. "If you're that good, why are you *here*?"

Much as Sam loved the department, he'd trade his badge for a guitar in a heartbeat…if he thought for a minute he could survive on a musician's salary.

"Somebody's got to teach you bunch of knuckle-heads how to get cats out of trees."

His students snickered.

"Fair warning—laughing at my bad jokes won't earn you extra credit, but showing up on time might." He dropped the pen on to the chalk ledge. "Any questions before we get started?"

"Were you injured putting out a fire?" the red-head wanted to know.

A flash of memory took him back to that night when the ceiling literally caved in on him, and he believed life as he'd known it was over.

"You know, your limp?" she continued when Sam didn't say anything. "Is that muscle or bone dam-age?"

She looked a little like Sophie—the only Marshall in generations born with auburn hair and brown eyes. Sam hoped the resemblance was purely physical, because his youngest sister's questions could drive a Tibetan monk to drink.

"What's your name, cadet?"

"Jasmine Epps, Captain." She sat at attention. "If I graduate, I'll be the first woman in my family to become a firefighter." She lifted her chin. "And there are a *lot* of firefighters in the Epps family."

Anyone who'd ever walked the long hallway down at headquarters recognized the name. But it didn't matter. For her sake and safety, Sam needed her to understand that her name would not buy preferential treatment, and that included off-track interruptions and distractions.

He straightened to his full six-foot height. "I'm here for the same reason you are," he said, addressing the entire class. "To whip you into mental and physical shape to become firefighters. And we only have three months to get the job done. You're all equals in here, so I'm not going to waste time worrying about the balance of male versus female pronouns." He met Epps's eyes. "You okay with that, recruit?"

"Yessir, Captain Marshall." She giggled quietly. "I'm surprised that you're so well acquainted with parts of speech. I have a degree to teach English, you know, so I'll have something to fall back on, just in case?"

Was she testing him, to see how much he'd let her get away with?

"That, people," he announced, pointing at her, "was the second—and last—self-deprecating comment allowed in this room. From this night forward, we operate on the assumption that at the end of this session, *every*one becomes a firefighter." Sam paused, to give the rule time to sink in. "Got it?"

Following the drone of yessirs, he picked up his clipboard and sat on the corner of his desk.

"Now, then, since we already know that Epps here has a closet full of big shoes to fill, let's find out who the rest of you are and why you're here."

While the guy in the far-right corner stated his name, age and marital status, Sam's cell phone buzzed. It was Mark, owner of The Meetinghouse and founder of the Marks Brothers. Upon arriving in Nashville, Sam had chosen his hotel for the sole reason that it was walking distance from the club, rumored to be a favorite of agents and producers. Although Sam had put everything into his performance there, no contracts materialized. The next best thing happened, though, when Mark asked him to sub for ailing or vacationing band members. And they'd been rock-solid friends ever since.

He made a mental note to return the call after class. Sam went back to focusing on the students, the last of whom had just finished his introduction.

"Look around you, people. These are the guys who'll have your back until the session ends…and maybe afterward, if you're assigned to the same house. Match faces with names. Memorize voices. Anyone care to guess why?"

The guy with the ditzy girlfriend said, "Face-mask drills? Might be the only way to tell who's who."

Sam was about to agree and elaborate when Epps interrupted. "Your turn, Captain Marshall. What made *you* become a firefighter?"

He stifled a groan and wondered whether to set her straight now or explain his expectations privately, after class.

Arms crossed over his chest, Sam said, "I was born 'n' bred on a Colorado ranch, and when I was sixteen, lightning started a brush fire. If not for some determined firefighters, we would have lost livestock, outbuildings, maybe even some ranch hands. I was impressed. Impressed enough that, first chance I got, I signed on with the volunteer fire department."

One student wanted to know what had brought Sam to town; another asked if the Nashville department had recruited him from Colorado. How would it look if he admitted that dreams of signing a recording contract—not the city's fire safety—had brought him to Tennessee?

Sam made a V of his first two fingers.

"One," he began, "starting right now, in the interest of time and efficiency, we'll do things like we did 'em in school. If you have a question or want to make a comment, raise your hand. Two—to answer your question—another thing that happened when I was sixteen was spending a week in Nashville with the family. I fell in love with the place and always said I'd come back." He shrugged.

Epps raised her hand, and when Sam gave her the go-ahead, she asked him how he'd become a captain.

In every training session, one student stood out from the rest. The joker. The know-it-all. The always befuddled. And the chronic question-asker. Oh, yeah, he'd have to nip this in the bud, stat.

"I kept my ears open and my mouth shut." He met every cadet's eyes. "Same thing each of you will do…if you hope to advance in the ranks."

Epps held up a forefinger and prepared to fire off another question, but Sam beat her to the punch.

"Pencils up, people. We have a lot of ground to cover, and I talk fast."

He instructed them to turn to the blank pages at the back of their workbooks, and after an hour of questions and answers regarding the preliminary qualifications for rookie firefighters, he dismissed class early. He erased the whiteboard as they filed out of the room. How many would he lose between now and the last class? One, if he had to guess: Epps. Her attitude made it pretty clear that she believed her family name would buy certain considerations. The minute she figured out how wrong she was…

His phone buzzed again.

"You know where The Right Note is, right?" Mark asked.

"The diner at the corner of 19th and 20th?"

"How soon can you be there?"

"Ten minutes, give or take. Why?"

"You'll find out soon enough. Bring an appetite. Supper's on me."

There had been a certain edge in Mark's voice, Sam reflected as he pulled into the parking lot. Hopefully, it wasn't because Eli had gone on another bender. "That'd be a sorry shame," he muttered. Mark's younger brother had been clean and sober nearly four years.

Mark was sipping a tall glass of sweet tea when Sam slid into the booth seat across from him. "I've been meaning to check this place out for years," he said, glancing around. "Most attempts at imitating a fifties soda shop fall flat, but I like this. I like it a lot."

Mark harrumphed. "Well, thank you, Frank Lloyd Wright. I'm sure the owner will appreciate your critique."

Sam chuckled as a freckle-faced teen stepped up and slid two plastic-coated menus onto the red Formica table. "Sweet tea for you, too, sir?"

"Sure. But hold the lemon, okay?"

The kid hurried off, and Sam pretended to read the dinner listings. "So why am I here?"

"We haven't even ordered yet. What's your hurry? Got a hot date or somethin'?"

"Matter of fact, I do…with a stack of lesson plans." Sam stretched out his sore leg and massaged the taut thigh muscle. Standing for extended periods always made it ache, but never more than when he paced the linoleum-over-concrete classroom floors. "Truth is, I'm curious. Every other time you've popped for a meal, I've had to work for it." He closed the menu. "So what can I do for you this time?"

"Sheesh." Mark shook his head. "You're such a cynic." He paused, then said, "I thought you were partial to blondes?"

The movements of a short-haired brunette had drawn Sam's attention to the kitchen. "With my luck," he said, averting his gaze, "she'll turn around and give me an eyeful of hairy moles and missing teeth."

Mark snickered, then pointed at Sam's leg. "You keep that roadblock out there, you're liable to find out. How long since the last surgery?"

Sam did the math in his head. He'd had two operations since the cave-in. "Going on three years."

"But it's still bugging you." Mark leaned back. "Are you gonna talk to somebody about it or keep playing the strong, silent type?"

"I'm talking about it now." He leaned back, too. "Unfortunately."

The waiter arrived with Sam's iced tea and, taking a pencil from behind his ear, asked, "You guys ready to order?"

Mark hadn't even glanced at his menu. "Turkey burger and sweet potato fries, house salad with light Italian on the side."

"Holy health food, Batman," the kid said. "What's got into *you*?"

"That crack is coming out of your tip, wise guy."

Sam read the boy's name tag. "Go ahead and laugh, Ted. I'll get the tip. It's worth every dollar to see this guy squirm." He tapped his menu. "I'll have a BLT, a side of fries and coleslaw." And when Ted walked away, he added, "So what's her name?"

Mark's eyebrows rose. "Whose name?"

"The woman who put you on a diet."

Waving the comment away, Mark said, "Can't a guy cut back a little without his friends jumping to crazy conclusions?"

"So I take it a best man invitation isn't the reason I'm here."

"Man. You're like a puppy with a bone." He shook a packet of sugar into his already sweet tea. "All right, Mr. Impatience, here's the deal—Duke Miller is taking Eli on the road."

"No kiddin'? Well, good for Eli. It's about time the guy caught a break."

After leukemia took his little girl, Eli's heartbroken wife had committed suicide, and he'd found comfort at the bottom of a bottle. Hard to tell how long he might have stayed there if Mark hadn't made him an offer he couldn't refuse: if Eli could shape up and kick the addiction, he'd make him a full partner at The Meetinghouse. Which he had.

"He leaves in two weeks. Just enough time to get his affairs in order."

"Will Torry replace him as manager?"

"Well, he's on the road more than he's here in Nashville."

Sam pictured Torry Martin, the big red-haired comic whose stand-up and movie career had taken off in the past year. "But Eli's still your partner, right?"

Mark shrugged. "Therein lies the rub, Sherlock."

"Wish I had a dollar for every time that line was botched."

Mark looked up. "Huh?"

"For starters, it's Shakespeare, not Sherlock Holmes… *Hamlet*, to be specific."

"Gimme a break," Mark kidded. "You know as much about the bard as I do. Which is zip."

"Says you." Sam launched into the story of how, back in high school, the object of his affections had signed up to play Gertrude in the annual winter pageant.

"Claudia's family owned the ranch just north of the Double M, and I figured she and I might have a chance to get closer if I drove her home from rehearsals."

"Closer, literally?" Mark leaned forward. "Or closer, figuratively?"

Sam ignored him. "Claudia loved attention. Positive. Negative. Didn't matter, long as people were looking at her. She was a cheerleader. Recited the pledge for the morning announcements. Faked migraines and fainting spells in the halls, so guys would have to carry her to the nurse's office."

"And you had a crush on a girl like that."

"I was young and dumb. What can I say? Anyway, it didn't surprise anyone when she snagged the female lead. I auditioned for the part of Horatio, thinking, fewer lines to memorize than Hamlet. But good old Mrs. Smith had other ideas."

"Hamlet? *You?* No way."

Sam nodded. "Yes, way. You should've heard my cousins, mocking every line as I prepped for that part."

"Well, at least you got the girl."

Sam took a deep breath, let it out slowly.

"No way," Mark repeated.

"Yup. I took all that razzing for nothing, since Claudia only had eyes for Bart Isaacs."

"Captain of the football team?"

"Nah. His dad was a big shot in Denver politics."

"Ah." Mark took a swig of his tea. "But I didn't fall off the turnip truck, my firefighter friend. No way you can convince me you played Hamlet!"

"Oh, yeah?" Sam sat ramrod straight, and began, "'To sleep, perchance to dream, ay, there's the rub. For in that sleep of death what dreams may come, when we have shuffled off this mortal coil, must give—'"

A breathy *oomph*, the shattering of plates and the clatter of silverware hitting the floor interrupted his monologue.

There on the floor beside him, amid broken dishes, tomato slices and a jumble of fries, sat the most gorgeous brunette Sam had ever seen. Dark, long-lashed eyes flashing, she glared up at him.

"Did it ever occur to you that sticking your leg out into the aisle might trip someone who can't see over a serving tray?"

CHAPTER TWO

THE GUY WINCED as he stooped to help her pick up the mess. "Man, oh, man. You're right, I wasn't even thinking. I'm really sorry."

The flash of pain on his face looked genuine enough to surprise her, even though *she* was the one sitting on her rump in the aisle.

Finn flicked a slice of bacon from her lap. "Yeah, well, accidents happen, I guess. Especially when we're distracted." She met his eyes. "Right… *Hamlet?*"

His cheeks flushed slightly, and despite herself, Finn thought it was charming.

"Sticking my leg out that way has become a habit since…" He ran a hand through almost-blond waves. "It's a bad habit, I'll admit."

He made a cup of his right hand and started dropping shards of glass and chunks of stoneware into it.

"Stop, please," she said, one hand up like a traffic cop. "I've got this. I can't afford a lawsuit if you cut yourself. Besides," she added, nodding at his leg, "you're already hurt."

"A lawsuit?" Blond brows drew together slightly. "Just ask Mark—I'm not sue happy."

"Sue happy…sounds like the title of a country song."

He got to his feet and held out a hand to help her up. When she put hers into it, Finn noticed that it was warm and strong…and callused. She'd overhead Mark say that he was a firefighter. Had he earned them on the job? And what about the limp? Had he earned it on the job, too?

Steady on her feet again, she thanked him, then dusted the knees of her jeans. A sliver of glass poked into her palm, and she drew a quick gulp of air through clenched teeth.

"Here, let me see that," he said, holding her hand up to the light.

He hadn't seemed tall, seated in the booth or kneeling beside her in the muddle of broken dishes. Bending slightly to inspect the cut, he towered over her, and something told her that even if he hadn't been wearing stack-heeled cowboy boots, she'd still feel tiny standing alongside him.

"If you tell me where to find some gauze and peroxide, I'll clean it up and bandage it for you. I'm a firefighter, so I have first-aid training."

He was talking a lot. Talking fast, too. Her snappish reaction to the fall—and the mess—had clearly unnerved him.

She wriggled free of his grasp. "It's just a little scratch. I'll clean it up later."

His pained expression told her his apology and the concern that followed had probably been authentic. But then, Finn could count on one hand the number of honest and decent men who'd crossed her path, and have fingers left over.

Well, at least he wasn't a musician, like his pal. Mark, band leader and owner of The Meetinghouse, was a regular customer. He often stopped by alone to hunch over sheet music or ledger pages. Other times, the rest of the Marks Brothers Band tagged along to discuss sets or work out four-part harmonies…much to her customers' delight. Her years as a waitress had taught her to accept their generous tips with grace and ignore their blatant flirtations without insulting them.

"You're sure? Because I'm happy to—"

"I'm sure. But thanks."

"Well, okay. But FYI, peroxide will foam up and help work out any glass particles that might still be in there."

She hid the hand in her apron pocket. "I've cut myself a thousand times, with things way bigger than a splinter of glass. So don't give it another thought. It'll be better before I'm married."

His left eyebrow rose slightly and so did one corner of his mouth.

What a stupid, stupid *thing to say!* she thought, making note of his dimples. Pete used to say, "Small talk won't kill you," but at times like these, it sure seemed as though it could.

"I'll just get Rowdy to, ah, redo your order."

"No need to go to all that trouble."

Other customers were watching and listening, so yes, she did.

"Hey, Teddy? Bring me the broom and dustpan, will you, please? And send Bean out here to help with this mess."

Discomfort sparked in his eyes as he shifted his weight from his bad leg to the good one. *He's a little careless*, she thought, staring into eyes as blue as cornflowers, *but he sure is easy to look at.*

She focused on Mark. "You guys sit tight, okay? We'll have your new order out here before this mess is cleaned up."

The kids appeared as if on cue, freckle-faced Ted carrying the broom and dustpan, tall, reedy Bean holding a plastic tub. The firefighter took a step forward, as if planning to return to his seat. Instead, he bent again and retrieved silverware and one unbroken plate. He eased them into the girl's tub, then relieved the boy of his broom.

"If you'll just hold the dustpan, son, we'll have this cleaned up in no time."

Finn was about to repeat, *Thanks, but I've got this*, when Mark shook his head.

"No point trying to stop him," he told her. "Ol' Sam here can't help himself—he's a public servant, through and through."

Funny. He didn't look like a Sam.

The cook stepped around the fragments—and the group of Right Note employees still gathered in the aisle—and delivered the replacement sandwich. "Here y'go. Just give a holler if you need anything."

"Thanks," Sam said as Rowdy, Ted and Bean made their way back to the kitchen.

"Well, don't just stand there takin' up space, Marshall," Mark said. "Take a load off, why don't you."

He slid onto the bench seat and gazed up at her. "When you bring the check, let me know what I owe you for the stuff I broke, okay?"

"That isn't necessary."

"I'll just have to guess, then."

"Things get broken in here every day." Finn shrugged. "So forget it. Really."

The slight lift of his chin told Finn that he meant to reimburse her no matter what she said.

"More iced tea?"

"Sure. Thanks."

Finn turned, picking up a few empty glasses on the way to the service counter. Did he practice that dimple-exposing grin, or was the guileless expression genuine?

She added the glasses to the washtub as Ciara waved from across the room, reminding her that it didn't make a whit of difference if Sam Marshall was interested or not, the real deal or as phony as a used car salesman.

Because *romance* and *Finn Leary* didn't belong in the same sentence.

CHAPTER THREE

SAM GLANCED ACROSS the diner, where the gal he'd tripped stood talking with the cook.

"You sure know how to make a first impression," Mark said, following his gaze.

"Yeah, well…" He squeezed a dollop of catsup on to his plate. "At the risk of sounding redundant, why am I here?"

"Good grief. You're about as patient as a kid on Christmas Eve." Mark rooted around in the briefcase beside him, withdrew a black ledger and slid it across the table.

Sam flipped it open, but peripheral vision told him that the pretty brunette was watching, making it all but impossible to concentrate on column headings, let alone dollar amounts.

"So what's her story?"

Mark scrubbed a palm over his face. "Her name is Finn Leary, and she owns this place. Now quit worrying about that mess and the lousy first impression you made. It's history." He tapped the ledger. "This isn't."

Sam did his best to focus. In the left-hand column, a list of monthly expenses—food and beverages, utilities, insurance, taxes—for The Meetinghouse. In the center, the club's employee roster and salaries. On the right, end-of-year profits split by Mark and Eli.

"Are these numbers accurate?"

"Yep."

"It's good to see how well you're doing—" he slid the book back to Mark's side of the table "—'cause it means you can afford to pay me in real dollars one of these days."

"Owners get paid last."

"Poor, poor, pitiful you," Sam teased. He pointed at the impressive after-taxes total. "My heart bleeds for you and Eli."

"Yeah, well, it'll be good news for you, too…if you say yes to my offer."

The girl with Finn laughed, too long and too loud. She looked perfectly normal, but her actions and reactions said otherwise. He ran down a mental list of possible explanations for her behavior. Autism. Asperger's Syndrome. Brain damage…

"I booked a flight on that rocket ship to Mars. How 'bout if I buy you a ticket, too?"

"Ticket?" Sam sat up straighter. "Wait. What?"

"Man. When you take a trip to la-la-land, you really *go*, don't ya?" He leaned forward, tapped the tablet again. "I'm trying to cut a deal with you, here, so quit gawking at Finn and pay attention, okay?"

"I wasn't gawking." But Mark knew better, so Sam humored him. "What kind of a deal?"

"Let me cut to the chase—while I still have your undivided attention. Eli asked me to buy him out of the business so he can use his share for a new guitar and amp, a mic and gooseneck stand, clothes to wear onstage."

"And you want *me* to take his place? As partner?" Sam laughed. "Maybe I need to show you *my* year-end total." He shook his head. "I'm a city employee. Trust me, it's nothing close to that!"

"I know it's last minute, so I don't need the whole shebang right now. I can deduct your share out of your weekly paychecks until you're full in. Or you can skip paychecks altogether and get there sooner."

Sam had some savings, but between fire department responsibilities, performing and auditioning for producers every chance he got, where would he find the time to comanage a place like The Meetinghouse?

"Business is booming," he told Mark. "Why not keep the profits all to yourself?"

"Workload, man. Workload. Takes hours to manage the place."

"Just how many hours do you need from me?"

"That's up to you."

"I'd still have time for the Marks Brothers?"

"Absolutely."

Well, that certainly sweetened the pot. The rumor he'd heard upon arriving in Nashville had proved true: agents, producers and other career makers often paid surprise visits to The Meetinghouse.

Maybe if he was in the club more often, one of them would make *his* career dreams come true.

"If help is all you need," Sam pointed out, "I can do that without the whole partnership thing."

"You know the old saying, in for a penny, in for a pound?"

Sam got it: Mark believed he'd work harder if he had more to lose.

"But why me? Torry already knows the business."

"True, but with the movie roles he's been getting, he wants the freedom to come and go as he pleases."

"He said no?"

"He said no."

Sam chuckled. "Not sure I like being second choice."

"Does that mean you're in?"

Finn stepped up to the table. "Do yourself a favor," she said, refilling their glasses, "and say no."

"Why?"

One perfectly arched eyebrow rose. "Because it sounds like a pipe dream, and *nothing* good ever comes of Nashville dreams."

Finn turned to leave, pausing just long enough to add, "The sandwiches are on the house."

Sam watched until she disappeared into the kitchen, then looked at Mark.

"What was *that* was all about?"

Mark picked up a sweet potato fry. "Y'got me by the feet, but don't look a gift horse in the mouth. You probably broke ten bucks worth of dishes." He took a bite. "So? What do you say? Can I count on you?"

Sam glanced toward the serving counter, where Finn was engaged in an animated conversation with the cook. She shot a glance over one shoulder and locked gazes with him. He'd read somewhere that according to Indian legend, when a man and wolf locked eyes, their spirits merged. In that mind-numbing, heart-pounding instant, he understood how that might be possible.

Somehow, he found the strength to look away.

"I thought *you* were picking up the tab...partner."

CHAPTER FOUR

FINN REFILLED MARK'S coffee mug. "How long have you known that guy you brought in here the other night?"

"Which guy?"

She could tell by the teasing look on his face that he knew exactly which guy.

"The firefighter you were in here with the other day."

"You mean Sam?" He grinned. "Guess you haven't heard that curiosity kills that cat, huh?"

"Then, I guess it's a good thing I'm not a cat." She winked. "So what's his story?"

"Story?"

Finn held the coffeepot over his lap, and Mark laughed.

"Okay, all right, I'll talk…if you sit down."

Sliding into the booth across from him, Finn placed the coffeepot on a napkin.

"Sam came to Nashville for the same reason as most of us did," Mark explained. "And when he couldn't find a label to sign him or a band to hire him, he parlayed his volunteer firefighter skills into a full-time job."

Part-time musicians, in her opinion, were more determined—maybe even desperate—to become full-time entertainers.

"Don't include *me* in your motley 'most of us' group. I was brought here—against my will, I might add—by parents who didn't give a fig about anyone or anything but a recording contract." Finn glanced across the way, where her younger sister was laughing and chatting with Rowdy. "Not even Ciara."

"But you made the best of a bad situation…"

True enough. Especially considering the after-effects of Ciara's head injury—the one she'd sustained in the accident that had nearly killed the entire Leary family. If not for the firefighters, on their way back to the station after a call…

Finn pictured Mark's friend in head-to-toe gear and wanted to know how he'd hurt his leg. Instead, she asked, "Is he any good?"

He smirked. "You're talking musically, right?"

"Of course, musically." What had she said or done to leave him with the impression that she was interested in anything else?

"Just making sure we're on the same page."

"What's his last name again? Maybe I've heard of him."

"Marshall. But it isn't likely you've heard of him. Sam's talented, but remember…he keeps a low profile. Besides, he spends too much time in front of a classroom to make a name for himself onstage."

A wannabe musician who didn't flaunt his talent at every turn? Finn didn't believe it for a minute.

"Where's he from?"

"Big ranch just outside of Denver."

"So no family here in Tennessee?"

"Not that I know of. I think he was the first Marshall who didn't devote himself to The Double M." He grinned. "You want his cell number, so you can interview him yourself?"

She came *this* close to saying yes, then heard Ciara giggle.

"Thanks, but no thanks." *My life is already complicated enough without adding another self-centered musician to the mix.*

Mark shrugged, as if to say it wasn't any of his business anyway.

"Did he say yes?"

"Did who say yes to—" Mark nodded. Shook his head. Sighed. "Oh. You mean Sam. And the partnership deal. Like I said, he's a very private guy, so that's something you'll have to ask him directly."

In other words, Sam had said yes. Her fleeting interest in him died. Entertainers were trouble enough, leaving shattered hearts and disappointment in their wake. It was one of the only life lessons her parents had taught her, and she'd learned it well. But a musician with access to all the power brokers who frequented The Meetinghouse?

Finn got to her feet, grabbing the coffeepot. "Coffee's on me this morning. Have a good one, Mark."

Head down and determined to blot the memory of Sam's arresting smile from her mind, Finn made a beeline to help the middle-aged couple at the cash register…

…and plowed right into Sam Marshall.

Big hands took hold of her shoulders and held on until she was steady on her feet.

"Good thing that's half empty," he said with a nod at the coffeepot, "or you'd have a burn to compound what happened the other night."

He was right, but Finn had no intention of admitting it.

Bean passed by with an empty tray. "Want me to take that off your hands, Finn?"

She put the pot on to the tray and winked at the girl. "Thanks, sweetie. Add five minutes to your a.m. break."

Bean had to stoop to dole out a thank-you hug. "You're the best, boss. The best!" she said, and hurried away.

Finn exchanged a few pleasantries with the couple at the cash register, and as they exited, two more diners entered. Bean raced up to lead them to a table.

"Meeting your partner for breakfast?" Finn asked him. Maybe changing the subject would change her attitude, too. She saw no reason to treat him any differently than any other paying customer.

Sam looked over her left shoulder and fixed his gaze on Mark, who seemed oblivious to his presence.

"I'm surprised he told you." He met her eyes again. "He's usually tight-lipped, especially where the business is concerned."

"Funny, he said pretty much the same thing about you."

"Did he, now? And yet he spilled the beans about our meeting."

"Actually, he didn't. I put two and two together."

"Don't defend him," he said, grinning.

"I wasn't—"

"Hey, Marshall," Mark called. "Is this block-the-aisle thing becoming a habit?"

Sam snapped off a light salute. "I'd better get over there before he takes a second whack at breaking the sound barrier."

She started a fresh pot of coffee, then leaned her backside against the stainless-steel counter. It was only ten o'clock in the morning, so why did it feel like midnight?

Ciara copied her stance. "Who-who-who's that man?" she asked, pointing at Sam.

"A friend of Mark's." Thankfully, the men were deep in conversation, and she could stare to her heart's content...for now.

"Is he—is he new to Nashville?"

"Mark says he's been here for a couple of years."

Her sister—a younger, shorter version of their once-beautiful mother—hid a giggle behind pink-and-black polka-dot fingernails. "I'd remember if he was in here before, because he's *handsome*," she said, drawing out the word. Shouldering Finn, Ciara added, "Is he one of those movie stars who lives in town?"

"I don't know anything about him, except that his name is Sam Marshall. His family has a ranch out west somewhere. He's a firefighter, and hurt his leg, probably on the job. He sings a little, and unless I'm mistaken, he's part owner of The Meetinghouse."

"Sounds to me like you know almost as much about him as his mama does," Rowdy teased, leaning his beefy forearms on the serving counter.

Ciara grinned as Finn pointed at the revolving order rack. "By my count, you have half a dozen orders to cook up." She grabbed her pad and headed for the dining room. "Better get busy, because I'll be back in a minute with a couple more."

Ciara feigned a look of disapproval. "Now, Finn, is that—is that any way to talk to your assistant manager?"

"Hey. Whose side are you on?" Finn wrapped her in a fierce hug, then finger combed Ciara's wavy brown bangs. "You have customers, too, sister dear," she said, turning her toward the counter. "You'd better get crackin', too."

Rowdy filled the twelve-slice toaster and pushed the lever. "Don't mind her, kid. Finn's old before her time, but it ain't her fault."

"I know," Ciara said.

Before the accident, her sister had been an athletic, straight-A student. Afterward, she'd become a stumbling, stuttering girl who didn't remember the drunken argument that had made their dad stomp on the gas until the already battered Jeep rolled end over end before coming to a screeching, grinding halt alongside the highway. She didn't remember spending weeks in the hospital, enduring six operations, the months of physical therapy that followed, or the fact that Misty and Connor had left town instead of dealing with their parental duties or taking responsibility for what they'd done to her.

But Finn remembered. And she'd never forgive them for it.

Shake it off, Finn. They'll never change. And, as Pete loved to say, *What's done is done, so just accept it.* Besides, she'd played a small role in the accident, too…

Finn stepped up to Mark's table. "What can I get you gents?"

"Sweet tea and a burger," he said. "Medium rare, with a side of fries."

"For breakfast?" Sam chuckled. "Broke up with the dietician already, did you?"

"Mind your own business, smart guy. This pretty young gal has better things to do than watch you poke your nose where it doesn't belong."

"Ah, but it *does* belong. As your partner, I'm concerned about your health."

Even Finn had to laugh at that.

"I'll have what he's having," Sam told her.

"When I deliver your orders," she said, winking

at Mark, "you'll have to tell me all about the woman who *almost* talked you into a health food diet." She pointed her pencil at Sam. "If he starts talking about her before I get back, stop him, hear?"

"Yes, ma'am. I mean, no, ma'am."

Ciara had been half right, Finn thought, clipping the order to a mini clothespin on the order wheel. Sam was handsome...but he had a sense of humor. In her experience, the two didn't coexist nearly often enough.

"I don't get it," Rowdy said, snapping the ticket from the rotating wheel. "Why does Mark eat two meals a day in here when he could eat free at his own place?"

"I know why," Ciara said, clapping like a school-girl. "Mark eats here because he's bored with the food on his own menu, that's why!"

Innocence radiated from Ciara's brown eyes, prompting Finn to draw her into another hug. "You are so smart!"

"Not as smart as you, but—but—but that's okay, because I'm the pretty sister."

Laughing, Finn said, "Yes, you sure are." She was lovely, even with the ropelike scar that started near her right nostril and disappeared in her hair... one more reason to resent their parents.

"Did I tell you that Mommy called me today?"

Finn took a moment to gather her self-control. "Really," she said through clenched teeth. A call from Misty could only mean one thing: trouble.

"She's coming to Nashville in a few months, and, and she wants to stay with *us*!"

There was barely room for the two of them in the apartment above the diner, even before Misty's suitcases exploded with clothes, shoes, makeup and hair products.

"I'll book her a room at a nice hotel. We'll all enjoy the visit more if we're not stepping on each other's toes all day and night."

"But, Finn… Mommy misses us. She said—she said she wants to snuggle and watch old movies together. And eat popcorn." Ciara raised both shoulders, smiling. "And drink cocoa!"

"It's August, Kee. Nobody drinks cocoa in August."

"Why not? We have air-conditioning."

Oh, if only she had Ciara's "keep it simple" gift!

"Did she say when she'll get here?"

"No. She, she need to make some arrange— arrangements."

"Aha." Finn recognized it as Misty speak for *I'll be there, eventually…unless someone makes me a better offer.*

"Promise me you won't be too disappointed if Misty can't come. You know how…busy she is."

"I won't be disappointed because she'll be here! She can sleep in my bed. I'll sleep on the couch."

Finn and Rowdy exchanged a wary glance.

"You'll see," Ciara added. "She'll come. You

won't—you won't really make her stay in a hotel, will you?"

"Maybe you ought to book a room for yourself," Rowdy told Finn.

But his joke fell flat as she recalled Misty's last spontaneous visit. A local newswoman had reserved the diner for a bachelorette party, and while Finn had worked, Misty had decided to treat Ciara to her first pub crawl. Not only had she forgotten that even one piña colada would interact poorly with Ciara's medications, but she'd left Ciara alone—supposedly "just long enough for a few dances." Alone, afraid and out of her element, Ciara had panicked and wandered off. If not for the elderly Baltimore couple who'd coaxed Finn's number from her...

Finn shuddered at the awful things that could have happened to someone as sweet tempered and naive as Ciara.

Rowdy shoved two plates onto the serving counter. "Order up."

"Can I deliver it, Finn? I won't drop anything. I promise."

She'd assigned Ciara the lunch counter to save her from having to walk while balancing food-laden trays. But this request seemed important to her, and what better way to let her sister prove herself than with two identical orders, delivered to two easygoing guys?

Ciara took a plate in each hand. "Two trips are

better than making a mess, right? I'll be right back for their—for their sweet tea."

Finn got a little teary-eyed watching Ciara approach the table, then engage in friendly conversation with Sam and Mark. She'd been through so much since the accident, but instead of coming out the other side bitter and self-pitying, Ciara woke every morning smiling, looking forward to the day. Finn plucked a paper napkin from a dispenser on the counter and blotted her eyes.

"Quit worrying about her," Rowdy said, patting Finn's shoulder. "She's a happy, well-adjusted young woman, thanks mostly to you."

Rowdy thought he knew the whole story, but he didn't. He meant well, though, so Finn sent him a feeble smile anyway. Keeping a roof over Ciara's head and food in her belly—well, anyone with a half a heart and a steady paycheck could do that much. Finn believed she owed her the rest. Whoever her sister was—and might become—was due to her own persistence and good-hearted nature. Finn wouldn't take credit for that.

Rowdy pointed. "Shape up, girl. Here she comes."

She picked up a clean cloth and spritzed disinfectant on the lunch counter. If Ciara saw her tears, Finn could blame the cleaning product.

"They changed their minds. They—they want sodas instead of sweet tea." Ciara scooped crushed ice into identical red plastic glasses. "You know, I think that Sam guy likes you."

"All of my customers like me," Finn teased.

"Yeah, but he's the only one who stares at you that way."

"What way?" Finn looked across the diner, straight into the big blue eyes of Sam Marshall, whose dimple appeared at the same time as his charming, slanted smile. It didn't seem rehearsed, like the flirtations of so many other rock star hopefuls who frequented The Right Note.

"See there?" Ciara wrapped her hands around the full, fizzing tumblers and started back to the table. "Told you he liked you."

Rowdy chuckled and went back to his over-easy eggs. "By Jove, I think she's right."

"Stow your bow, Cupid." Finn returned the cleaning supplies to their shelf and faced him. "You're wasting perfectly good arrows, shooting at the likes of me."

He put down his spatula and, wiping enormous hands on a corner of his apron, stepped up to the service counter.

"Finnegan Ula Logan Leary..."

She hated Misty's silly reason for choosing the mostly male names that appeared on her birth certificate: "Your initials spell FULL, and that's what I want your life to be!" If she'd been the least bit sincere, would she have made choices that left Finn feeling empty and afraid...and alone?

"...why are you determined to make life so hard for yourself?"

Of all people, Rowdy should know the answer to that. He'd been there when Pete had provided a home for her and Ciara after Misty and Connor had taken off.

"Times like these," Rowdy continued, "I wish Pete was still alive. He's the only one who could ever talk sense into you."

She couldn't deny it. But Pete Maxon had earned the right to scold and advise her since, at the dawn of his golden years, the never-married Pete had accepted the mantle of friend and father to her and Ciara. And he'd done a far better job of it than Connor ever had.

"You have a right to a normal, happy life, Finn. Husband. Kids. A home of your own. *She* wants that for you, too." Using his chin as a pointer, he drew her attention to her sister, laughing and joking with a family in the corner booth.

Ciara turned, as if she sensed they were talking about her. When their eyes locked, Finn saw pure childlike love in her sister's expression. That was what had prompted her to devote herself to Ciara, no matter what. Well, that, and her role in the accident. If doing right by Ciara meant foregoing the white-picket-fence scene, so be it.

"I did some checking," Rowdy was saying. "Sam hails from a big, tight-knit family out west. Could be just the type who'd love that girl almost as much as you do."

Ciara stacked dirty plates in her arms and made

her way back to the counter. The effort needed to keep things in balance showed on her face. Finn took a step forward, thinking to relieve her of the burden.

"Don't," Rowdy said, anticipating her intentions. "She's doing fine."

Ciara proved him right by easing the soiled dishes into a tub. And without a word or fanfare of any kind, she carried the whole mess into the kitchen.

"Look, Teddy! I brought—I brought you a surprise!" she announced, sliding the tub onto the dishwasher's conveyor belt.

Grinning, the boy rolled his eyes. "Gee, thanks. You're my new best friend."

Heart swelling, Finn fought tears of joy and pride.

"You ought to smile more," a DJ-deep voice said from behind her. "Because you're mighty pretty when you do."

Turning, she met the smiling eyes of firefighter, musician and comes-from-stable-stock Sam Marshall...

...and hoped he couldn't hear her hard-beating heart.

CHAPTER FIVE

"IF YOU'RE INTERESTED, make a move!"

Sam tapped the mic to test the amp's volume. "See, that's your trouble. You make moves without thinking. I'd rather look a few moves ahead."

"Your chess analogy isn't lost on me." Mark leaned his forearms on the edge of the stage. "But Finn isn't a game player, dude. I've known her a while. Watched her interact with people at the diner. She's different around you. So I say go for it."

Yesterday, Sam had complimented her smile, and he still hadn't figured out if her reaction had been more shock or suspicion.

"Thanks, but no thanks. One trip-up with her is one too many."

"That's a sorry excuse if ever I heard one. Broken dishes and stuff spilled on the floor is all part of the restaurant business."

Maybe, Sam thought, but he'd never been one to repeat a stupid mistake. At least, not if he could help it.

"So you'll be okay without me tonight?"

Mark nodded. "Yeah, Torry's gonna open with

a comedy set, then we'll play for a couple of hours and he'll close the show."

The comic waved Sam and Mark closer. "Little birdie told me a hotshot Hollywood producer is in town," Torry whispered. "You'd better believe we're gonna give it all we've got tonight."

Mark patted his wallet and started walking toward the office. "I'm only interested in making this fatter, so knock yourself out."

Torry pulled his thick, carrot-red hair into a ponytail. "He'll sing a new tune when one of us gets signed to costar in the next blockbuster movie."

Sam chuckled. "Not to rain on your parade, but I thought Hollyweird talent scouts went the way of the dodo bird."

Torry's exaggerated gasp sent him backward a step. "Silence! You'll jinx it!" A mischievous grin lit his dark eyes. "Hollyweird, huh? That's funny enough to use in my act." He winked. "I may or may not give you credit."

He climbed onto the stage and shaded his eyes from the spot. "I hate those things. Why do we need searchlight wattage?"

"So the audience can key into your facial expressions. Besides, the audience can't distract us if we can't see them."

The comedian lifted one shoulder. "See, there's the difference between what you do and what I do. I don't need them to see the nuance of my facial expressions. What I need is to see *their* faces, so I can gauge their reactions to my jokes."

"How long have you known Finn Leary?"

"Whoa. I had no idea you were an award winner."

Sam didn't get it and said so.

"Where should we hang your Change the Subject Fast award?"

"How about right beside your Avoid the Subject plaque?"

Torry narrowed one eye. "This club ain't big enough for two comics. I have a contract, you know." He squinted at Sam. "Now, what were we talking about?"

Sam opened his mouth to repeat her name, but Torry beat him to it.

"I've been chowing down at The Right Note for as long as I can remember. All the way back to the days when Pete still owned the place. So I've known Finn for years. Literally." Arms folded over his broad chest, he frowned. "Why?"

"No reason, really. Just curious."

"About what?"

"About what happened to her parents, for one thing."

"Mark didn't tell you?"

"Nope."

The comedian sat on a tall stool. "Well, there was a wreck six or seven years ago," he began. "Bad one. Nearly killed her whole family. Everybody came out of it more or less okay, except for Ciara's head injury."

Nodding, Sam pictured Finn's younger sister. "How old is she?"

"I dunno...twenty-two, twenty-three." He held up a hand. "Wait. I thought you were interested in Finn. You can't hit on Ciara. She's too sweet and innocent for the likes of you!"

"I agree. The little sister is a sweetheart, but I..." *Shut up, Marshall. You've already said too much.*

"Now that you're management," Torry said, fingertips drawing quote marks around the word, "you'd better learn how to take a joke." He leaned forward. "'Cause *I'm* the comedian, remember?"

Torry studied Sam's face for a moment, then continued with his story. "Okay, so here's what I know. Her parents were addicts. Nix that. *Are* addicts. Which might explain why nobody—not even Finn and Ciara—has a clue where they are most of the time. Pete, who pretty much built The Right Note from the ground up, never married, never had kids—" he gave Sam a playful elbow jab "—that we know of. Anyway, when the Learys split, Pete took pity on the girls and put 'em up in the apartment above the diner. Gave 'em odd jobs to do so they'd feel like they were earning their keep. When he retired, he made Finn his manager, and when he died, he left everything to her."

"Huh," Sam said. Under similar circumstances,

would he have the backbone and generosity to take care of two nearly orphaned teenage girls?

"Well…?"

Sam looked at Torry. "Well, what?"

"You don't want to know if she's married or not?"

"I didn't see a wedding band."

"That doesn't mean diddly. Safety regs and all that, y'know?"

Yeah, Sam had considered that possibility.

"Well?" Torry repeated.

Seemed to Sam he could save a lot of time by just asking, straight out, whether or not there was a man in Finn's life.

"So is she available?"

"I thought you'd never ask!" The full-bodied laughter echoed throughout The Meetinghouse. He whistled. Flapped his arms. "She's free as a bird." And then his expression turned serious. "Not that it's gonna do you much good. She's turned down a *lot* of guys like you."

"Guys like me? What does that mean?"

"You know. Cowboy types." He pointed at Sam's pointy-toed boots and Western-style shirt. His hands formed a rectangle, like a photographer lining up a shot. "More specifically, guys who want to see their names on the marquee at the Ryman and the Opry house. Wannabe singers with big Nashville dreams. She's antimusician. *Big-time* antimusician."

"Oh?"

"Her folks have been in the business for decades."

The Learys must have done far more than crash a car to inspire her opinion that all musicians were bad news. Frankly, Sam didn't know if he wanted to learn the details. He already had way too many demands on his time. Besides, how did that old saying go? *Take care when trying to fix a broken person, because you might cut yourself on their shattered pieces.* Good advice, especially for a person who still bore the scars of saving others.

"Thanks, man. And don't worry. Mum's the word."

Torry got to his feet and made his way down the stage stairs. "I wasn't worried." He paused on the dance floor to add, "Except maybe about your sense of humor. Need I repeat, I have a contract?"

Sam returned his smile. "I'm not nearly smart enough to write and deliver jokes night after night."

"And don't you forget it…*boss.*"

He left Sam mulling over an either/or decision: ask Finn for the rest of her story, or find a way to stop thinking about her.

Her likeness flashed in his mind.

An instant—that was all it took for him to realize the latter was next to impossible.

He glanced at his watch. *If you don't lollygag, you'll have time to head home for a shower and a shave before you go onstage tonight.*

Lollygag. One of his dad's favorite words. It made Sam a little homesick, and he made a mental note to call home first thing in the morning.

"Better come up with some kind of a script before

you dial the folks' number," he muttered. He needed ready answers for his mom's predictable questions: "Are you getting plenty of sleep? You're not eating those horrid frozen dinners every night, I hope?" And his favorite, "Are you seeing anyone yet?"

As usual, he'd tell her that he wasn't.

But he sure would *like* to be.

CHAPTER SIX

SAM LEANED INTO the deck rail, marveling at his view of the river. After witnessing the aftermath of the 2010 flood, he considered himself lucky to be on the fourth floor, safe from rising waters should the Cumberland overflow its banks again. He was mildly surprised at how quickly he'd adjusted to life in a nine-hundred-square-foot condo after spending most of his life on a sprawling ranch in the shadow of the Rockies.

The hardest adjustment had been sleep patterns. Back at the Double M, he'd turned in early, bone tired from long days of hard labor. Got up early, too, ready to dig in to the demanding work all over again.

Since injuring his leg, Sam rarely got to bed before three, either because he put so much effort into his lesson plans, lecture notes and handouts, or because of a performance that lasted until two. Lack of sleep was one of the only negatives to life in Nashville.

Except for the occasional bout of homesickness. Fortunately, the cure was simple enough…

According to his watch, it was six in the morning, Mountain Time. He could picture his folks at the kitchen table, fully dressed and with breakfast behind them, his dad thumbing through the morning paper while his mom scribbled her to-do list for the day.

Sam refilled his coffee mug and carried it to the balcony, leaned back in his deck chair and propped both boot heels on the glass and steel railing.

"You must have ESP," his mom said. "'Call Sam' is at the top of my list today!"

"Oh? What's up?"

"Let me put you on speakerphone, so Dad can talk with you, too."

"Hey, son. 'Bout time you touched base. Your mother cries herself to sleep every night, wondering if you're all right. Sprained her wrist wringing her hands, too."

He heard a giggle, then a quiet slap. "Clay Marshall, none of that is true and you know it."

Sam chuckled. He'd always loved watching his parents interact. To the rest of the world, Clay Marshall seemed tough and gruff. But when he gazed at his wife of many years, the rough edges softened. Victoria's eyes overflowed with indisputable adoration, too. If Sam could find a woman who looked at him that way, he'd—

"Coming home for Thanksgiving and Christmas?" she asked.

"Don't think I can manage both."

"I had a feeling you'd say that. But I wouldn't be

your mother if I didn't try. Besides, you know if I have a choice, I'll take Christmas every time. The whole family will be here!"

With the exception of Sam, the entire Marshall clan showed up for *every* holiday. A few of the family's celebrations were so grand, they'd earned the attention of local media. The slower pace of Thanksgiving had always been more to his liking, but since moving to Nashville, he'd spent the week between Christmas Eve and New Year's at the Double M. It gave him plenty of time to catch up with extended family.

"Already booked my flight." And God willing, he wouldn't face weather or mechanical delays as he had in years past. "So what's new?"

"Same soup, different day," his dad said.

"Listen to him," his mom put in. "We had another cougar running around here for weeks, giving us all nightmares."

"Yeah, but we took care of him, same as always."

He'd talked to Zach and heard all about it. "Too bad she took so many horses and cows before you got her." *But unfortunately, that's life on the Front Range.*

"How's Aggie?" his mother asked.

During their few visits to Nashville, his parents had met his cantankerous landlady. "'Same soup, different day,'" he quoted. Then he chuckled. "Still bragging that she's a descendant of Andrew Jackson. If you want my honest opinion, the reason she never married is because she'd have to give up that famous last name."

"Hard to imagine any right-minded man popping the question. That woman would try the patience of a saint."

"Oh, now, Clay, that isn't very nice!"

"The truth hurts sometimes." He quickly changed the subject. "How's your leg, son?"

"Fine." It wasn't, but they didn't need to know that. Funny, the way his dad asked about it more often than his mom. Sam wondered how much of that was due to a fear of the answers...

"Have you talked with your cousin Nate lately?"

Sam heard a smile in his mother's voice, and unless he was mistaken, it meant she was about to disclose a big secret. More accurately, what *she* considered a secret. During their last phone call, Nate had told him that he'd asked Eden to marry him... and she'd said yes. But why spoil his mother's fun?

"We talked a while back. Why?"

"He and Eden are officially engaged, and they're planning a June wedding. Though why they want to be like every other couple out there is anybody's guess. At least they won't have to worry about a venue. A very good thing, since they still haven't chosen a date." She lowered her voice to a near whisper. "I'm not supposed to know, so if he confides in you, mum's the word."

Sam heard his father's good-natured groan. "The boy knows better than that, Vicky."

He considered telling them that he'd bought into Mark's club, then thought better of it. The announcement would be less confusing when delivered in person.

The sound of chair legs squawking across the hardwood told him his dad was on his feet. The man was a lot of things, but subtle wasn't one of them. Laughing to himself, Sam said, "I'd better get to work and let you guys do the same."

"Call soon," his mom said. "And remember, you haven't heard a thing about the wedding!"

He promised to keep Nate's news to himself, even though in his opinion, secrets—even small ones—took folks into dangerous territory.

Long after hanging up, Sam remained on the balcony, watching the September breeze rustle going-gold leaves as sunlight flickered on the water's surface. The shrill call of a bald eagle drew his attention skyward. No doubt it was one of those released along the river a few years earlier. The bird circled as it descended. It had probably hoped for a fat white bass but bagged a crappie.

"Better than nothin', I guess," he muttered, getting to his feet. He'd barely had time to lock the slider when the phone rang.

"Hey, young'un!"

He'd recognize Nate's teasing voice anywhere. "Your ears were ringing, huh?"

"Uh-oh. Who's been talking behind my back?"

"Just spoke to my folks."

"Ah. Does Aunt Vicky still think she's the only one who knows about the wedding?"

"Evidently, 'cause she made me promise to play dumb if I talked to you."

"I'm not touching that line!" Nate laughed. "Mothers. I think they're all cut from the same cloth."

For a reason he couldn't explain, Finn's mother came to mind. *Not all of 'em*, he thought.

"So what's up, cousin?"

"I was scrolling through my contacts," Nate said. "When your name went by I said, 'Give that boy a call.'"

Nate was ten months older than Sam, but to hear him talk, years separated them.

"You guys took down another cougar, huh?"

"Yeah. That's something those foster kids living in Eden's grandparents' house will remember for a long, long time."

He'd met Eden's boys twice. Once during a summer visit to the ranch, and again after the fire that nearly killed Nate.

"Will Eden keep her job after you two swap I do's?"

"Yes and no."

Sam knew if he waited, Nate would explain.

"We cut a deal. Her greedy landlord sold Latimer House, so she moved them into her grandparents' place. It beats being homeless, but the house lacks the space they need for classrooms and whatnot.

Sooner or later, they'd outgrow it, and those boys need stability. So I made her an offer she couldn't refuse. Soon as we're married, the whole kit and caboodle of 'em will move into my house." Nate chuckled. "They're over here most of the time anyway."

"Mighty generous of you, cousin."

"Nah. It's the right thing to do. They're good kids, for the most part."

For the most part? Something in Nate's voice told Sam it was best to let that one slide. At least for now.

"How do their parents feel about you and Eden assuming the mom-and-dad roles in their kids' lives?"

"Most are out of the picture, either in prison or dead. Eden and I are working with the state to become legal guardians."

"For all of them?"

"All but the one."

No doubt he was referring to Thomas, the kid who'd set fire to Nate's barn, nearly killing himself, Nate and four of his horses. If Sam closed his eyes, he could still see how pale and weak his big, burly cousin looked after his release from the hospital. The only time he'd seen him in worse shape had been after the accident that had ended his major league career. Sam would have worried a whole lot more about Nate…if not for Eden.

Sam didn't ask what had become of the boy. That,

like news of the partnership, could wait until he got back to the Double M, and they could talk in person.

"Real reason I called," Nate said, "was to ask if you'll be my best man."

"Of course I will! Does that mean you guys have set a date?"

"No, not yet. But you'll be one of the first to know when we do." Nate paused. "Speaking of dates and stuff, are you seeing anybody?"

"Nah." Finn's image flashed in his brain, and he slapped a hand to the back of his neck. "No time for stuff like that."

Nate laughed, but his tone changed when he added, "What was it you told me when I said that?"

"When the right one comes along, you'll *make* time."

"It was good advice then, it's good advice now." There was a moment of silence on the line. "What do you want in a woman anyway? Perfection? If that's the only reason you're still single, well, you're old enough to know there's no such thing."

"Present company excluded, of course."

"Well, that goes without saying."

"To be honest, I never gave much thought to what kind of woman I'm looking for. A hard worker, I guess. Independent. Good sense of humor. Five foot two or three, big brown eyes, dark curly hair..." The words stuck in his throat. He'd just described *Finn*.

"Whoa, dude. That's pretty specific for a guy who hasn't given it any thought. You sure you aren't seeing somebody? I wouldn't tell a soul. Not even Zach. Trust me."

"I trust you, and if there was something to tell…"

He diverted the conversation back to the wedding, and while Nate elaborated on the plans, Sam came to an undeniable conclusion. It was time to figure out why he'd allowed a near stranger—no matter how gorgeous and appealing she was—to dominate so many of his thoughts, and take up such a big portion of his heart.

CHAPTER SEVEN

"MAN. IT IS *pouring* out there." Mark shook rainwater from the brim of his Stetson as the door swung shut behind him.

Torry slid a tall black stool to the center of the stage and leaned into the mic. "Weather dude says we're in for a long, bad night."

His foreboding tone reverberated through the nearly empty club, inspiring a chuckle from Dirk, the Marks Brothers' drummer.

"Long as the river doesn't rise again, I can handle it." Mark hung the damp ten-galloner on a gooseneck mic stand, and bent at the waist to adjust knobs and dials.

Sam remembered when more than thirteen inches of rain fell during a two-day period, breaking decades-old weather records and sending the Cumberland over its banks and into the streets. The whole town had become a murky water world, and the flood had damaged homes, businesses and historic buildings…including the Grand Ole Opry.

"The leg's bothering you, eh?"

Until Torry mentioned it, Sam hadn't realized he was massaging the thigh. "Nah. It's fine." In truth, it almost always ached to one degree or another. Complaining didn't make it hurt less, so he'd taught himself to stay busy enough to ignore it.

"Y'know, I don't think I ever heard how it happened."

At first, Sam couldn't talk about the accident that had taken him off the truck and put him into the classroom. Then he talked until people's eyes glazed over. These days, he simply delivered the well-rehearsed speech that summed up the whole miserable event in less than a minute:

"House fire was out of control when the truck rolled up, but neighbors said the owner was still inside, so I entered through a basement window and found the woman unconscious in her kitchen. I'd just handed her off to EMTs when the ceiling collapsed, trapping me in the grid work. When I came to, I was in the ICU, covered in bandages, and found out I'd lost a quarter of my calf and thigh muscles."

Torry's eyes widened. "Whoa."

Sam summed up with his usual closing line. "The old lady is still kickin', and so am I—not as high, but kickin'—so there's a lot to be thankful for."

"Still, that's rough, dude. Sorry you had to go through it. But hey, maybe with some practice, you could turn that limp into a wicked swagger." Torry crossed the stage and demonstrated. "I mean, that's what I'd do."

"Like this?"

Torry cupped his chin, watching as Sam attempted the strut. After letting out an exaggerated sigh, he shook his head. "Well, at least you can sing."

"Speaking of singing…"

Sam and Torry turned and met Mark's glare of disapproval.

"The show starts in half an hour," the club owner said. "Are you guys ready?"

They exchanged a puzzled glance. It wasn't like Mark to snap the whip. In fact, he was more likely to goof off than anyone at The Meetinghouse. Sam wondered what had happened in the past few minutes to prompt the out-of-character grimness. It could be anything from concerns that the roof would leak to a breakup with his latest lady to a band member calling in sick.

Sam made his way to the steps leading down from the stage. "We're good to go," he assured Mark.

Rain sheeted down the windows, and lightning flashes brightened the club's dim interior. Standing beside Mark, Dirk glanced at the ceiling. "Good thing you reroofed the place after that last storm."

"Yeah." He walked toward the bar. "C'mere, Sam. There's something I want to show you."

Torry drew a finger across his throat and mouthed, *Uh-oh* as Sam followed.

Mark climbed onto a stool and thumped the newspaper that lay open on the counter. "Take a gander at this article."

Sam settled on to a stool. "Which article?" he asked, picking up the issue.

"The restaurant review column. That guy gave The Right Note five stars. *Five.* For a diner!"

He scanned the piece, making note of the writer's opinions on the menu, service, cleanliness and ambiance. Was there a diplomatic way to tell Mark that he agreed? Sam didn't think so.

"So you're saying we should make some changes in food? Or keep our emphasis on folks who come in for the music?"

"That pricey neon sign outside says Food and Entertainment to Feed Your Soul." Mark leaned forward, lowered his voice. "If we improved the menu, we could easily double our profits." He tapped the newspaper again. "But not unless we change *this* guy's mind."

The "Eat or Run" syndicated column had earned an audience of millions—thanks to the writer's blog and regular TV appearances. He could make or break bars and restaurants with one great or ill-timed review. While he'd praised the waitstaff and performers, he'd given the club's menu just three stars.

Mark moved to the other side of the bar and tossed the newspaper into the trash. "Here's an idea… It's no big secret that you're smitten with Finn Leary. Why not see if you can turn that into something bottom-line good?"

It was true that Finn had been popping into his

head at all hours of the day and night, but he'd hardly label himself *smitten*.

"What do you mean…something good?"

"It's pretty clear she's taken with you, too. Maybe if you plied her with some compliments, she'd drop a hint or two about her customers' favorite menu items. And we could rustle up some similar recipes."

"Whoa. Wait a minute, here. That's way too James Bond for me, pal. You know as well as anyone that my face is an open book. Even if I was willing to go all double agent for you—and I'm *not*—I could never pull off something like that. Besides, why are you worried? The Right Note is a diner. This isn't. No competition."

"Says you." He smirked. "Maybe I'll do it."

Sam laughed. "You're crazy, you know that?"

Torry cleared his throat. "Uh, sorry to interrupt, guys, but there's a young lady here to see you, Sam."

Epps stepped out from behind him. "Hi, Captain Marshall. If you aren't busy, I wonder if I could have a moment of your time."

Every time his dad had caught him red-handed at one sort of boyhood mischief or another, he'd say "You look like the cat that swallowed the canary." That was how Epps looked right now.

"We're about to go onstage," he told her.

She glanced around. "And play to an empty room? Ugh. That's gotta be a major bummer."

Mark frowned at her. "We'll just consider it a dress rehearsal."

Epps gave his paternal tone a second's worth of consideration before facing Sam again. "Do you mind if I hang around? I'd like to talk to you between sets."

He had a notion to tell her he minded—minded a lot. Instead, he gave the G key of his MacCubbin Sitka guitar a tweak, then ran a thumb over the bronze-wound strings.

"Nice," Mark said, strumming his Epiphone Hummingbird. "What say we organize a dueling-guitars night, see which one the audience likes best."

Sam's fingers flew over the fret board as he worked out a short lick of their opening number. "You're on, pal."

Epps applauded, then beamed up at him, resembling every groupie who'd stood at the foot of the stage, their wide, bright eyes making it known that they'd do just about anything to gain the attention of the Marks Brothers. If *Finn* had gazed at him that way, Sam would be in trouble. Big trouble.

Days ago, Epps had hinted at needing a tutor to help with the math and memorization portions of the upcoming exam. That very afternoon, Sam had sought out his captain's advice. It had taken a full minute for the man to list all of Epps's high-ranking department relatives. If Sam agreed to help her—and the sessions proved successful—he might earn a few brownie points. But if things went sideways? Well, an unhappy Epps meant an unhappy family. A well-connected, powerful, unhappy family. Next day, he'd made it clear that one-on-one sessions wouldn't be fair to the others. Not clear enough, evidently. Tonight, he'd nip it in the bud. The biggest challenge? Saying no without hurting or embarrassing her.

"So it's okay if I stay, then?"

Sam sent her a careful, controlled smile. "If you were my kid, I wouldn't want you out this late on a stormy night, but I can't tell you what to do."

"Are you sure?" Mark gave her a quick once-over. "'Cause after that lukewarm review, last thing we need is the cops marching in here, writing up citations and doling out fines because we're serving underage kids."

"Forget that article," Sam advised. "Most people won't even read it, and the few who do won't let it keep them away. It's apples and oranges, remember? And you can quit worrying about the Age Police showing up, too. Epps here is one of my new recruits."

"That's right. And Captain Marshall knows I'm of age because I had to include a copy of my birth certificate with my application to the academy." Epps giggled. "Which way to the ladies room?"

Mark pointed and, once she was out of earshot, said, "I don't know how you do it, dude." He glanced in the direction Epps had gone. "Old, young, married, single—women fall all over themselves when you're around."

All but *one*. "You're crazy."

"Hmph. If you were a *real* friend, you'd tell me your secret."

Sam had known Mark long enough to realize the futility of arguing the point. So he faked a big laugh. "This is the perfect example of the old 'I could tell you, but then I'd have to kill you' scenario."

"Oh, man," Torry said. "It's gettin' deep in here." He backpedaled toward the hall. "If you need me, I'll be in the office, changing into my waders."

The men's laughter echoed through the club.

"What's so funny?" Epps asked as she returned to the stage area.

"Private joke. Guy stuff," Sam said by way of explanation.

The adoring glint in her eyes reminded him how essential it was to set her straight tonight.

What were the chances that someday Finn would look at him this way?

CHAPTER EIGHT

"CAN YOU BELIEVE this wind?"

"The rain is falling *sideways*!"

"You don't think we're in for another 2010, do you?"

Ciara, Bean and Ted stood side by side at the window, staring out at the street.

Rowdy used a meat mallet to hammer on the service counter. "Get away from that window, you bunch o' goofballs. If this storm spins into a tornado like it did in '98…"

The trio exchanged worried glances.

"You'll be safe back here, washing up this mountain of dishes. And there's a shipment of canned goods to unbox and shelve. Don't make me count to ten, or—"

Finn watched all three hustle into the kitchen and get right to work, smiling because they knew as well as she did that Rowdy's paternal glare was 100 percent bark, zero percent bite.

Jimmy stopped loading the dishwasher. "What happens if he gets to ten?"

"You ride that conveyor belt," Rowdy answered.

"And get the insubordination washed outta ya, that's what!"

Ciara laughed. "You're such a big silly, Rowdy. Everyone knows—everyone knows Jimmy can't fit through that machine."

Smiling, Finn went back to the stack of invoices on her desk. Oh, how she loved the people who'd become more family than employees! She and Ciara might not have the most normal parents in the world, but they had a whole lot of other things to be thankful for. A roof over their heads. Over-stuffed closets. More than enough to eat. And a thriving business that would—

An earsplitting crash drowned out the kitchen sounds, followed by the unmistakable tinkle of glass shattering.

"I *knew* they should've cut down that old tree!" Rowdy shouted.

"What?" Finn was on her feet and beside him in an instant, staring, slack-jawed, at the still-dripping leaves and branches that filled the entire right side of The Right Note.

Rowdy ordered the diners and staff to stay put, then dialed 911.

Finn glanced around. At still-spinning red-vinyl stools, bent at awkward angles near the snack bar. At bench seats and tables torn from the bolts securing them to the black-and-white-tiled floor. At shards of glass and bits of metal that glittered like diamonds all around her feet. At the neon signs—

one designed to resemble a staff and music notes above the words The Right Note Cafe, another that sputtered and buzzed in its futile effort to say Welcome—that hung precariously from their anchors.

Half a dozen customers had decided to wait out the storm in the diner.

"Is everyone all right?" Finn asked.

Nodding, they huddled in The Right Note's far corner.

"That guy doesn't look so hot," Rowdy whispered.

Sure enough, an elderly gent stumbled from his booth.

"Call 911 again," she whispered back. "He could have a heart condition or something."

As Rowdy dialed, she put an arm around the man. "Better stay put until the EMTs get here," she said.

"I'm fine," he growled, waving her away.

Clearly he wasn't, as evidenced by his halting, unsteady gait.

Finn guided him back into his booth. "Please, sir, just sit tight. I wouldn't want you to trip over any of this…" She gestured toward the tree and debris.

He fumbled through his pockets, then cursed under his breath. "Now, where's that infernal cell phone? I want to call my daughter, let her know I'll be late."

She glanced around, saw it in the middle of the table. Finn was about to hand it to him when she noticed his dilated pupils. Pete had insisted that she take CPR classes, so Finn recognized the symptoms of shock: trembling, cool yet clammy skin, bluish fingernails and lips.

"Here's your phone," she said. "Would you like me to call her for you?"

Rowdy draped a tablecloth over the man's shoulders as the red-and-blue strobes of emergency vehicles whirled around the diner's interior. A moment later, the place filled with first responders.

A burly firefighter approached. "What's up?" he asked Finn.

She described the man's symptoms.

"Good job. Thanks. Everybody else okay?"

She looked toward the out-of-town guests huddled in the opposite corner. "Yes, scared, but everyone's all right."

He squatted and signaled the nearest paramedic.

"Okay if I get those people into the back room?" she asked, pointing to the rest of her diners.

"Bob!" he bellowed. "Okay if these folks head to the back?" In a softer voice, he told Finn, "He's just checking for structural damage. Wouldn't want the ceiling to cave in on you."

Bob moved closer. "Things look okay out here." Using his ballpoint as a pointer, he asked, "Gas stove back there?"

"Yes…"

"Just let me make sure the connections are intact and there are no leaks before anybody goes anywhere."

After poking and prodding, he gave the thumbs-up sign, and Finn waved her customers closer.

"Let's get some dessert into you," she said, guiding them to the big stainless table in the storeroom. "What's your pleasure? Cake? Ice cream? Pie?"

"That's very kind of you," a young woman said, "but my husband and I would rather get back to our hotel."

Members of the other family agreed. "Thanks for the offer, though," the dad said. "Hope you'll be back in business soon. We've enjoyed all our meals here."

A cop approached and suggested they leave through the back door. Finn rounded up a few of the umbrellas left behind by former diners and passed them out.

"Sorry for the disturbance," she said, grinning as they departed.

"Wasn't your fault," the mom said.

"Guess even the mighty oak has its limits," the young woman's husband said.

"You might want to round up some plywood," the cop suggested. "And call your insurance agent."

Finn exhaled a shaky sigh. He was right.

"A city inspector will come by in the next day or two, let you know what he thinks needs to be fixed." He handed her a business card. "If you get Rick Martin, tell him I said hello."

Frank Martin, the card said.

"He's my brother. A real straight arrow. He won't make reopening any harder than it has to be."

Finn pocketed the card. "Thanks, Officer Martin."

An hour later, the engine of a tow truck churned as it dragged the tree from the diner. One by one, the emergency vehicles drove off, leaving Finn and the staff to contemplate their next steps. They came together in a group hug.

"We're all safe," she told them. "That's the most important thing. Once we clean up this mess, things will look a lot better."

"She's right," Rowdy said. "So let's get crackin'." He disengaged from the huddle and meted out assignments. "Bean, grab a broom. Jimmy, you get the dustpan. Ciara, you bring the trash can over here so—"

"No, I think you should all go home. Get some rest, and we'll talk about who does what tomorrow, okay?"

One by one, they agreed.

"I'll go upstairs," Ciara offered. "And make us— make us some tea. That always calms you down."

"That's a great idea." Finn hugged her tight. "But don't make mine just yet. I need to call our insurance agent."

"You won't be too long, will you?"

She checked her watch. "I hope not, but if I'm not there by ten, you go ahead and get into bed, okay?"

Ciara popped a noisy kiss to Finn's cheek. "Okay. Love you, big sister!"

"Love you *more*!"

It was a game they'd played for years. Ciara had no way of knowing how much Finn meant every word.

When Ciara was gone, Rowdy asked, "What can I do for you, kiddo?"

"You can go home and put your feet up. Something tells me there will be plenty for you to do tomorrow."

"No way I'm leaving you here alone with that gaping hole in the wall. Anyone with a mind to raid the cash box could just waltz right in and—"

Sam entered, as if summoned by a fairy godmother.

"Holy debris, Batman," he said. "What happened in here?"

After Rowdy brought him up to speed, Sam got on his phone and, pacing, spoke quietly into the mouthpiece.

"Mark and the guys will be here in a few minutes," he said, hanging up. "They'll bring everything we need to close up this wall."

Glass crunched under his boots as he paced, checking out the damage.

"We?"

Sam stopped walking and turned to face her. Finn blamed the events of the past hour—and not his caring expression—for her accelerated heartbeat.

"Of course *we*." He gestured toward the gap. "Not even a superwoman like you can fix this all by yourself."

"Superwoman, indeed," she huffed. But he was right, of course, and rather than admit it, Finn said, "I'm surprised you heard the sirens over your blaring music."

He grinned, and her heart thumped harder still.

"I'll have you know," Sam said, cocking an eyebrow, "we do not *blare*. We merely test the limits of the noise code. Things were slow tonight, and I heard the alert on my cell. Recognized the address and came right over."

Finn was suddenly thirsty. Very thirsty. She went into the kitchen and fetched two bottles of water from the walk-in cooler. "So you're still in the loop with the fire department?" she asked, handing one to him.

"Thanks." He unscrewed the cap. "And yeah, I guess you could say that."

She held out the second bottle to Rowdy, but he declined it. "Sounds like you're pretty well set, here. If it's okay, I think I'll take you up on your offer to head home early."

"Feel free to sleep in," she told him. "There's no point in going to the farmer's market at the crack of dawn."

The big man gave her a sideways hug. "Y'know, I might just do that…if I remember how to sleep past four!"

The place fell silent, save for the *drip-drip-drip* of rain plopping into the puddles just outside the broken window.

"I've seen a lot of destruction," Sam said. "This looks way worse than it is. It'll take some time, but you'll be back in business before you know it."

"And we'll help," Torry said, leading the parade of band members, each toting a four-by-eight-foot sheet of plywood.

"This stuff was left over from when we redid the bathrooms," Mark said. "So don't look at me like that. You're doing us a favor, getting it out of the way."

Regardless of where it came from, Finn intended to repay Mark for every last sheet. *Mark and Sam*, she corrected herself, since he was an owner now.

While the men hammered and sawed, boarding up the opening, Finn shoved aside stools, tables and benches and swept up glass and bits of metal and plastic that had held the big window in place. Already she could see that Sam had been right. It would take time and patience, but the diner would be good as new before long.

The Right Note had been providing for her since Pete had hired her at the tender age of fourteen. When he'd learned that the Learys were facing eviction, he'd given her a raise, more than enough to keep the wolf from the door while her parents spent the rent money on recording studios, drugs and alcohol. Two weeks after Ciara's release from the hospital—and three days before Finn's eighteenth birthday—Misty and Connor had left in the middle of the night. *Gig in Chi-town*, their note had said. *Be good girls while we're gone!* Connor had signed *Daddy*, though neither she nor Ciara had used the term in years, and left two hundred dollars on the table. He hadn't provided a phone number, address or the name of the club that had hired them. Two months later, when Pete found out what they'd done, he'd moved her and Ciara into the upstairs apartment. And when the Learys returned eight months after that, expecting to pick up where they'd left off, he'd made it clear they would *not*.

"Good ol' Pete," she muttered, remembering the tongue-lashing he'd given her folks.

"What's that?" Sam asked.

"Oh, nothing." She faked a grin. *Stop looking so sympathetic, Sam Marshall*, she thought, *or I'll lose it*. Finn hated few things more than blubbering in front of people, strangers in particular.

What would Pete say if he were here? "Look for the silver lining, cupcake. There's always a silver lining." Her eyes misted with tears. Oh, how she missed him!

"Well, we're done," Torry said, rapping on the plywood wall. "That'll hold ya until your insurance agent cuts you a check."

"Thanks, guys. You're all entitled to free meals just as soon as we're open for business."

Torry took her aside. "Are you *crazy*, offering this

motley crew free food? They'll eat clean through to the kitchen, and you'll have to start all over again!"

Laughing, the guys made their way out through the back door.

All except for Sam.

"I know a couple good contractors," he said. "Recruits turned firefighters who used to work for family businesses. So, just say the word, and I'll hook you up."

"Thanks." She glanced into her office, where the still-unpaid invoices sat on her desk. "I have a couple of phone calls to make."

"Insurance agent?"

Finn nodded. "Thanks for rounding up that work crew. You're right. No way Rowdy and I could have done all that alone. Especially not so quickly."

"Happy to help."

It was what everyone said, but it rarely sounded more heartfelt.

Sam handed her a business card. "If you need anything, you know, while you're waiting for the agent to get back to you, call me. Any time. Even if it's just to talk." He looked around the place. "Because I'm guessing this hit you pretty hard."

Why, oh, why, did he have to seem so sincere? Tears stung her eyes, and Finn held her breath. *You will not cry. Do.* Not. *Cry!*

Sam took a step closer, stooping slightly to study her face. Why didn't he just leave? She'd ask him to go…if she could speak around the sob in her throat.

"Aw, hey, it's okay. You're safe now," he said, and extended his arms.

If anyone had told her she'd so willingly step into them, she would have called them insane.

But that was exactly what she did, and safe was exactly how she felt.

CHAPTER NINE

SAM HAD COMFORTED women before. Not so unusual
for a guy in his line of work, especially one with a
mom, grandmothers, sisters, an assortment of aunts
and nieces and a weepy ex-girlfriend or two. Some
wailed, others sniffled, a few hiccupped…over lost
loved ones and pets, poignant movie plots, thoughtful gifts. But not one had held on so tight he could
feel her heart beating against his chest. If not for
the tears dampening his shirt and the quaking of
Finn's petite body, he wouldn't have realized she
was crying.

His leg was killing him, thanks to hefting and
steadying the plywood while Torry, Mark and the
guys had nailed it in place. He could go home, el-
evate it and apply heat, swallow an aspirin or two
and feel relief in no time. But he'd rather endure the
pain than let her go.

Common sense told him that useless platitudes
were the last thing she needed to hear right now.
So he stood quiet and still, and let his presence do
the talking.

Thanks to Mark and Torry, he'd learned a bit
about Finn's history. The terrible accident. Absentee

parents. Full responsibility for her sister. Employees who relied on her for a steady paycheck. Sam thought of his own mom and dad, whose unconditional love showed in everything they said and did.

The contrasts made him hug Finn a little tighter. She'd grown up without any of that, yet she'd taken on the role of mother, father and older sibling to her special needs sister. If she'd been raised by parents like his, how much *more* terrific would she be?

Finn pressed both palms to his chest and gazed up at him through long, tear-spiky eyelashes. His pulse pounded when a faint, sheepish grin lifted one corner of her mouth.

"I'm not usually such a big whiny baby. Sorry."

When she looked away, it felt as if someone had flipped a switch and turned out the light in his heart. Sam lifted her chin on a bent forefinger, gently guiding her gaze back to his eyes.

"You're not a big whiny baby, and you have absolutely nothing to apologize for."

Finn bit her lower lip to still its trembling, and he admired her all the more for the effort at self-control.

"I meant what I said."

Dark eyebrows lifted slightly.

"You really *are* safe with me. Safe to cry or stamp your feet or put a fist through a wall." He grinned. "Although I don't recommend that last one."

"Right...the place has sustained enough damage for one night." She took a deep breath and let it out slowly. "Besides, tears and tantrums are a waste of time and energy."

Sam read between the lines: she hadn't come by that mind-set the easy way. How many other hard-earned lessons had life taught her? He fought the urge to pull her close again.

"Don't know about you," he said, "but I could go for some strong coffee and a slice of pie."

She smiled, and the light in his heart went on again.

"Cherry or apple?"

"Doesn't matter."

He followed her into the kitchen, where she grabbed two plates from the shelf above the long stainless counter.

"Sorry it isn't homemade, but it's not half bad warmed up in the microwave and topped off with ice cream."

Sam considered reminding her there was nothing to apologize for. Instead, he said, "I'd offer to help, but, *man*, you made quick work of slicing that pie!" Chuckling, he balanced on a wheeled stool. "Remind me not to startle you when there's a cleaver in your hand."

She used the tip of the wide blade to point at a row of knives and scissors stuck to a magnetized strip above the counter. "*That's* a cleaver. This is a chef's knife. It'll slice, chop, dice, mince or mash—as in garlic cloves. Most useful kitchen tool ever invented."

It was good to see her more relaxed. "Aha. So that's why you have half a dozen of them."

One shoulder rose in a dainty shrug. "Rowdy uses them, too. Sometimes we're in here together, plating up customers' orders. Nothing less appetizing than for customers to hear the crew bickering over cutlery."

He wanted to keep her talking—about anything *but* the damage out front—so he said, "Ever heard of Aggie Jackson?"

Finn laughed and slid their plates out of the microwave. "Who *hasn't* heard of her?"

She dropped a scoop of ice cream on top of each wedge. "How do you know the woman whose main claim to fame is that she's a descendant of Andrew Jackson?"

Sam thanked her for the pie and reached into one of the bins at the end of the counter, helping himself to a fork. "She's my landlady. One of these days, I'll meet someone who *doesn't* know she's the great-great…" He handed her a fork, then cut into his pie. "How many generations back do we need to go to get the right number of 'greats'?"

Finn sat on the empty stool beside him. "Gosh. I'd need a calculator—or a time machine—to go back that far in history."

Laughing, Sam made his way to the cooler, doing his best not to limp. When he returned with a carton of milk, she nodded toward his leg. "Overdid it tonight, I see."

He grabbed two glasses from the drying rack near the dishwasher. "No biggie. It'll be fine by the time I'm married."

She'd just taken a bite of pie, and her mouth froze, midchew. Her expression reminded Sam of his cousin Zach's boot camp graduation photo, stern and no-nonsense. He'd meant it as a joke. *Looks like the joke's on you, Marshall.* He handed her a glass of milk, then hid his embarrassment by taking a long, slow gulp from his own glass.

Her laughter started soft and low, then escalated until it bounced off every hard surface in the kitchen. Sam loved the sound if it—rich and throaty and wholly feminine—and his pulse pounded harder.

"Guess it'll be a while before you let me live that one down, huh."

Her question implied they had a future together, and Sam liked that. Liked it a lot.

She toasted him with the tumbler. "This was a good choice, by the way. It'll be hard enough to sleep tonight, even without caffeine floating around in my system."

Sam doubted he'd sleep well, either…because Finn would be floating around in *his* system. But she looked tired and understandably stressed.

"I should probably hit the road so you can—"

"How long have you been in Nashville?"

"Going on six years now. Seems half that…" *At times like this.* "And twice as long."

Finn nodded. "I know exactly what you mean. My family landed here when I was thirteen."

"Musicians?"

"My parents are singer-songwriters, and play about half a dozen instruments apiece. But that's true of a big chunk of the city's population. Connor and Misty tried all sorts of gimmicks but couldn't find the one that set them apart from the competition."

Based on her faraway expression, she was thinking of a far less pleasant time. She'd already gone through a lot tonight, and he felt bad, having opened an old wound. Sam covered her hand with his. For a moment she sat nodding, lost in her thoughts, and he was glad she hadn't pulled her warm little hand away.

"It's a rough road," he admitted.

"Road?"

"The one that leads to a recording contract."

One eyebrow rose, and she wasn't smiling when she said, "And you know this because..."

"Because I've walked it a time or two myself."

Coincidence that she chose that moment to take back her hand? Sam didn't think so.

"It's nowhere near the top of my priority list anymore, though," he quickly added. "Family, the department, the academy, then music, in that order. Performing is more a hobby now than anything else."

She turned on the stool to face him head-on. "Hypothetical question—if somebody with clout heard you perform and offered a contract, would you sign it?"

"Well, sure."

He'd answered truthfully, but it wasn't what she wanted to hear, as evidenced by the almost angry spark in her dark eyes. Finn got up, stacked his plate atop hers and grabbed the flexible hose dangling above the dishwasher. She rinsed both plates and stood them in the wash rack, then returned for their glasses. After rinsing those, too, she crossed both arms over her chest.

"Well, it's late, and I have a lot of phone calls to make in the morning. I appreciate everything you did tonight."

Sam put all his weight on the good leg as he stood. "No thanks necessary. I was happy to do it. I'd do it again in a heartbeat." The word reminded him that he could have counted her heartbeats just moments ago.

Her expression softened slightly. Because she remembered, too?

She uncrossed her arms and walked to the back door. "Are you parked out front?"

"Yeah…"

"Sorry about that. Now you'll have to walk all the way around the building."

"Don't be sorry. It isn't your fault that Mother Nature decided to park a tree in your diner."

She held open the door. "Hope the leg doesn't keep you awake all night."

It wouldn't be the leg keeping him awake.

"Easier said than done, I know," she continued. "But try to get some sleep, okay?"

She glanced into the back lot and thanked him again. *Subtle, Finn.* Sam grinned. *Real subtle.* He'd given her his card. Should he repeat his offer to help anytime?

The harsh glare of the street lamps exaggerated the worry lines and weariness on her lovely face. Had he thanked her for the pie? "Thanks for the pie," he said, just in case. "You were right. It was great, especially warmed up and topped off with ice cream."

She hid a yawn behind her free hand. "I still owe you a meal, though."

"Aw, Finn, you don't owe me a thing. I mean it."

Several seconds ticked by as those big dark eyes studied his face. Looking for proof that he was just another musician who said things he didn't mean? If that was the case, Sam had no idea how he'd prove otherwise. But he wanted to try...

"Lock up tight," he said, "and I'll see you soon."

Her lips said, "Okay," but her eyes said, *Not if I see you first.*

The door clicked shut, and he listened as the bolts slid into place. Head down and hands pocketed, Sam splashed through puddles as he headed for the front lot. He'd heard about women with more baggage than an airport luggage carousel. Considering Finn's background, her suspicious nature was understandable. That didn't make it easier to deal with, though.

His mind went back to the moment when he'd quoted her "better before I'm married" comment, and the roundabout reply that hinted she saw him as something more, something better than a self-centered, music-first jerk. Sam slid behind the steering wheel and started the pickup. While adjusting the rearview mirror, he noticed the almost dry evidence of Finn's tears on his shoulder. Man, she'd felt good in his arms.

Good enough that he might just start lifting weights again, so he could help her carry that baggage.

CHAPTER TEN

FINN'S INSURANCE AGENT walked through The Right Note, jotting notes and muttering as he shook his head.

"It's a mess, all right, but don't you worry. Soon as you get me quotes from three licensed contractors, I'll cut you a check."

She hated the idea of browsing the internet for reputable companies, then making appointments so they could come out to estimate the cost of repairs. More distasteful still was having no idea how long it would take them to get back to her with quotes. Last night, she'd dropped Sam's business card into the waste can beside her dresser. Hopefully, Ciara hadn't yet gathered the trash, because if he could save her time by recommending his friends...

"Thanks, Dave," she said, walking the agent out. "I'll email you as soon as I have some prices."

"Good, good. And don't forget to get me an estimate of your own...projected losses for every day you're closed while construction is going on."

She thanked him again, then headed straight upstairs to look for Sam's card.

"Ciara," she muttered into the empty can, "sometimes you're too efficient for my own good."

"What—what do you mean?"

"I threw something in here, then realized I need it."

"What was it?"

"A business card."

"Sam Marshall's business card?"

"Yes…"

"I read it. And—and I remember what it said."

"You're amazing, you know that?" Finn smiled and prepared to type his information into her cell phone. "Go ahead. Tell me what it said."

Eyes closed, Ciara began with, "It had a little shield in the top corner. Under that, it said Nashville Fire Department. Then, then it said Sam Marshall, Captain. And under *that* it said Academy Instructor. And *then* in the bottom corner was—was his phone number and email address."

She recited the digits as Finn typed them into her contacts list, and although it wasn't likely she'd need it, she added his email, too.

"Thanks, Kee. You just saved me calling around to find out how to get in touch with him."

"You—you could have called Mark…"

"When you're right, you're right, but now, thanks to your excellent memory, I won't have to!" She glanced at her watch. "How would you like to join me for lunch? We'll go to Puckett's, and after we eat, you can get something from their little store."

"But I thought you hated the crowds over there."

"Today, I'll make an exception, just for you."

"You're the best, Finn!" Ciara hugged her, then headed to her room. "I'm going to wear my new sundress. I hardly ever get to wear pretty clothes!"

Finn had to admit she was right. For work, they wore jeans and red T-shirts under white aprons that bore The Right Note's logo. It might be fun to put on something dressy and feminine for a change.

But first things first.

Finn dialed Sam's number and counted the rings. If not for needing his recommendations, she wouldn't have called him at all. So why did she feel disappointed when his voice mail picked up?

"Sam Marshall here. You know what to do. Thanks, and I'll talk with you soon."

She waited for the beep, then left a message asking if he could put her in touch with his contractor friends.

Moments later, the phone rang.

"Good thing I have caller ID…"

She would have recognized that smooth, DJ-deep voice anywhere.

"…because you forgot to leave your number."

"Oh. Right." She rolled her eyes. "Sorry about that."

Finn cringed and waited for him to say she didn't have anything to apologize for. She'd been reciting the phrase so often and for so long, it was the first thing that came to mind any time things weren't perfect. *Maybe you should see a shrink to find out why.* Then again, it made no sense to waste money and time on therapy when she already knew the answers: Misty and Connor.

"If I had a dollar for every time I didn't leave my number," Sam said, "I could buy you dinner at the Watermark."

One of Nashville's top-ten restaurants? Good thing he was kidding; she didn't have a thing to wear to a swanky place like that. The cliché complaint threatened to turn her grin into a giggle.

"Those contractors you mentioned last night... My insurance guy says the sooner I get him three bids, the sooner he can cut me a check. Which means I can reopen, well, sooner."

"I, ah, I'm in the middle of a class right now."

Of course he was. What was she thinking, calling during business hours! Last night's craziness must have rattled her more than she realized.

"Oh, wow. I'm so sorry, Sam."

There you go again, "I'm sorrying" all over the place. And then she remembered that he'd returned her call.

"Don't give it another thought. I'll dole out a writing assignment, look up those names and numbers and call you right back."

Before Sam hung up, Finn heard a cacophony of laughter, mixed with good-natured cries of "Attaboy" and "Way to go, Captain." His students wouldn't have reacted that way if they didn't like him. She pictured Sam, alternately lecturing and writing salient points on the chalkboard, probably while wearing the department uniform—creased navy trousers and a light blue shirt, open at the collar.

Finn hit her phone's end button and opened her closet door. Among shirts, skirts, jeans, sweaters and dresses that hung in order of hem and sleeve length, she chose a pale yellow sundress. Strappy white sandals and a cross-body purse completed the outfit, and she placed them all at the foot of her bed.

She'd just kicked off her shoes when the phone buzzed on her nightstand.

"Wow," she said, tidying the doily, "when you say you're going to get right back to someone, you aren't kidding, are you?"

The sound of his rumbling laughter made her smile. Her amusement disappeared, though, when she caught sight of herself in the mirror, finger combing her bangs and grinning like a love-struck schoolgirl.

"Got a pen and paper?"

Her hurried search through the nightstand drawer produced a small tablet and a pen, but a few squiggly lines proved it was dry. "Figures," she muttered. "If the pen writes, there's nothing to write *on*."

"Or the other way around."

"Exactly! Okay. I'm ready. Finally. Sorry to waste your time. I know you're busy."

"No busier than you. And believe me, Finn…time with you is never a waste."

It was what anyone would say to a chronic apologizer, right? So why had his simple statement made her misty-eyed?

As promised, Sam provided three names. "Will you let me know who ends up doing the work?"

"Ah, so you can collect your finder's fee, huh?"

A moment of silence preceded a hoarse sigh. "I, ah, I'd better get back inside before they start throwing spitballs or something. Catch you later."

He hung up before she got a chance to thank him. A pang of guilt shot through her. She hadn't intended to insult him, but apparently, that was exactly what her sorry excuse for a joke had done.

And there it was again: *sorry.*

You're sorry, she thought, dropping on to the foot of her bed. *A sorry mess.*

"Instead of sitting here wasting time," she told her reflection, "get busy."

She dialed the first number from Sam's list, and while waiting for an answer, Finn remembered something he'd said. "Time with you is never a waste."

Bet he doesn't feel that way now!

Logic told her his opinion shouldn't matter so much.

But when it came to Sam Marshall, she felt anything but logical.

CHAPTER ELEVEN

WHEN AGGIE HEARD why he was limping more than usual, she clucked her tongue.

"I think you know what I'm going to say."

He didn't, but Sam played along.

"No woman is worth all that pain."

She was clever, that landlady of his. He'd stopped by to drop off the rent check, but by not accepting it, she'd more or less trapped him there on her ornate red velvet sofa. *Never should have told her what happened at The Right Note*, he thought as the lecture continued.

"Finn Leary is a gorgeous little thing, so I'm not the least bit surprised that a man like you is attracted to her."

A man like him?

"But nothing you do or say will soften that hard heart of hers. Oh, don't get me wrong, she's friendly enough…if you're a paying customer. I don't know what her type is, but you're not it!"

"Oh, you're great for a guy's ego, you know that?"

Aggie ignored his comment. "I've seen that girl smile like a beauty queen, all the while telling handsome singers and musicians to buzz off. She doesn't say it in so many words, of course, but they get the message, believe you me!"

"Well, at least she softens the blow with a smile."

"My advice? Save yourself a lot of misery and aim those gorgeous blue eyes of yours elsewhere." She adjusted the hem of her sparkly red skirt. "And wipe that look off your face."

"What look?"

"That cow-eyed, hopeful look. It's useless with a woman like her, I tell you. Useless!" Aggie picked up a store-bought cookie and took a bite, oblivious to the crumbs that rained to the floor. "So tell me, how are the classes going this time around?"

"Good. Fine."

"But you're still hoping to get back on a truck someday, aren't you?"

"Nah, I accepted the hard facts long ago."

"Probably for the best, considering…" She pointed at his left leg. "You're satisfied with the teaching position, then?"

Sam nodded. "I get far more out of it than I put in."

"I imagine it's very fulfilling, knowing your instruction will help keep those youngsters safe out there on the job, and that once they're trained, they'll save lives and property."

She pointed at the cookie plate, his unspoken invitation to take one.

Sam held up a hand. "Just had a sandwich, but thanks."

"So tell me, Sam, are you *happy*?"

"Well, sure. Yeah." What a strange question, even from Aggie. "Why do you ask?"

"Because you don't look it. Oh, you can flash that dazzling smile till the cows come home, but you're not fooling *this* old broad." She leaned forward and patted his knee with long-taloned red fingertips. "You're a good and decent man, one of the best I've had the pleasure of knowing—and at my age, you should take that as an enormous compliment—and you deserve all the joy this life has to offer."

She took another bite of her cookie, then used the remaining crescent as a pointer. "That's why I don't want to see you getting tangled up with that girl. She's a big, fat heartache waiting to happen."

He remembered Finn's wisecrack—about him getting a finder's fee for recommending the contractor—and wondered how close to the truth Aggie's warning might be.

"Have you talked to your folks lately?"

"Yeah, and they send their love." They hadn't, but Aggie had no family, so what could it hurt to let her believe they'd been thinking of her?

"You really ought to visit them more often. Man only gets one family, you know."

Sam agreed, then told her about his cousin Nate's upcoming wedding, adding that he planned to spend Christmas at the Double M.

Aggie exhaled a soft sigh. "Bet Denver is beautiful in the wintertime, with all that snow and the mountains in the background…"

"Yeah. It's a sight to behold, all right."

"But I'll bet it doesn't compare to Nashville at Christmas."

The city did a great job trimming lampposts, storefronts and municipal buildings, but Sam preferred nature's decorations.

His landlady launched into a recitation of the city's history, starting with the cable cars that once clanged through the streets, ending with the story of the great fire of 1916. She wasn't old enough to remember any of that firsthand, and he wondered where the conversation would lead.

"I'm thinking of going to one of those jazz-fest things down at Riverfront Park. You wouldn't want to go with me, would you?"

She was lonely, which explained why just about anyone who showed up at her front door could expect to stay at least thirty minutes. Sam had never been a jazz fan and didn't like the idea of lumbering down that steep hill on his bum leg to search for a flat spot in the lawn near the amphitheater.

And yet, he said, "Maybe, if I don't have to work."

Aggie threw back her head and cut loose with a laugh that sounded more like a roar. And with her mane of wild red hair, it fit.

"All right, get on out of here, you big-hearted goofball, you. I know you have a to-do list as long as my arm, but you're sweet as rock candy for trying to placate an addle-brained old lady." She waved him closer and hugged him tight.

"You're about the least addle-brained person I know," he said, handing her the check.

He was halfway to the door when she grabbed his arm. "Take some time to prop up that leg, first chance you get." She stood on tiptoe to plant a big kiss on his cheek, then jabbed an arthritis-crooked forefinger into his chest. "And remember what I said about that Leary girl, you hear?"

Nodding, Sam headed for the parking lot. What would Aggie say if she found out that her warnings had made him more curious than ever about the people and events that turned Finn Leary into the most intriguing woman he'd ever met?

IT COULD HAVE been frustrating that none of the contractors could stop by today. But Finn decided to follow Pete's advice and look for the silver lining. She and Ciara had the day to themselves.

When she broke the news, Ciara clasped her hands. "For—for *real*?"

"For real. Now put on something pretty, and let's hit the bricks, kiddo."

"No stocking shelves?"

"And no scrubbing floors."

"No wiping sticky stuff off the menus?"

"And no refilling condiment dispensers."

"Or napkin holders…" She grinned. "I'll be ready in—in two shakes of a lamb's tail!"

Another Pete-ism. Once, when Finn had asked how many adages he might have in that white-haired head of his, he'd imitated Humphrey Bogart: "Schweetheart, I probably have about a million of 'em. More than a million, maybe."

Pete fooled a lot of people with his gruff, growly manner, but he'd never fooled Ciara. Within ten minutes of their first meeting, she'd figured out that deep in that barrel chest beat the heart of a softie. "His eyes sparkle when he talks," she'd told Finn, "just like Grandpa's." That was before the accident that changed everything—except her sister's uncanny talent for finding the good in people, even the parents who came and went like one of Pete's proverbial bad pennies.

Finn squeezed her eyes shut. *Forget about it. Just forget about it.* It wasn't as though rehashing the ugly scenes would turn Connor and Misty into caring, responsible parents. Besides, she and Ciara were safe now. And they had Pete to thank for that.

"Are you almost ready, Kee?"

"Almost."

Finn slid her wallet into her purse. As she prepared to drop her cell phone in beside it, she saw Sam's number in the recent calls list. Ciara liked him, so he couldn't be *all* bad, even if he was a musician.

She snapped the purse shut and whispered, "Wonder what Pete Maxon would think of you, Sam Marshall?"

Ciara appeared in the doorway. "Aw, you look adorable, sweetie!"

"You said that yesterday."

"It's just as true today. So are you ready for another day of fun?"

"You mean not just eating and shopping at Puckett's again?"

"Oh, we'll do that and a whole lot more."

"You're the best sister ever, and the prettiest, too!"

For the moment, she *felt* pretty. Almost as pretty as when Sam told her she ought to smile more often.

"So—so where are we going first?"

Finn linked arms with her sister. "Today, young lady, you and I are going to do everything the out-of-towners do!"

They started out at Riverfront Park, where they boarded a trolley packed with tourists. It took them downtown. When they grew tired of walking Music Row, they'd hop a trolley going back the other way.

The sisters toured Fort Nashborough, the Old Spaghetti Factory and its dozens of Victorian antiques, the Ryman Auditorium, the Tennessee State Capitol and Printer's Alley.

"Are your—are your feet tired, Finn?"

"To be honest, *all* of me is tired!"

"Then, can we sit down and eat now?"

It wasn't in Ciara's nature to complain. For her to admit she wanted to take a break spoke volumes.

"You bet we can. It's just a short walk from here

to Church Street. After lunch, we'll ride home from Puckett's in a taxi."

A deep voice behind them said, "No need for that. I'll take you home."

Ciara squeezed Finn's arm. "Look, Finn, it's Sam! Sam Marshall!"

"So it is." Just as she'd suspected, he looked good in uniform. Real good. "So what are you doing on this side of town, Sam?"

"Errands, mostly. You?"

Ciara grabbed his hand. "Finn said we could be tourists today, since we didn't have to fill catsup dispensers."

He winked, then met Finn's eyes. "I think that's a great idea. All work and no play—"

"—makes Jack a dull boy," Ciara finished with him.

"Mind if I join you at Puckett's?"

"Oh, oh, can he, Finn? *Can* he?"

Her tone reminded Finn of the day last spring, when Ciara had found a half-dead baby bird. "Can I keep him, *please*?" That day, she'd had no choice but to say no. Now, she didn't have to. It was nearly two; the worst of the lunch rush should be over, meaning they'd get in and out quickly.

"Sure, sweetie. I think it'd be real nice if Sam joined us."

Ciara glanced from Finn to Sam and back again. "Hey, Finn. His eyes sparkle when he smiles, just like—just like Pete and Grandpa."

"So they do," she agreed, accepting his extended elbow.

Sharing a meal with him would be a lot of things, but *boring* wouldn't be one of them.

CHAPTER TWELVE

CIARA LEANED FORWARD as far as the seat belt would allow and squeezed Finn's shoulder. "Wasn't that just—just the most fun day, *ever*?"

"Yes, sweetie, it was." Finn gave her hand an affectionate pat. "Now sit back, okay, so you'll be safe...and so Sam won't get a ticket."

"Oh. Oh, yeah. Right." She squeezed Sam's shoulder, too. "We don't want that, do we?"

"Nope, we sure don't want that."

He glanced into the rearview mirror and saw Ciara sitting ramrod straight and barely able to contain her excitement.

"This was the best day ever!" she repeated.

That was exactly how she'd sounded when a dog walker had led a motley assortment of mutts past the truck window. He liked seeing her happy, excited, enthused. Seemed to him that after all she'd been through, Ciara had a right to all the pleasure life could offer. If half a dozen shaggy pups could inspire giggles and finger-pointing, how much more would she enjoy a trip to the zoo?

"The fun doesn't have to end yet, y'know."

From the corner of his eye, he saw Finn's "What

are you up to" expression, and suddenly, the surprise didn't seem like such a great idea after all. Another peek in the mirror told him that the sightseer-stuffed trolley parked beside them at the traffic light had fully captured Ciara's attention, and he used the moment to run the concept past Finn.

Nashville Zoo? he mouthed.

Tension furrowed her brow, but all it took was a quick glance at Ciara to erase it.

"Oh, why not? It'll be fun." She faced the backseat. "Sam wants to know if we'd like to go with him to the zoo."

"The zoo? Really?" Ciara bounced up and down. "You're right, Sam. The fun doesn't have to end yet! Finn and me, we haven't been to a zoo since we were really little. Where was that one, Finn?"

"Chicago, I think. Or Baltimore." She shrugged. "I forget."

He couldn't imagine living in so many places that what should have been standout childhood memories blurred into each other. Sam turned to Ciara. "So what's your favorite animal, kiddo?"

"Oh, the giraffes for sure. I just *love* watching them walk around on those long, skinny legs of theirs." She craned her neck to look out at the sooty sky. "Do you think we'll get rained on?"

Half a dozen sentences in a row without the halting, without word repetitions…

"The weatherman said we might get a storm after

supper," he said, "but we should be okay through the afternoon."

"Oh—oh, no. I—I hope it doesn't storm." Eyes shut tight, Ciara covered her ears. "I don't—I don't like thunder!"

Finn looked directly at her sister. "When we get inside the park, keep a lookout for a snack cart. We'll get you some peanuts to feed the giraffes."

Ciara picked up on her calm demeanor. "Okay, okay! That will be fun!" She giggled. "Remember the time when a giraffe tried to eat your hair?"

"*Tried* to eat it? I had a bald spot the size of a quarter for months!"

Sam turned off the radio because in his opinion, there was no sweeter music than Finn's laughter.

The threesome chatted amiably for the remainder of the drive to the zoo, then entered through a temporary entryway. Just beyond the Pardon Our Dust and New Entrance Opens Soon! signs, Ciara pointed out the peanut vendor. The brown paper sacks looked pretty small, so Sam bought two and handed one to Finn and the other to Ciara.

Half an hour into their tour, he noticed that Ciara was moving more slowly than usual. Finn must have seen it, too, for she slowed her pace and lingered longer than necessary at every enclosure on the Jungle Loop—even those that housed sleeping animals. His own leg felt pretty good for a change, but then, he'd taken ibuprofen before leaving the house.

He pointed north. "How would you ladies like to

ride the Wilderness Express? I read an article that said it'll take us places we can't see on foot."

Ciara considered the train and, frowning slightly, said, "But—but does that mean we have to walk all the way back to the gate?"

"No, ma'am. I took care of that when I got our tickets." He patted his shirt pocket. "Just so happens I have six tokens right here."

She held out her hand, and the instant he dropped two into her upturned palm, she planted both feet on the colorful Now Boarding train icon painted on the pathway.

"We're first in line for the next ride."

"Yup."

"I saw it go by before. I want to sit in the yellow car."

"Okay."

Her smile vanished, her expression taking on a blend of dread and worry. "Do—do you think our engineer will be drunk?"

Finn answered in his stead. "Drunk? Kee, what are you talking about?"

"I saw it on the news. The driver lady fell down and—and the passengers told her boss on her. They said the reason she fell down was—was because she was drinking during her lunch break. You know, Finn, *drinking*. Like Mom and Dad used to do."

Sam could have sworn he heard Finn mutter, "*Used* to?"

"I do *not* want to be in another crash," Ciara continued, "because of drunk driving!"

Sam silently cursed the parents, whose addictions were chiefly to blame for her condition and for her fears. Finn had been paying the price, too, for what happened that night. It didn't seem fair that the Learys got off scot-free.

"Don't you worry, kiddo," he said. "I saw that news story, too. The zoo fired the driver, so we're perfectly safe."

She worried her lower lip. "Are you—are you sure?"

"One hundred percent."

"Well, okay…if you say so…"

Ciara searched his face, no doubt seeking proof that she could take him at his word. He wanted her to trust him, and as he helped her into the yellow car, an unfamiliar mood descended, one he could only describe as *paternal*. He blamed it on his recent talks with Zach and Nate, who'd found happiness in life mates and impending parenthood.

Fatherly was the last word he'd use to explain his feelings for Finn, who could have walked a designer's runway in that pink dress. It brought out the pink in her cheeks…and accented every womanly curve.

He sat behind her, and since there was no chance she'd catch him staring, that was exactly what he did. He'd dated a brunette or two in his day. Had they been blessed with gentle waves that sparkled with strands of gold? If so, he hadn't noticed. The color of her hair reminded him of the chestnuts his grandmother used to oil up and roast on Christmas Eve. Her skin glowed, too. He'd give anything to find out if it felt as smooth and soft as it looked.

The train rounded the curve at the tiger enclosure, and every passenger leaned left to get a better look. Sam shook his head. *Get a grip, Marshall, or you're liable to fall outta this rig.*

By his guess, Ciara stood three inches taller and outweighed her older sister by twenty pounds. Seemed to Sam that if the powers that be intended Finn to carry such heavy burdens, they should have given her broader shoulders, instead of that petite, feminine physique.

Ciara leaned her head on Finn's shoulder. "How much farther to the giraffes?"

Finn pressed a gentle kiss to her temple. "Not much longer, Kee."

Sam leaned forward. "Are you wearing a watch?" he asked Ciara.

She wrapped her fingers around her left wrist. "Not today. It—it didn't match my outfit."

Chuckling, Sam removed his wristwatch. "Here," he said, handing it to her. "You keep an eye on the little hand, and when we get there, you can let me know how many minutes it took to reach the giraffes."

Finn smiled. "Now, why didn't I think of that?"

Three, maybe four inches separated them, and

the light was bright here, despite the awning over the train car. If those long, thick eyelashes had been the result of mascara, he'd know.

"Maybe because you're human and can't do everything all by yourself?"

Ciara laughed. "That's pretty funny, Sam."

"Oh, yeah? Why's that?"

"Because Pete used to tell her the same thing *all* the time. Didn't he, Finn?"

"Yes. Unfortunately, he did."

And from the sound of things, she hadn't enjoyed hearing it.

After snacks at the Snake Bite Café, the threesome headed for the zoo's parking lot.

Finn took Ciara's hand, then looked up at him. "Thanks, Sam, for making a good day even better."

"It isn't over yet," he repeated. "I need to get you two home before that sky opens up. But...but what would you say to dinner before I drop you off?"

She glanced at the darkening clouds. "You've already done too much. The Right Note is around the corner, and Ciara is exhausted."

He'd noticed, too. Much as he hated to see their time together end, Sam nodded.

"I have an idea..." Finn said.

"Oh?"

"Come to the apartment tonight and have supper with us."

"Tonight?"

"Mmm-hmm. We're having my homemade spaghetti and meatballs."

He licked his lips. "Spaghetti?"

Finn laughed. "We need to call the *Guinness* people."

"The *Guinness* people?"

"This has to be a historic event…an echo, in the great outdoors."

Ciara laughed. "That's a good one, Finn! An echo, 'cause Sam was—Sam was repeating everything you said!"

Smiling, he opened the passenger door and gave Ciara a hand getting into the back. "Buckle that seat belt now, hear?"

"Because we don't want you getting a ticket?"

"No…because we don't want you getting hurt."

Her grateful smile warmed him to the soles of his boots. But that couldn't compare to the heat he felt when he gave his hand to Finn, and she held on just a little longer than necessary, gently squeezing his fingers.

For the duration of the six-block drive to The Right Note, Ciara chattered about the things she'd seen at the zoo while Finn smiled, and Sam nodded. He parked in the back lot, and as Finn started to get out, he held up a forefinger.

"Let me flex my chivalry muscles, okay?"

She stayed put, those big eyes following every step as he walked around to her side of the pickup.

"So what time's dinner?" he asked, helping her down.

"We call it supper," Ciara corrected him, joining Finn on the blacktop. "Dinner is for Sunday. And Thanksgiving and Christmas."

"Ah, I see." He closed both passenger doors. "What time should I come back for supper?"

"Six."

"What can I bring?"

"Just your appetite."

"Hey," Ciara interrupted, pointing at the tiny landing at the top of the stairs.

Finn's eyes widened, and she whispered something, and he couldn't decide if she sounded more terrified or disgusted.

"Finn! There's a stranger up there, sleeping on our lounge chair!"

"I know, sweetie. I know." She ran a shaky hand through her hair. "Give me a minute to figure out what to do, okay?"

And then Sam heard her whisper, "Connor."

Ciara pointed again. "Don't worry, Finn. It isn't a stranger. It's Dad!"

Before she could respond, Connor stood and leaned into the railing. "I thought I heard voices down there," he called, waving.

Sam looked up at the man who'd neglected and abandoned his daughters. He glanced at Finn. She bit her lower lip. Was it resignation or defeat that darkened her eyes? He hated seeing her this way.

Wanted to *do* something to erase the past or, at the very least, make the present easier to bear.

"You gonna be okay?"

"Yes."

"We can reschedule…"

"No. Nothing should change just because he's here."

"Six o'clock, then?"

Finn nodded and left him alone near the truck. Frustration and helplessness swirled in his heart as she and Ciara joined Connor at the top of the stairs. He hoped Aggie had been wrong, because if she hadn't?

If she hadn't, it was already too late to save himself.

CONNOR STEPPED OVER his duffel bag. He pulled Ciara close and kissed both cheeks, then held her at arm's length. "Let me look at you, girl. My, my, my. You get prettier every year."

"Have you—have you been waiting long, Dad?"

"Two, maybe three hours." He made eye contact with Finn, who was standing at the edge of the landing. "Wouldn't have had to wait out here in the heat…if I had a key to the apartment. Where *were* you?" He drew her into the hug too. "When I saw the shape the diner is in, I got really worried!"

"I gave you a key last time you were here."

"Yeah." He sent her a sheepish grin. "Guess I lost it."

The way he'd lost the other five? And their cell phone numbers?

"I'm making spaghetti for supper," she said, unlocking the door.

He kick-shoved the duffel into the living room. "What time do we eat?"

"Six."

"But it's only three thirty…"

"It's okay, Dad," Ciara said. "I'll—I'll make you a sandwich to tide you over."

"That'd be great, honey." He followed his daughters into the kitchen, and as Finn washed her hands, he said, "I sure could go for a nice cold beer."

He knew she never kept alcohol in the house, and he knew why.

"I've got the drinking thing under control. Honest."

How many times have I heard that *one?*

"We have soda and iced tea," Ciara said. "And— and lemonade."

"Still making it from scratch?"

"Finn *always* makes it from scratch. I'll get you a glass."

Connor and Ciara sat at the table, talking about the weather while Finn opened cans of tomato paste, tomato sauce and diced tomatoes.

"I don't think I've ever seen you looking prettier," he said as the butter melted in Finn's Dutch oven. And as she chopped the onion, he complimented her sister's fingernail polish.

"You painted all those tiny dots, all by yourself?"

"No, Finn did it for me. She does it every week."

Finn added spices to the pot and told herself it was the onions, not Ciara's grateful little smile that made her eyes sting.

"I'm going to change into jeans," Ciara said.

Connor followed as far as the kitchen door and stood for a long time, silent and staring and shaking his head.

"She's come a long way, hasn't she?"

The lid hit the pan with more force than she'd intended. "Ciara works hard, and it shows."

"I think we both know who works hardest." He returned to his chair. "That crack earlier, about wanting a beer… It was a dumb thing to say."

For as long as she could remember, Connor had been saying things he didn't mean.

"I've been clean and sober for two months now." He held his right hand in the air. "Honest."

"You're back in AA, then?"

"Went to meetings every day…until I left to visit my best girls."

"Speaking of leaving, how did you get here? I didn't see a car out back."

"Hitchhiked, mostly, but I walked some, too. When I got to town, I looked up a pal. She fed me and…" Connor sipped his lemonade. "Then she dropped me off."

It hurt, hearing that he'd stayed in touch with his *pal* but not her and Ciara.

He propped one boot heel on the rung of Ciara's chair. "Heard from Misty lately?"

Ciara returned in time to say, "She's in Atlanta. She—she got a job singing, and—and playing guitar in a hotel lounge."

"Alone?"

"That's what I asked," Ciara said, grinning, "and she said, 'Just me and Gibson.'"

"Hard to believe she still has that beat-up old guitar."

Finn emptied a bag of salad fixings into a bowl. "How long has it been since *you* talked with her?"

"Not since that gig in Mobile. Seemed dumb, both of us trying to survive on one paltry paycheck and sharing that crummy room management put us up in. So I called a buddy in Orlando, and he hooked me up."

"How long were you in Florida?"

"Oh, I dunno, three months I guess, give or take a week."

"And you never thought to call, tell us where you were?"

"You've got my cell number," he said matter-of-factly. "So does Ciara. I figured if you needed me, you knew how to get in touch."

"Last time I tried calling, some random guy said I had the wrong number."

"Oh. Yeah. That must have been when I forgot to pay the bill."

She could have pointed out that providers didn't

reassign numbers after customers missed just one payment, but why put him in the position of telling yet another lie?

Ciara pulled a chair up close to Connor. "I'm so glad you're here, Dad. I really, *really* missed you!" She rested her head on his shoulder, and again, he kissed her temple.

"Missed you, too, Kee."

Kee? That was *her* special nickname for Ciara. How dare he waltz in here after months and months without so much as a postcard, and behave as if he'd never left!

He held up his tumbler and shook it until the ice cubes rattled against the glass. "Why don't you get your old dad a refill, honey?" he told Ciara. "Everybody knows how much your sister hates to be interrupted when she's busy."

"She—she does?" Ciara stopped halfway between the table and the fridge. "You do?"

She aimed a stern glare in her father's direction. "You, sweet girl," she said, softening as she faced Ciara, "have never been an interruption."

Ciara grabbed the lemonade pitcher. "I'm—I'm glad. I wouldn't want to be a bother."

"A bother? Impossible! You're my best friend!"

"You're my best friend, too!" Beaming, she refilled Connor's glass. "There you—there you go, Dad."

Did Connor ever feel guilty? Finn wondered, listening to Ciara's halting, repetitive speech, knowing it was *his* fault? She peeked over her shoulder. Evidently not, she thought, watching as he sat, one snakeskin boot resting on the opposite knee, nodding like a proud papa as his special-needs daughter accomplished the simple task.

Pete used to say Connor could charm the leaves from the trees. Would he fool Sam the way he'd fooled audiences from California to New York? Finn wasn't sure she wanted to find out.

She lowered the flame under the sauce pot and put the lid in place. "I'll be right back."

"Where are you going?"

"To change my clothes."

Behind the safety of her closed bedroom door, Finn dialed Sam's number, thinking to take his advice and reschedule the visit. Why draw the innocent guy into Leary family drama? She got a busy signal and decided to try again after she'd swapped her dress for jeans and a T-shirt.

Finn had just finished lacing up her sneakers when Connor barged in, closed the door behind him and sat on her desk chair. "Can I talk to you for a minute, honey?"

Dread settled over her. What bad news would he deliver, and why had he felt it necessary to hide it from Ciara?

Finn folded her sundress, put it into the hamper and sat on its lid.

He ran a hand through salt-and-pepper hair. "I,

ah, would it be all right if I crashed here with you girls for a while?"

"How long is a while?"

He shrugged. "Couple weeks, a month, maybe?"

"Okay, out with it. What happened in Orlando?"

Connor hung his head. "Lost my job."

Connor speak for *fired*. "Why?" As if she didn't know.

"Showed up late a few times. More than a few, actually."

Late, drunk and, if she had to guess, one too many creditors appearing, demanding to be paid. His story about attending AA meetings had been just that, Finn decided, and she was tired of his lies. Tired of his excuses. But he was her father, and like it or not, she couldn't very well turn him out into the street…even though he'd pretty much done the same to her and Ciara…

Finn got to her feet. "After supper, I'll make up the bed and clear some space in my closet and drawers for your things."

"Aw, honey, I can't put you out of your own room. I'll bunk down on the couch." He snickered nervously. "Believe me, it'll beat some of the places I've slept."

She didn't doubt that for a minute. But there was a method to her so-called generosity: if Connor took the couch, he could sneak out for booze any time he pleased; if he slept in her room, she'd catch him at it.

"I'd feel better if you stayed in here until you get a job and a place of your own."

"Speaking of jobs, I was kinda hopin' you'd find something for me at The Right Note."

Last time he blew into town, he'd talked her into letting him run the cashier's stand, and the cash drawer had been nearly two hundred dollars short when he blew out again.

"I haven't even interviewed contractors yet. It could be a month before we're up and running again. And, come on, you hate not being busy."

"Touché." Grinning, he got to his feet. "So you're really okay with it? Me staying with you guys for a while, I mean?"

"On two conditions…"

He pocketed both hands and waited.

"One, you'll look for work. *Really* look. And two, you'll go to meetings. Every. Single. Day."

"Well," he drawled, "First, I'll need to find out where—"

"AA is exactly where it was last time you were in town, and the meeting schedule hasn't changed, either." Finn knew, because every now and then, she attended an Al-Anon for-family-members gathering.

"Oh. Well. Good to know."

"Is it?"

"Sure, sure. Beggars can't be choosers, they say."

A glance at the alarm clock on her nightstand reminded her to try Sam again. Finn didn't leave a message this time, either. Just as well, because what could she say? Based on what little she'd heard about his family, he wasn't likely to forget *this* meal any time soon!

"I need to set the table and get the pasta water boiling. We're having company for supper."

He opened the door and stood aside as she walked into the living room. "Anyone I know?"

"I don't think so."

"Have you been seeing him long?"

"I only met him a few days ago. And I'm not *seeing him*. Sam and I are...friends."

In the kitchen, she saw that while she and Connor had been talking, Ciara had set the table and finished the salad. She stood, wide-eyed and shoulders up, waiting for Finn's approval.

"Aw, Kee! Everything looks terrific!"

Finn didn't mention that she'd mixed up the silverware placement. Or that the lettuce chunks were three times larger than any human mouth. Ciara had understood what needed doing, and she'd done all on her own.

"I wanted to—wanted to surprise you."

"Well, you sure did!" Finn drew her into a hug. "Thank you for helping. Now I'll have time for a cup of tea before I start the pasta."

Ciara pointed. "I filled the pot. Didn't turn it on, because I wasn't sure when to put in the noodles."

"You're amazing," Finn told her.

"Do you—do you think I did a good job, Dad?"

Finn realized he was about to point out Ciara's mistakes; she couldn't let him do that.

"Of course he does. She's something else, isn't she?"

Connor met her eyes, nodding as understanding dawned.

"Yup, you're something else, all right," he said, winking. "I'm mighty proud of you."

The doorbell chimed, halting any chance for him to say more and mess things up.

Finn turned Ciara toward the door. "Will you let Sam in and bring him to the kitchen?"

The minute she was out of earshot, Finn said, "Sometimes Ciara gets things backward. And sometimes she goofs them up entirely. But she tries real hard, so let's not point out her mistakes."

"If we don't, how will she ever learn the right way to do things?"

Oh, great...lessons in doing things the "right" way, from the man who's done everything wrong!

"I've figured out how to teach her without embarrassing or frustrating her, without any help from anyone but her doctor. I know you mean well, but unless she's in danger, let me handle things, please?"

"There's no denying you've done a great job with her. Why, last time I was here, she wouldn't have attempted anything like this."

Ciara, hand in hand with Sam, walked into the kitchen.

"This—this is Sam, Dad. He's our new friend.

He's a firefighter, and, and he teaches firefighters how to *be* firefighters. He took us to the zoo today. And isn't he handsome? He's a singer, just like you. And Rowdy says he's one of the bosses over at The—"

"Whoa, girl," Sam said, "you're gonna give me a swelled head."

Smart move, interrupting her, Finn thought. Because if Connor found out about The Meetinghouse partnership, he'd hit Sam up for a job, rob him blind and disappear. What would become of their friendship then?

"If I ever need a publicist, I'll know who to hire." Sam winked at Ciara, then extended a hand to Connor. "Good to meet you, sir."

"Good to meet you, too… Handsome Sam."

He'd turned on the charm full bore, from the big friendly smile to the hearty handshake. She had no idea how long he'd been in town before his *pal* dropped him off earlier; it was entirely possible that Connor was already aware of Sam's involvement with the club.

"And, please, call me Connor."

So it begins, Finn thought. *Don't fall for it, Sam. Please don't fall for it.*

CHAPTER THIRTEEN

"I MADE—I MADE the salad, Sam," Ciara announced. "And I set the table, too."

Winking, Sam gave her a thumbs-up. "Excellent work, kiddo. Excellent!"

"I did it to help Finn." She looked toward the sink, where Finn was draining the pasta into a colander. "So she could have an important talk with—with Dad." Hands clasped under her chin, Ciara squealed softly. "He's going to stay with us for a while. Right, Dad?" She beamed at Connor.

"Right, honey."

Somewhere under that machine-made tan, Connor blushed. Sam made note of the guilt in his dark eyes, too. From everything he'd heard, the man had good reason to feel guilty.

"How long will you be in town, Mr. Leary?"

His daughters waited with wide-eyed expectation for his answer.

"Connor, remember? Mr. Leary was my dad."

Ciara seemed disappointed by the nonanswer. And Finn? Finn rolled her eyes and turned back to the stove.

Connor propped his booted feet on a nearby chair and leaned back.

"Anything I can do?" Sam asked, joining Finn at the sink.

She leaned in close and whispered, "You can leave, save yourself from having to witness the Leary family drama."

Yet again, her situation reminded him how lucky he was to have parents and a family like his.

"And miss out on that?" he asked, pointing at the saucepot. "Not a chance."

"In that case, you could get the salad dressing out of the fridge."

He opened the door and inspected the bottles lining a lower shelf. "Any particular flavor?"

Ciara waved her hand like a girl in school. "French for me, French for me!"

Connor chimed in with "Italian."

Sam put their choices on the table. "And you, Finn?"

"Ranch, if there's any left."

"A girl after my own heart. Where have you been all my life?"

"She's been right here," Connor said. "Holding down the fort while her mom and I worked."

Finn shook her head—if Sam had blinked, he would have missed the quick, silent gesture that said it all: *save it, Dad.*

While Sam dropped ice into each glass, Connor bent at the waist and whispered to Ciara. "The forks belong on the left side of the plate, and the butter knives and spoons go on the right." He moved the utensils into their proper positions.

Finn whirled around and branded him with a stern glare.

"Aw, I'm sorry, Finn," Ciara said. "I thought, I thought, I thought the forks went—"

"You did a great job, Kee, and the table looks fine."

"But I wanted to do it *right*."

Finn wrapped her in a hug, then cupped her chin in a palm. "Would you pour the iced tea for me, sweetie?"

The distraction instantly changed Ciara's expression from hurt to delighted. Finn sure knew how to handle that girl, Sam thought.

"She'll be a wonderful, loving mother someday, don't you think?" Connor asked him, nodding at Finn.

If she gets the chance, with you and her mother putting up roadblocks.

He decided to change the subject. "I hear you're a songwriter?"

"That's right, Handsome Sam, and I hear *you're* a singer."

He didn't want to start out on the wrong foot with Finn's father, but if the guy didn't drop the stupid nickname...

"You *look* like a singer."

Now, how was he supposed to respond to *that*?

"You into sparkly suits and ten-gallon hats, or baseball caps and torn jeans?"

The other night in the diner, over pie and milk, Finn had underscored Mark's assertion that she didn't think much of musicians. Now that he'd met her father, Sam thought he understood why.

"I live by the KISS rule when I can," he said, hoping that would be the end of it.

It was not.

"How long have you been at it?"

"Got my first guitar for my twelfth birthday." Sam grinned slightly, remembering the wrapping paper with horses and cowboy hats—and the yards of blue ribbon—that his mom had used to cover the case.

"You play for pay, or just for fun?"

Finn was mixing sauce into the pasta, not nearly distracting enough to keep her from hearing his reply, so Sam chose his words carefully.

"I get onstage when I can…long as it doesn't interfere with my teaching."

Connor leaned back as Finn plopped a thick pot holder onto the table.

"I just got in from a gig in Florida, myself. Needed a change of scenery."

There was more to it than that. A whole lot more, if Finn's raised eyebrow was any indicator.

"So I thought, why not spend some time with my beautiful daughters while I wait for the next offer to roll in?"

Gut instinct warned Sam to exercise extreme caution when dealing with Connor Leary. He'd met the type before: good-looking, reasonably talented, likable enough to bluff his way through just about anything, with just about anyone.

Anyone but Finn, that was.

No sooner had she put the spaghetti pot in the center of the table than Connor grabbed the fork and served himself. "Hey, Kee, pass the Parmesan, will ya?"

The girl happily obliged as Sam filled her plate, then Finn's. And as she joined them at the table, he grasped the sisters' hands. "Mind if I say a quick blessing?"

"I think—I think that's a great idea, Sam!" Ciara gushed.

Finn answered with a happy, surprised smile.

As for Connor, at least he had the common sense to stop stuffing his face.

"We're thankful for this meal and the beautiful women who prepared it—" he gave Finn's fingertips a gentle squeeze "—and for friendship."

Connor, not to be outdone, added, "And for a roof over our heads and clean sheets on our beds. Good food, good meat, good God, let's eat!"

Sam didn't think he'd ever met a more self-centered man. His daughters might have to treat him with deference, but *he* didn't.

"So you never got around to telling us how long you'll be in town, Connor."

"That depends entirely on the generosity of my eldest daughter." He patted Ciara's hand. "Right, Kee?"

With what Sam could only call complete clarity, Ciara said, "Finn always—always does what's right. Finn always does what's best. Because she loves everyone more than herself." She looked at Connor to add, "It's what Pete said *all* the time." She sent a loving glance to her sister. "And he was right."

Finn's eyes welled with tears, and she smiled. "Sam, would you pass the ranch, please?"

When he handed it off, their fingers touched for a split second...long enough for a slight tremor to pass from her to him. The urge to pull her to her feet and gather her near washed over him like a tidal wave.

"Sam?"

He looked at Ciara. "Hmm?"

"Why are—why are you staring at Finn that way?"

Sam pretended to flick an eyelash from her cheek. "There. That's got it." He picked up his glass, and as he drained it, he wished it was big enough to hide him from the three pairs of dark eyes watching him. Closely.

Connor snickered. "Why, I do believe Handsome Sam here is sweet on our Finn."

"What does—what does that mean?"

"It means," Sam said softly, "that Finn and I are friends. Good friends."

Ciara's shoulders slumped.

"Aw, why do you look so sad, Kee?"

"Because, Dad, I was hoping they'd fall in love. And get married."

Finn's big eyes locked on Sam's. "Oh, wow, I'm… I'm *so* sorry."

"Me—me, too, Sam."

He patted Ciara's hand, then turned to Finn. "So tell me, maker of the best spaghetti I've ever tasted, what's for dessert?"

He had a feeling he'd carry that wide-eyed, grateful look with him for days.

And nights.

CHAPTER FOURTEEN

"YOU HAVE NO idea how good it is to hear your voice, kiddo."

"Uh-oh, what mess have you gotten yourself into this time, big brother?"

He propped his boot heels on the railing and settled back in the deck chair. "No mess. Just missing home a mite more than usual."

"Then, pack up your guitar and get back here! You know we'd all love that...none better than Mom and Dad."

"Can't just bail on my students." Or Mark, he thought. And with Connor Leary in town—

"So how are things out there?" his sister asked. "You seeing anyone?"

"Nope." At least, not in the traditional sense. "Are you?"

Sophie laughed. "Yes and no."

"If he's making you miserable, I can be there in three hours."

"He's fine. It's me who's making *him* miserable."

Sam sipped his iced tea. "A quiet, demure, easy-going gal like you, making a man miserable?" He chuckled. "I find that hard to believe."

"Save your sarcasm for someone who appreci-
ates it."

"What's his name?"

"Ben."

"Not too-nice-for-his-own-good Ben Stewart..."

She sighed. "One and the same."

"He's a good kid."

"I know."

"A gentleman."

"I know."

"From a good family."

"I know, I know, I *know*!"

"So what's the problem? Isn't he tall enough for
you?" Sophie was nearly as tall as Sam, measuring
in at five feet ten and a half inches.

"He's six-three."

"Too fat, then?"

"He has a terrific physique."

"Well, it can't be 'cause he's a slacker. He's still
VP of his dad's hardware chain, right?"

"It isn't his work ethic. Or his looks. Or his family ties. Ben is wonderful."

"Then, I repeat—what's the problem?"

"I'm high maintenance. Everybody says so. Ben
shouldn't have to work so hard at, well, at making
the relationship work."

"Then, stop making him work so hard."

"That's not my point."

"Still, seems to me that's the simplest solution to

your problem." He paused to give her time to think on that. "Right?"

Sophie sighed. "I suppose."

"You know what Mom would say if you put this issue on *her* table?"

"'If you live by the Golden Rule, you'll never need another,'" they said together.

"She's right, Sophie."

"I know."

This time, it was Sophie who paused. "So what's her name?"

"Whose name?"

"The woman who put you in such a funk."

"I'm not in a—"

"Please. I haven't heard you sound this way since you broke up with Miss Priss."

"Suzanne."

"Whatever."

"And I didn't break things off—she did." Sam pictured Suzanne as she'd looked that night...tall, buxom, blonde and blue-eyed, and all wrapped up in the arms of J. D. Caruthers.

"If you think I'm hanging up before you tell me who she is, you're sadly mistaken."

High maintenance or not, Sophie had always been a good listener. Sympathetic when a situation called for it, to the point when she needed to be. What could it hurt to tell her about Finn? Might be nice to get another viewpoint on things—a woman's viewpoint.

Sam started by describing her, then eased into an explanation of how they'd met and the events that had led up to her ownership of The Right Note. "Then, a couple nights ago, a tree fell on her diner and—"

"Not that big beautiful tree on Broadway, where all the musicians take turns entertaining the tourists!"

"One and the same. The city has been nursing it along for years, but that storm the other night was more than it could handle."

"That must have been scary. And upsetting."

"Yeah, but she took it on the chin. It's what she does."

"I like her, sight unseen!"

"She's antimusician."

"All of them? Even *you*?"

"Even me."

"Hmph. I like her a little less now, passing judgment without giving you a chance."

"Well, in all fairness, I sort of understand her reservations. I haven't met her mother yet, but I got more than my fill of her dad tonight. He's a recovering alcoholic."

"Did she tell you that?"

"Didn't have to. I know the signs."

"Ah, because of Mark's brother, Eli. But…"

"But what?"

"Are you worried about that?"

"Why would I be? Finn drinks coffee and tea, but I've never seen her touch anything stronger."

"Think maybe she's on the wagon?"

He thought about Finn's long list of responsibilities. "No way."

"Avoiding temptation, then, in case she inherited her folks' tendencies?"

"Never gave it a thought," he admitted. "But if that's the case, I admire her for making that decision."

"What about the sister?"

"She's a sweetheart. You'd love her. Not a mean bone in her body. Not even toward that so-called father of theirs."

"He didn't beat the girls when he was drunk, I hope."

"No, I don't think he did. But Ciara's brain injury is his fault. Got hammered one night and drove the family car off the highway and into the trees. She was barely out of the hospital when both parents hit the bricks, leaving Finn to keep a roof over their heads and food in their bellies. In my book, that's abuse of a different sort."

"Wow. Just...*wow.* And exactly where are these Parents of the Year?"

"I have no clue where their mother is. Their father—and I use the term loosely—just rolled into town after months without a word, hoping to sponge off Finn until he finds, and I quote, 'a new gig.'"

"Wow," she said again. "That's some rough stuff."

He heard a *but* in her tone and expected her to recite a different version of Aggie's warning. Nothing could have surprised him more than when Sophie said, "Have you told *her* how you feel?"

"No, because I don't know how I feel."

"Give me a break. The way you were talking about her just now?" Sophie harrumphed.

"She's a great gal."

"So you said."

"Gorgeous, too."

"Uh-huh."

"With a heart bigger than the Double M."

"So…"

"So…what?"

"Is she a good kisser?"

Sam licked his lips.

"You came close a time or two?"

The memory of Finn all wrapped up in his arms the night of the storm hit him hard. "A time or two, I guess."

"Answer me this, brother dear—how many women have made you feel this way?"

"What way?"

Sophie growled into the phone. "Sam Marshall, are you being obtuse on purpose?"

"Obtuse?"

"You can be *so* exasperating!"

Sam chuckled, imagining her face puckered and fists clenched, maybe even stomping one big foot as she spoke.

"Wait just a minute here," she said. "Didn't you tell me that she mistrusts musicians? Is *that* what's bugging you? You think she'll reject you because you yodel and pluck the guitar strings now and then?"

"Holy smokes, Soph, give a guy a little credit, will ya?" Sam laughed. "I do a bit more than *that*."

"Okay. All right. So you've written a few tunes—pretty good ones, I'll admit—and you were blessed with stage presence and a decent voice. Now that you own part of a nightclub, you'll get to prove it any time you please. And I'll bet my beautiful new Reinsman saddle Finn doesn't know any of that, does she?"

Sam could only shake his head. "See, this is the trouble with having a sister who's one of your best friends. She can read you like a book."

"*One* of your best friends?"

"Well, there's Mark, but he's a guy."

"Wait until Mr. Flirty hears that!"

"You won't tell him."

"Oh, I won't, huh?"

"Because then he'll know you were talking about him. Guys love knowing cute girls are talking about them. You think he was flirty last time you visited… just wait…"

She giggled. "Speaking of, what does *Mark* say about Finn?"

"Not much." Because he didn't know much, Sam was forced to admit.

"Oh, good grief. You just met this Finn person, didn't you?"

"Leary. Her name is Finn Leary. And of course I didn't just meet her." It had been weeks since he tripped her in her own place of business.

"Oh, good *grief*," she repeated. "Would you believe Ben just pulled up out front?"

"Golden Rule," he reminded her.

"Seems to me you ought to take your own good advice."

"Huh?"

"How would you like it if Finn kept a bunch of secrets from you?"

"Secrets? What secr—"

"You'd hate it, that's what. So take her to dinner. Someplace nice. Spell it all out. If she takes it well—including the part about your partnership with Mark—you're good to go. If she doesn't, you'll spare yourself a world of hurt." Sophie paused. "Why doesn't she know about the partnership anyway?"

"She does, sort of, I think."

"Oh, good grief. You're giving me a headache. I need to go, big bro. But we'll talk again real soon. I *promise*."

He knew what that meant: Sophie aimed to check on him, maybe even nag him if necessary, until he came clean with Finn.

"But before I hang up… You gave me some good advice, earlier, so let me repay you in kind—you and Finn *both* deserve to hear the truth. Even if it hurts. The longer you put things off, the more painful it'll be if she rejects you."

If Finn rejected him, it would be more than painful—whether he waited or not.

He heard the doorbell, and she finished with, "Love you, Sam. Be happy, okay?"

"Love you, too. And ditto."

What Sophie had said made a lot of sense. Especially that part about the folly of prolonging the inevitable, good or bad.

Sam glanced at the clock. Only a little past nine. Finn didn't seem the type to hit the hay early. The only question remaining, really, was whether he should call first, or just show up.

CHAPTER FIFTEEN

"BOY, CIARA SURE was tuckered out. You and Sam must have walked her poor legs off today."

"Don't worry. We took breaks. Rode the train. Had a nice, leisurely meal." When Finn had checked on her sister earlier, she'd been fast asleep and smiling. If anyone deserved sweet dreams, it was Ciara.

"Sam seems like a nice guy."

Finn put away the spaghetti pot. "He's nice enough. But let's not forget, Connor, he's a *musician.*"

He cringed. "First of all, it isn't fair to judge 'em all by your mom and me. And second, do you have to call me Connor?"

"What do you suggest I call you?"

"Oh, I dunno…" He made a silly face. "How 'bout *Dad*?"

The last time he'd behaved like a father, Finn was ten and Ciara four. He'd found a rusty old swing set at a yard sale and spent the better part of a weekend assembling it in the backyard. After supper every night of the following week, he'd pushed them until she believed her toes might pierce the clouds, then twisted the chains until the world became a dizzying blur. The week had ended on a sour note as he and Misty announced they were moving to Abilene.

A grueling ten-hour drive had brought them to a dark, dingy dive, where a wheezing old man had grumbled that for every five hours they worked, he'd give them twenty dollars, all the booze they could drink and cigarettes they could smoke, and the keys to a room behind the bar. The door had creaked, and so had the floor, both lumpy double beds and every drawer in the cockeyed dresser. The place had smelled like dirty ashtrays and sweaty socks, and the black-and-white TV had pulled in just one snowy channel. If not for the wild-haired, tattooed waitress who sneaked them burgers and sodas and chased off the boozers who mistook their new home for the bathroom... Finn shuddered, considering what might have become of her and Ciara.

"You're awfully quiet."

His voice brought her back to the here and now—a decidedly better place, despite the route it had taken to get here.

"Ciara would love it if you called me Dad."

How like him to use poor, sweet Kee to get what he wanted.

"She told me it makes her sad when you call me Connor."

Finn believed it, but only because Ciara had told her the same thing.

"Okay, then, let's strike a deal—you stay sober for a month, and I'll call you Dad." It would be an easy promise for him to keep, because if things ran true to course, he'd leave before the week was up.

He pulled her into a hug. "Deal."

The too-familiar scent of whiskey wafted into her nostrils. Finn stepped back and glared at him. "Where did you get the booze, *Dad*?"

He hung his head. "Brought it with me."

She jogged into the living room and rooted through his duffel until she found the bottle, then marched into the kitchen and unscrewed its cap.

"Hey, hold up there, honey. I barely cracked the seal on that."

He looked as if he might cry as the whiskey went *glug-glug-glug* on its way to the sewer…where it belonged.

"Finn, honey, be reasonable."

She dropped the empty bottle into the trash.

"Our agreement begins right now—you're welcome to stay…as long as you keep your promise."

Connor groaned, driving all ten fingers through his hair. "Yeah, all right, okay."

He seemed sad. Broken. Pathetic. And none too pleased with her tendency to treat him like a son, rather than a father. *Well, guess what,* Dad, *I don't much like it, either.* But what choice had he left her? The rules were as much for his well-being as for hers and Ciara's. If he couldn't see that…

Finn didn't like feeling resentful one minute, guilty the next. Despite Connor's faults and failings, she loved him!

Finn had been about nine when her parents had cut their one and only record together, a remake of a 1950s hit. She'd memorized every word, and for some strange reason the maudlin lyrics comforted little-girl Ciara when storms rattled the windows or a scary movie made her believe in monsters under the bed. A week or so ago, Finn had caught herself humming the melody, but for the life of her, she couldn't remember the lyrics. Except for the last line, which went something like "all I'm guilty of is loving you."

"I'm going to do it this time. I know you've heard that before, but things are different now. *I'm* different now."

He looked every bit like a penitent little boy, and she felt guilty about that, too.

"I love you, Dad." She hugged him. Tight. "I've missed you like crazy, and I'd like nothing more than to have you stay with us permanently…" Tears threatened, and a sob formed in her throat. "I don't want to lose you to that stuff," she said, holding him at arm's length. "So I hope you mean it this time. If not for your sake, for Ciara's. And mine."

There were tears in his eyes, too. "You've got my word, baby girl. This time, I'm really gonna try."

She understood that it was Connor's way of telling her he'd stay clean…until he couldn't. She'd drive herself insane trying to fight this battle for him.

She put her hand on his shoulder. "Traveling all

day took its toll on you. Let me put some fresh sheets on the bed so you can get some shut-eye."

"I told you, I'll be fine on the couch."

And have you sneak out to buy another bottle while I'm sleeping? No way!

"I haven't taken care of you in ages." *Because you haven't been around.* Finn backpedaled toward the hallway. "So let me do this for you."

Connor's smile, sad and slow, touched a long-forgotten chord inside her. She didn't have much reason to believe that he'd get clean and stay that way, but without hope, what did she have?

He followed her into the bedroom, and together, they stripped the bed.

"I have to interview contractors tomorrow, one after the other, starting at nine. You can come with me if you like, let me know what you think of them."

"That might be fun."

Fun was hardly the word she'd use.

"After they've delivered their quotes, we'll grab a bite to eat. We can bring my laptop so you can start looking for work."

He snorted. "And end up communicating with some creep online?"

"Well, if that doesn't appeal to you, you'll just have to pound the pavement, check out pubs in person to see if anyone's hiring singers or guitarists. *Or,*" she emphasized, "you could do something different."

"Like what? I'm only good at one thing."

Two things, she thought. *Drinking and breaking your promises.* Unfortunately, nobody would pay him for that.

"Something will turn up," Connor said. "It always does." He shooed her from the room. "If you insist on giving up your bed, the least I can do is make it. Now git. Put up your feet. Find an old Western on the TV, and soon as I'm through here, we'll watch it together."

The way they had when she was small…

"Let me do this for you, please?"

He shrugged and nodded, then said over his shoulder as he left the room, "Might be too little, too late, but I'm going to make things up to you and Ciara."

When Finn returned to the living room, she found him stretched out in the recliner, dozing while some show about Alaska flickered on the screen. She relieved him of the remote and gave his shoulder a gentle nudge.

"You're all set."

He dropped the footrest and got up, yawned and stretched, then chucked her cheek. "Thanks, honey. You're an angel. Dunno what I ever did in my miserable life to deserve a kid like you, but if I figure it out, I'm gonna do it over and over and over again."

Finn pretended she hadn't heard it all a hundred times before. "G'night, Dad. Sweet dreams."

As her bedroom door clicked shut, Finn flapped a sheet over the couch. She hoped it wasn't a mistake, allowing him back into their lives. How many more disappointments could Ciara handle?

"Who are you kidding?" she muttered, shaking a pillow into its case. "*You* can't handle another disappointment, either."

She'd barely dropped the pillow on to her make-shift bed when a soft knock sounded at the door. The clock said nine twenty. "Oh, please, don't let it be Misty," she whispered. "*Please*, don't let it be Misty."

Parting the gauzy curtains covering the window beside the door, Finn peered outside...and directly into the big blue eyes of Sam Marshall.

She opened the door a few inches. "Did you forget something?"

"No."

So then why was he here?

Sam pocketed one hand. "If you have a few minutes, there's something I'd like to run past you."

Finn opened the door a little wider. "Oh?"

Moths, drawn to the porch light, circled his head. Squinting, Sam batted at them. "If you're not gonna let me in, would you mind turning off that beacon?"

Finn opened the door all the way. "We'll have to keep our voices down. Ciara and Connor are asleep. Well, Ciara is asleep. I have no idea what Connor might be up to in there." She gestured toward her room.

"Kitchen?" he asked, easing the door shut.

Finn led the way. "What can I get you? Pie? Tea? Soda?"

"Water will do." He patted his flat stomach. "I'm still stuffed from supper."

"Ah, a quick learner, I see."

One eyebrow rose slightly.

"Ciara's definition of dinner?"

He smiled. Not a forced Connor-type grin, but a genuine, full-faced smile that warmed her all the way through. Ciara was right: his eyes *did* sparkle.

She considered apologizing again for Ciara's off-the-wall comments about love and marriage, but thought better of it. If she still kept a diary, as she had as a girl, that moment would go down as one of the most embarrassing of her life.

"Your contractor friends seem conscientious," she told him.

"Yeah?"

"They'll all be at The Right Note tomorrow morning. Nine, nine thirty and ten o'clock." She handed him a bottle of water. "Do they know one another?"

"Al and Jerry were in the same class at the academy. Don't know about Paul."

"So if the appointments overlap, a fistfight won't break out?"

"Nah. They're good people. At least, they were good in class. What kind of businessmen they are when they're not fighting fires…" He shrugged.

She sat across from him. "I kind of got the impression they'd worked for you."

"For Mark. At The Meetinghouse. Which is one of the things I wanted to talk with you about."

"The Meetinghouse?" Finn pictured the club's two-story brick exterior, the exposed-beamed ceiling. "I've only been there once. And only in the daytime. One of his guys—the drummer, I think—was getting married. I made and delivered a couple of platters for the bachelor party."

"Sometimes Mark is a goofball. Why would he hire a caterer when he has a fully staffed kitchen and a well-trained staff right there?" He winced. "Not that I begrudge you the work. I'm sure the food was great."

Finn smiled. "I have to admit, I wondered the same thing. But I've never been one to pass up a job. Especially one that could bring me future business."

"And did it?"

"No, but I'm not surprised. Musicians are…" Finn had already hit him with that particular hammer. What good could possibly come from whacking him again?

She was grateful that Sam changed the subject. "Your dad said he was in Florida. Miami? Tampa?"

"Orlando. Misty was down there with him for a while, but she got a better offer from somebody in Atlanta. Not that I heard any of that firsthand, mind you."

"Misty…your mother?"

"Yeah, I guess you could call her that."

His expression changed from mildly curious to surprised. *That's what happens when you share private family business with a stranger.*

"You grew up in Denver?"

"The family's ranch is twenty-some miles southwest of the city."

"We spent a whole week on a ranch when I was about twelve. Somewhere in Montana. Or maybe Idaho."

"Sounds like you moved around a lot."

"No more than your average army brat. It wasn't all bad, though. I met some great people, saw some beautiful sights." She sipped her water. "How about you? Did your family move much?"

"Nope, never. My ancestors settled the land during the 1800s, and the Marshall clan grows deep, deep roots."

His expression softened, making it clear that he loved the place and the people who called it home. Just one more bit of proof in her mind that musicians weren't to be trusted. Nothing—not even a beloved home and family—would stand in the way of their dreams of stardom.

Finn envied him a little and tried to imagine what it would have been like, living in one place for decades, instead of weeks or months. And thanked the good Lord that she'd had Ciara to make it more tolerable.

"Do you have brothers and sisters?"

"Three sisters, two older and one younger. And two cousins who've always been more like brothers to me. Zach and Nate and I spent every spare minute together as kids." Another quiet laugh, and then, "We got into some crazy situations. Crazy enough that everybody for miles around would see us and say, 'Lock up the good china…here come those Marshall boys!'"

Finn couldn't help but smile at the obviously fond, fun memories…even though she envied him, just a little bit.

"And they all stayed at the ranch?"

"Zach joined the marines after graduation, did a couple tours of duty in Afghanistan. He lived in Vail for a while, teaching women how to defend themselves against predators, but he's home now. He and his wife just had a baby. Nate left for a while, too. Spent a few years on the East Coast, pitching for a major-league baseball team. But he's home now, too, making plans to marry Eden. She's a counselor of some kind…teenage boys. After the wedding, they'll adopt the lot of 'em."

"How many are there?"

"Twelve, thirteen? I forget. Good kids, though. Especially considering what their lives were like before Eden got hold of them."

Finn wouldn't mind meeting the couple who'd saved a dozen wayward kids. Wouldn't mind meeting the boys, either, because there had been plenty of times when she'd almost taken the wrong fork in the road.

"How did you end up in Nashville, of all places?"

"Same as most folks, I reckon. Had a knack for stringing words together and matching them up with notes and chords." He shrugged. "Not well enough to earn a living at it, though. I'd been a volunteer firefighter back home, so I took a chance that what I'd learned there would give me an in here, with the NFD."

"And it did."

"Not right away. Had to go to school, as they say. Pay my dues. Put in the time."

"How long were you on the job before you were injured?"

It must have been the weight of memories that turned down one corner of his mouth. Turned off the sparkle in his eyes, too. It made Finn wish she hadn't asked the question.

"Are you sure you wouldn't like a slice of pie?"

"I'm sure."

He twisted the water bottle's cap—on, off, on, off—without removing it. It dawned on her that Sam had come here tonight to tell her something. Or ask her something. And her inquisition had gotten in the way of that.

"So you had something to run by me?"

"Oh. Right. That." He slapped a hand to the back of his neck, then leaned forward, hands clasped on the table. "This thing you have about musicians…"

It wasn't a *thing*. It was a decision, made years ago, after her parents and their so-called friends, not to mention Finn's so-called boyfriend back then, let her down. Big-time. And repeatedly.

"Is it a hard and fast rule for full-time professionals? Or is there some wiggle room for guys like me, who only…dabble?"

"You'll have a hard time convincing me you *dabble* at anything."

He stroked his chin. "Not sure I follow you."

She liked him. Respected him, too, not only because of his career choice, but because he'd back-burnered his Nashville dreams to stick with it. Ciara stuttered and stammered far less around him, and Finn had learned to rely on her sister's "good people" barometer. Sam could become a friend to both of them…if she didn't blow it by lumping him in with others who'd proved themselves untrustworthy.

"Let's just say I admire your sticking power."

"Sticking power?"

"I haven't met very many people in this town with that quality. So if you're here to ask if you and Ciara and I can be friends, the answer is yes."

He traced the swirls on the red Formica tabletop. And he still wasn't smiling.

"So what was it like, growing up in the shadow of the Rockies?" she tried.

"Humbling."

She'd expected him to describe the vista. The wildlife. The ever-changing weather that defined the mighty mountain range. Instead, with just one quietly reverent word, he'd acknowledged how insignificant and powerless he felt by comparison. It gave her yet another reason to respect him.

"How's this for an idea… I was planning a trip home over the Christmas holidays, but my sister talked me into going for Thanksgiving instead. Why don't you and Ciara come with me? My folks have a guest room with twin beds. And I have a boatload of frequent flier miles racked up."

Well, *that* came out of the blue! "As wonderful as that sounds, I have a business to run."

"Aw, Rowdy can handle things for a couple of days, can't he?"

He probably could…if she'd let him.

"Well, November's a long way off yet. You don't have to decide right now."

"Are you kidding? It's nearly September, and you know how time flies!"

Sam got to his feet, and she followed suit.

"There's something else I need to tell you…"

Please, don't say you just signed a record deal!

"Do you know Mark's brother?"

"Eli? Yes, I've met him a time or two." An alcoholic musician, he reminded her of Connor, so she'd kept her distance.

"He's going on tour with Duke Miller and wanted out of The Meetinghouse partnership. That left Mark in the lurch, so he asked me to buy into the business."

So he'd said yes to Mark's offer that day in the diner. He wasn't "just" a musician anymore. Surrounded by others who shared his dreams, night after night, how long before he followed Eli's example?

"Are you a full partner?"

"More or less. Mark and Torry are old hands at running the place. My job is to make sure the amps and mics are plugged in, see to it no one can trip over the wires. The guys know, of course, but that's it…and I'd like to keep it on the down-low. Last thing I need is a bunch of hopefuls hanging around, hoping I can get them an audition with agents or producers."

"Because if you had the power to do that, you'd do it for yourself, right?"

In the silence that followed her question, Finn had a horrible thought: if Connor found out, they'd all pay a price, but none more than Sam.

"I need to ask you a favor, Sam."

"Anything."

Judging by that look on his face, he meant it, even before hearing what she might ask of him. Oh, to have some assurance that Sam was as good and decent as he seemed!

"Promise me you won't tell my father that—"

Connor padded into the room on white-socked feet, scratching his head with one hand, his chest with the other.

"Don't tell your father what?" he said around a

yawn. After helping himself to a bottle of water, he faced Sam and frowned slightly. "Don't tell me *what*?"

"That I, ah, that I'm taking your girls out for a night on the town. Dinner at Old Hickory and a show at the Opry. Next week. I only had three tickets, though, and Finn didn't want you to feel left out."

"It'll take one heckuva lot more than missing dinner and a show to hurt this old buzzard's feelings. Besides, it'll be nice having the apartment all to myself for a couple of hours."

He must have realized how ungrateful that sounded because he quickly said, "That's really it, honey? You thought I'd feel left out?"

"Pretty much, yeah."

Finn added another item to her Reasons to Resent Connor list: he'd put Sam in the awkward position of lying to spare his feelings, which forced her to compound the lie with one of her own.

Faced with this new bit of information, Connor adopted a concerned, contrite expression. He put down the water and gave her a sideways hug.

"This nose-to-the-grindstone girl of mine could use a night out. So thanks." He let her go and re-trieved the bottle. "Don't stay too late, Sam. Finn has big, important decisions to make first thing in the morning and needs her sleep."

When he was out of sight, Finn hung her head.

Sam crouched to meet her eyes. "I mean no disrespect, because he's your father, after all, but I've met his type before. So don't worry."

Interesting word, *worry*.

"I hope you're a Garth Brooks fan, because I have it on good authority that he's in town next week."

He had the most soothing voice, deep and mellow and mesmerizingly slow. If she didn't know better, Finn would say Sam was trying to hypnotize her. *If you're not careful*, she warned herself, *that'll happen whether or not you* let *it.*

"Garth Brooks, performing at the Opry," she repeated.

"Shh...it's a surprise guest spot. Only reason I know is because I'm pals with the band that's his opening act."

"He's Ciara's favorite entertainer."

"I'd call that a lucky break."

She hid a yawn, and he said, "Your dad made a good point—you have lots to do tomorrow, so I'll let you hit the hay."

Side by side, they walked toward the door. "We'll work out the details later," he said. "Just be sure you wear something pretty, like you did today."

The implied compliment made her heart flutter. *Stop it, you ninny. Stop it right now.*

"So you're serious, then. That story wasn't just something you cooked up on the spot for Connor's benefit?"

"Trust me, okay?"

To start a mad scramble for last-minute tickets?

"I thought you needed reservations weeks in advance at Old Hick—"

Sam pressed a fingertip to her lips, effectively silencing her. "Such a suspicious little thing." He took a step closer.

As Finn looked up at him, his arms went around her. And she didn't fight it.

"Even if that were true, *some* dabbling musicians have connections."

"Oh?"

He bracketed her face with big, tender hands. And she let him.

He drew gentle circles on her cheek with his thumb. It had been a long time—too long—since she'd felt safe and cared for. Finn liked the feeling. Liked it far too much.

"So, it's a date then?"

She shrugged one shoulder. "Who could say no to Garth Brooks?"

His lips were touching hers when he said, "Garth who?"

Then he kissed her, soft and long and sweet…

…and she let him.

CHAPTER SIXTEEN

"WHAT'S WRONG, KEE? Another headache?"

Ciara sat on the couch, rubbing her temples. "Yeah. It isn't—isn't as bad as last time, though." She sent Finn a feeble smile. "Hey. There are two of you. That's pretty funny, huh, Finn?"

Finn did her best not to show her concern. "Two of me? Before my first cup of coffee? I'm surprised you didn't say scary instead of funny!" She sat beside Ciara. "How long have you been seeing two of everything?"

"Just, just since I woke up." She pointed. "Two TVs, two recliners, two *Starry Night* prints on the wall..." Ciara laughed softly, then hugged her knees and hid her face in the crook of one elbow. "Ugh," she said. "It makes—it makes me kinda dizzy."

Finn grabbed her cell phone and scrolled to Ciara's doctor's number. While waiting for the call to connect, she wondered what test he'd missed. In her quest to solve the puzzle of Ciara's recurring headaches, Finn had pushed for every imaginable analysis to rule out food allergies, vision problems and eyestrain, and reaction to her antiseizure medications. She'd been vigilant about protecting her sister from stress, bright lights, too much TV.

It didn't surprise her when, immediately following the fallen-tree episode, Ciara had voluntarily turned in early, or that when Connor showed up from out of the blue—after nearly eight months without a word—she'd asked for an ibuprofen. But double vision? That was a new and disturbing development.

Finally, a nurse answered, and because Ciara sat close enough to hear every word, Finn matter-of-factly explained the problem. Some might call her overprotective, but she didn't care. If Ciara so much as sniffled, she saw the doctor. Finn sensed the unease in the woman's voice.

"I'm sure Dr. Peterson will want to see her ASAP. I'll call you back, Finn, just as soon as I find a way to squeeze her in."

Hours later, following a thorough exam, Dr. Peterson called ahead to the Vanderbilt University Medical Center and ordered an immediate MRI *and* a CT scan. "Mostly as a precaution," he whispered to Finn. "Double vision might be as simple as scar tissue putting pressure on the optic nerve." But she'd gotten to know him well, too, and picked up on the apprehension in his voice: the symptom could be a lot more serious than that.

Now, as she listened to the radiographer's fingers tapping his computer keys, Finn tried not to fidget. From her vantage point near the back wall, she watched her sister on the monitor, eyes closed and humming along with the music wafting from her headphones. Much as she detested sedatives, Finn agreed that the mild tranquilizer would help Ciara remain still throughout the tests.

During the ten-minute drive between the hospital and home, Ciara leaned forward in the passenger seat and pointed skyward.

"I can't—can't believe it's going to rain *again*." She exhaled a long, shaky sigh. "I'm tired of rain." Turning slightly, she added, "Can cloudy weather cause headaches?"

I sure hope it's that simple. "I suppose." Finn reached across the console and patted her sister's hand. "In a few days, the results from all those tests will be back, and we'll have a better idea what's going on in that pretty little head of yours."

"Maybe. And—and maybe not." She sighed again. "Remember what Dr. Peterson said?"

"He said a lot."

"He said—he said, 'We'll do everything we can to get to the bottom of this. But don't put all your hopes in a couple of—of test results.'"

How had she heard Peterson's warning through the closed door of the changing room?

"You barely touched your scrambled eggs this morning. Bet you're hungry now, aren't you?"

"Yeah—yeah, I am."

Relieved to hear Ciara still had an appetite, Finn said, "We'll grab a couple of burgers, take them home and eat while we watch an old movie. How's that sound?"

"Like—like we did when I was little?"

"Yup, just like when you were a little girl."

It hurt like crazy to admit it, but Ciara would always be a little girl, thanks to the brain damage she'd sustained in the crash.

"Can we get a hamburger for Dad, too? He loves them. It will make him so—so happy."

Only Ciara would consider the happiness of the man who'd caused her problems.

"Sure, we can." *And he'd better act like he enjoys it, even if he isn't hungry*, Finn thought, *or else!*

When he heard about their morning, Connor would act out a concerned-father show, and upset Ciara even more. In her present condition, no good could come of that. Finn decided to wait until the test results were in, when she could report that an adjustment to her meds would bring everything back to normal. Or as normal as possible, considering her injury.

Finn guided Ciara up the stairs and got her settled on the sofa.

"Where's—where's Dad?" she asked as Finn draped a throw over her legs.

Hopefully not out looking for whiskey. "Oh, he probably got bored and went for a walk." She handed Ciara a stack of DVDs. "Are you still seeing two of everything?"

"No. I'm a little bit—little bit dizzy still. But except for that, I'm better."

"Good. You choose a movie for us while I bring the food upstairs."

Finn started for the door but paused in the opening. She'd only be outside a few minutes…more than enough time for Ciara to succumb to a dizzy spell and…

"Do you need to use the bathroom or anything?"

"Nope."

"Are you thirsty?"

"Nope."

"Good. You sit tight, then. Don't get up, not for any reason until I get back, okay?"

Nodding, Ciara began flipping through the plastic cases.

Finn hurried down the back stairs. She'd barely gathered up the bags and kicked the car door shut when, from out of nowhere, an all-too-familiar voice said, "There's m'girl!"

"Good grief, Connor—I mean, Dad! You scared me half to death!"

"Sorry, sweetie." He relieved her of the drink tray. "Where have you guys been all morning?"

Remembering her fears that he'd make a fuss, Finn said, "Ciara was feeling a little off, so I took her to see Dr. Peterson. It's probably just a twenty-four-hour bug."

"You don't know what a relief it is to know you're always there for her."

He entered the apartment ahead of her, and as Finn doled out the meal, Connor sat beside Ciara.

"You don't feel feverish," he said, pressing a palm to her forehead.

"Feverish?" She glanced at Finn in confusion.

"I just told Dad we went to see Dr. Peterson to make sure your headache isn't because of a virus." She hoped Ciara wouldn't mention the tests or anything else related to their busy morning because the expression on their father's face was proof that he'd overdramatize things.

"I picked—I picked *Sound of Music*," Ciara said, unwrapping her burger. "When the songs come on, will you sing with me, Finn?"

"You bet I will." She passed Connor his meal.

He held up a hand. "I'm not the least bit—"

"Ciara wanted to make sure we brought you a burger because she knows how much you love them. Isn't she the sweetest, most thoughtful little thing?"

Fortunately, he got the message. After popping a fry into his mouth, he said, "Ran into your boyfriend downtown."

Finn felt the beginnings of a blush creeping into her cheeks. "Boyfriend? I don't have a boyfriend."

"You mean—you mean Sam?"

"Yup."

"Then, Finn's right, Dad. She doesn't have a boyfriend. Sam is a man. So you have to say, 'I ran into your *man* friend.'"

Ciara meant well. Ciara *always* meant well. Still… *Please, Kee, don't try to help me.*

"When you're right, you're right." He chuckled and faced Finn. "Your man friend said to tell you hi, and that he'd call you tonight." He paused to take a bite of his burger. "Something to do with date night, I think."

Ciara perked up. "You and—you and Sam are going out on a date?"

"It isn't a date. It's just three friends, spending an evening together."

"Three?"

"You don't think I'd see Garth Brooks without you, do you?"

"Garth *Brooks*? For *real*?"

"Sam got tickets," Connor said. "And he's taking you to some big fancy restaurant before the show. So you two will have to get all dressed up, like a couple of Hollywood movie stars."

Ciara stared at Finn. "He is? We are? I *do*?"

Finn laughed. She didn't know which question to answer first, so she said, "Yes, yes and yes!"

"What, what day?"

"I'm not sure."

Connor pulled the straw in and out of his cup, and Finn cringed at the *hee-haw, hee-haw* sound.

"I reckon that's why he's calling Finn tonight, sweet girl, so he can firm things up."

A wistful, dreamy smile lifted the corners of Ciara's mouth. "I like Sam. I like him a lot." She met Finn's eyes. "Do you like him a lot, too?"

She liked him more than anyone she'd met in years. *Don't forget...he's a musician. And the boss of musicians.*

"He's a very nice man."

Connor cleared his throat. "Did I ever tell you girls that when I was a boy, I spent a lot of time at my grandpa's Texas farm?"

Together, the sisters said a bored, "Yes."

"So you know that they had mules named Maw and Paw?"

"Yes," they droned.

"And that they were the most stubborn, ornery critters in the barnyard?"

Did he really crave attention that badly? Or was this his way of controlling them, if only for the moment?

Ciara tore the corner from a catsup packet and squirted some onto her fries. Finn wondered if Connor realized she'd already lost interest in his mind game.

"Finn reminds me of those critters," he said, unfazed by their lack of enthusiasm.

She rolled her eyes and made no attempt to hide it. "Gee, thanks. No chance I'll get a big head with you around... *Dad.*"

"Didn't mean it as an insult, honey. Just stating a fact to help Ciara to understand that if you don't want to talk about something, you're not gonna talk about it. No matter what either of us says or does. At least, not until you're good and ready."

It was nice having him here, where she could see and hear that he was all right. But his presence also reminded her of the hurtful things he'd done, and everything he'd neglected to do. The back-and-forth emotions underscored the need to keep Ciara's situation under wraps. Because at the conclusion of his Father of the Year performance, he would hit the road—probably before the ice melted in his soda. And that would break Ciara's heart.

As if on cue, Connor scooted closer to her on the couch.

"You forgive me, don't you, Kee, for staying away so long?"

"Sure, Dad."

"And you know I would have called you, if I could?"

"Um, yeah..."

He slid an arm over her shoulders. "I love you to pieces. You know that, right?"

Ciara squinted one eye as he pressed a kiss to her temple. "Me, too, Dad."

Finn cringed when he looked in her direction. If he thought she'd respond in the same accepting, tolerant way to his lies as Ciara always had—

"Don't ever play poker," Pete used to say, "because every thought in your head is written on your face." There must have been more truth in his words than she realized, because Connor quickly averted his gaze. She'd lived most of her life making sure Ciara always felt safe, protected and happy. If putting up with Connor for a while ensured that, so be it.

"Finn, honey?"

So. She'd misread his expression and demeanor, had she? For an instant, she almost envied his acting skills.

Almost.

She clamped the soda straw between her teeth. "Hmm?"

"What's it gonna take for *you* to forgive me?"

Dozens of times, he'd vowed to get clean and sober and hadn't. Held up his right hand and promised never to leave them again and had…usually without bothering to scrawl a goodbye note. What would it take to forgive him? A magic spell, perhaps, to erase her memory of every time he'd broken Ciara's heart. Or a miracle, so she could believe he had the capacity to become a man of his word.

Unfortunately for Connor, it had been a long, long time since Finn believed in magic or miracles.

Ciara waved her hand, like a child in school. "Finn? Oh, Finn? Dad asked you a question."

Only one answer would satisfy her sweet, innocent sister. And to deliver it, Finn needed time. Time to come up with something other than a bald-faced lie.

Her cell phone rang, startling her. One of the contractors, she hoped, calling back to reschedule the walk-throughs she'd postponed.

Saved by the bell, she thought.

"Bet you five of these that it's Sam," Ciara said, holding up a French fry like a dueling sword.

Finn didn't recognize the number and almost didn't take the call.

"Finn, darlin'! It's so good to hear your voice!"

Should have followed your instincts, she thought as Ciara leaned closer to Connor.

"Why does—why does she look afraid?"

"Don't rightly know."

"Well, it can't be Sam. She *likes* talking to Sam."

Finn tightened her grip on the phone...and on her self-control, too.

"I have an audition next week with This Side Up Records, and I'd love to spend some time with you while I'm in town. Do you still have that pull-out sofa?"

"Yes, but that's where I've been sleeping. Temporarily."

Connor pursed his lips and ground out, "*Now* I know why she looks like she's seen a ghost."

Ciara glanced from Finn to her father and back again. "Why?"

"Because," he said slowly, "she's talking to your *mother.*"

CHAPTER SEVENTEEN

"SO LET'S RECAP," Sam said, walking between the tables. "You'll be expected to recall street names, numbers, people's names, floor plans of buildings and houses. Who can tell me the point of all this memory stuff?"

"Gotta get to a fire before we can put it out," said one student.

Another agreed. "Dispatch won't repeat addresses over and over, so we need to remember where the fire is."

"And once we get inside," said a third, "we'll need to pay attention to where the doors and windows are. Escape routes…"

Sam nodded. "Excellent." He distributed handouts. "Print your name at the top. You'll have five minutes to read this paragraph. When the timer dings, turn the papers facedown and answer the first set of questions on the back."

Sam set the device for five minutes and the students fell silent, reading. All but Epps, who muttered and fidgeted like one of his cousin Emily's elementary-school-age kids. He stood beside her desk, hoping his presence would be enough to settle her down before she distracted those seated near her.

It wasn't.

He should consider himself fortunate; of the hundreds of recruits who'd gone through his classes, Sam could count the jakes on one hand. The timer buzzed, and he instructed the class to turn their papers over.

"I hope you took your time, absorbed every detail from that paragraph. Because I'm going to reset the timer, and this time, you'll have ten minutes to answer the second set of questions."

"Aw, bummer," someone complained. "These are multiple choice. I've never been very good at multiple choice."

Sam chuckled. "Not my favorite, either. But we do what we have to, right?" He paused. "Ready?"

Unenthusiastic nods and yeses floated around the room. Sam watched them, hunched over their papers, some gnawing on their pencils, others frowning as they tried to recollect details provided in the paragraph that described which extinguishing agent was effective against a propane fire, and whether faulty brakes or hydroplaning had caused a fiery highway accident.

When they finished, Sam collected the papers and gave them another set of questions.

After gathering up the fourth handout, he reiterated lessons on mechanical aptitude and asked them to call out the various tools a firefighter needed on the job. Calipers and depth gauges, combination squares and spring dividers. A dozen types of saws, a variety of hammers and screwdrivers, wrenches, pliers and even belt sanders. In all, there were nearly a hundred hand tools that might be used in fighting a fire or assessing its cause afterward…and to pass the exam, they had to be able to identify—and use—them all.

"The written test isn't easy," he stressed, "so we're going to take practice exams. Two, six, ten… however many it takes you to feel confident when it's time to sit down for the real thing. I've put you through your paces, mentally and physically. On the day of the physical exam, most of you will be able to lift a sixty-pound ventilator fan from an overhead bar, to the floor and back again. You'll have very little trouble carrying unconscious citizens because you've done countless arm curls. You've hefted that eighty-pound pipe up all seven flights of the training tower in one minute flat—and know better than to call it a hose. And although a timed trial wasn't required, most of you ran up the aerial ladder in your firefighter coats and masks—carrying full air tanks—in record time."

Epps raised her hand. "Do we *all* have to crawl through that tunnel maze?"

"Yup."

"What about scaling the wall? Do I have to vault over it without a rope or a ladder?"

"Yup."

She studied her palms. "But…what if I can't connect and disconnect the hose couplings in under a minute?"

"Then, you take the test again, until you can."

"And breaking into somebody's house or office building." She groaned. "Is that really a requirement?"

He tried not to acknowledge her classmates' eye-rolls and sighs of frustration, tried to ignore it when someone whispered, "What a jake."

Here on the East Coast, the term was reserved for quality firefighters. Where he came from, it was an insult. Sam gave a nod to the student…a guy from Detroit, where oddly, they spoke the same language as Colorado firefighters.

"We've been all through this, Epps, more than once. Those are the rules, for your sake and for the benefit of the civilians you'll serve."

A voice from the back said, "So you really think we're ready for the exams, Sam?"

He avoided looking at Epps. If anyone failed the test, it would be her, and for no reason other than that she rarely tried and always expected special treatment.

"Would you mind going over the oral interview one more time?" a student asked.

"Don't mind at all." He rifled through his lecture notes and slid a page from the folder. "The questions will be all over the place," Sam reminded them. "Things like why you decided to become a firefighter, for example."

"Because I want to help people," one guy said.

Another chimed in with, "And make a difference in people's lives."

"Good," Sam said. "Real good. Now, how do you know you're qualified for the job?"

"Because Captain Sam Marshall was our instructor."

Amid the quiet laughter, Sam said, "Too bad flattery isn't worth any points on the test." He sat on the corner of his desk. "But on a more serious note, you need to sum up your training in three, four sentences, tops—tell the panel how many hours you spent studying for the written exam. How many you put in working on the strength and dexterity stuff. And—without sounding cocky—how well you did during training exercises. Make it known that you've worked hard because the job was worth the effort and because you understand how important it is to be ready when that bell rings in the station house."

Some students made notes, some sat nodding…

…and Epps drew curlicues on the cover of her notebook.

"They're going to ask you to talk about yourself, too. Not résumé-type stuff…they'll have your application for that. So tell them things that prove you're well-rounded. That you're a good communicator. That you're a team player who has no problem taking orders. They might ask about a previous boss. Even if he was an incompetent jerk, you're not going to admit it. Instead, you'll say that he taught you the importance of prioritizing tasks, that he pushed you to work harder and meet goals you didn't even know you had. And you'll cite an example or two."

Now Epps inspected her fingernails. While chewing a wad of gum. "Where do you see yourself in five years?" he asked her.

"Retired. Or maybe doing *your* job!"

The guys laughed, and she smiled.

But Sam found no humor in her reply. "What if the panel wants to know what you see as your greatest weakness?"

She sat blinking then said, "Well, I'm terrible at answering stupid questions."

Sam was still not amused, and he stared hard at her until she responded.

"Math. Math is a *huge* weakness. I hate it."

"Because…?"

"Because, well, when am I ever gonna need *geometry* to douse a fire or rescue a person?"

The guy beside her shook his head. "Basic math is important, Epps. Everybody uses different levels of oxygen, especially under stress. If you can't do basic math, your tank could run out while you're in the middle of a rescue."

"Great point, Burke." Sam faced the class. "Here's a favorite question of the panel—what are your salary requirements?"

The students recited annual earnings expectations, and when they quieted, he shook his head. "Do your homework. Find out what the going rate is for someone in your position. Go into that interview expecting an appropriate income amount, based on your work history, your exam scores, your hopes for a future with the department. And when they ask why they should hire you instead of some other candidate, what will you tell 'em?"

"Because my grandfather is Jack Epps."

"You might think that's funny," Sam told her, "but, trust me, the panel won't." He wondered if she really believed she could waltz in there and walk out with a seal of approval simply because of her surname.

But he'd already given her more time than she'd earned. Sam faced the class again and laced his fingers behind his back. "They're going to ask what you see as your biggest flaw. So be prepared to tell the panel how you're working hard to overcome your stickler-for-details tendencies. Or maybe you're a workaholic. You habitually show up early and leave late. And if they want to know what your friends think of you, don't give 'em some vague answer like, 'They like me 'cause I'm fun.' Be specific."

"What about…I have a pickup truck so I'm always available to help them move?" a guy at the back chimed in.

Sam joined his students' laughter. "That's not a

bad answer, actually. It shows you're willing to help folks, even when you're off duty. Talk about your hobbies. Your favorite sports. Maybe you volunteer at a local soup kitchen, or you helped a political candidate hand out fliers on Election Day. See where I'm going with this?"

"Yeah," Epps said drily. "We lie."

Silence fell over the room, and it must have unnerved her because she added, "Um, we make sure the panel understands that we're well-rounded individuals, like you said."

He erased his notations from the whiteboard. "Questions?"

When no one spoke up, he said, "See you next time, then."

Everyone left, except for Epps.

"I'll never pass the tests," she said, wringing her hands. "I really *am* awful at math, and my memorization skills are even worse. I can't bench-press a box of chicken nuggets, and I run out of steam halfway up the aerial ladder." She stamped one foot. "I'll be the first Epps to flunk out of the academy."

"Maybe that's not such a bad thing."

She looked hurt and shocked and angry, all rolled into one.

"You can't be serious. They'll disown me!"

"I doubt that. They're family. They want you safe. And happy. You don't seem to have any interest in the profession, so I don't understand why you're here." He stuffed his teaching materials into his backpack. "It's pretty clear you'd rather be anywhere else."

"Oh, so you're a mind reader, are you?"

He ignored her surly tone. "No, but I've been at this long enough to pick up on the cues."

"Maybe that's the problem."

"What is?"

"You've been teaching so long that you're just going through the motions."

"Says the only student who ever fell asleep in my class."

"Is it my fault that your classes are boring?"

Sam zipped his bag.

She stamped her foot again. "I think you're treating me this way, singling me out, because I'm a woman."

"You're kidding, right?"

Epps bristled slightly under his hard stare. "Okay, maybe that was uncalled-for. But I'm desperate for your help. That isn't a crime, is it?"

The crime, as Sam saw it, was twofold. He'd allowed himself to get so sidetracked by her childishness that he never saw it coming: she was about to hit him with the tutoring nonsense again.

"I've tried every way I could think of to get you to help me, to teach me, one on one." She smirked. "So much for you being able to pick up on cues."

Oh, he'd noticed the pitiful pouts. The flirty glances. Her tendency to laugh too long and too hard when he cracked a joke. And the snide, borderline-disrespectful remarks.

"Listen, Epps. I don't have time for this right now." *Because I need to call Finn, let her know what time I'm picking her up tonight.* "Can we talk later?" He slung the backpack over one shoulder, thinking maybe he'd just stop by the apartment.

"How much later? The longer you put it off, the behinder I get."

If he'd been thinking straight, Sam would have suggested talking after their next class. When there were plenty of witnesses to back up his story that he'd turned her down gently, and with good reason. But Sam hadn't been thinking straight since that kiss.

The mere memory of it stirred something deep in his chest. He cleared his throat.

"You know where The Frothy Monkey is?"

"It's only one of my favorite cafés!"

"Meet me for coffee." He didn't know how late spoiled brats slept, so he said, "Tomorrow at nine, if that isn't too early for you."

"It isn't."

She grabbed her purse and backpack and hurried out the door without another word. If he had a lick of sense, he'd catch up with her and cancel.

"If you had a lick of sense, you would have nipped this in the bud by now."

Tonight, after dinner and the show with Finn and Ciara, he needed to come up with two plans. One that would help Epps understand, once and for all, why the whole tutoring thing was a bad idea. And one that would secure his future in case that backfired and she decided to sic her big-shot relatives on him.

Sam climbed into his pickup. It wouldn't be the end of the world if they fired him. He had a big, loving family back in Colorado, and if there wasn't room for another volunteer at the fire department there, he'd help Nate and Zach run the Double M full time.

Two former students had climbed the department ranks, and either one could do the instructor's job. Torry and Mark had managed The Meetinghouse for years without his help. And any day now, The Right Note would reopen and would get along fine without him.

But would he get along fine without Finn?

CHAPTER EIGHTEEN

IT WASN'T EASY keeping his eyes on the road. Not with Finn in the passenger seat looking like a cover model, anyway. Sam fiddled with the radio and made small talk about the weather, the I-40 bridge project, the latest politician caught with his hand in Joe Q. Public's pocket. But that didn't help him focus on driving, either.

He glanced in the rearview mirror. "You're awfully quiet tonight, kiddo. You okay back there?"

"Yeah, just a little—just a little tired is all."

Tired? Judging by Finn's concerned expression, lack of sleep wasn't the problem. Maybe Ciara had just picked up a bug. In the short time he'd known her, he'd started thinking of her as a little sister.

"Well," he said, "tired or not, you look mighty pretty tonight. Did I tell you that?"

"Yes—yes, you did. Twice."

Her smile eased his worries somewhat.

"This is—this is a new dress. Finn took me shopping just for tonight." She leaned forward to pat her sister's shoulder. "She's the best sister ever."

"She sure is."

"Do you think Finn looks pretty? She bought herself a dress, too. And also shoes."

It touched him that she'd bought a new outfit for their date. "No," he said, chancing a peek in Finn's direction, "I don't think she looks pretty."

Ciara gasped. "But, Sam!"

"Your sister looks beautiful tonight. More gorgeous than a model. Or a movie star."

Finn fiddled with the hem of her skirt, then folded her hands in her lap. "Please, sit back, sweetie. Is your seat belt buckled?"

"But it'll wrinkle my dress."

"No, it won't."

He glanced into the rearview in time to see Ciara pouting. Unless he was mistaken, she wasn't convinced.

"Is your seat belt buckled yet?" Finn insisted.

"No, but Sam is a good and safe driver. Why do I need to buckle it?"

"We're definitely safe with Sam. It's all the other crazy drivers I'm worried about. You know what a worrywart I am, so humor me, okay?"

His heart beat a little faster, hearing her admit that she felt safe with him. If only he could protect her from trees crashing into her diner, less-than-paternal parents…and whatever was going on with Ciara.

At some point tonight, he needed to tell them that circumstances might force him to move home. By his estimation, they had a good ten minutes before arriving at the steak house.

"I need your advice, ladies…"

Ciara giggled. "Hear that, Finn? Sam called me a lady!"

"You *are* a lady," he said before continuing. "A very lovely lady, I might add." He winked at her in the mirror and continued. "So I have this student, right, who comes from a long line of firefighters. She's having a hard time with some of the lessons and asked me to tutor her. But I can't do it. Wouldn't be fair to the rest of the class. If I say no to her, though, that family of hers might—"

"I never saw a *girl* fireman, except on TV."

Someday, he'd tell Ciara the difference between a fireman and a firefighter. "I've taught a couple dozen female students. They worked hard, real hard, and gave it their all." Sam shrugged. "Some of them are firefighters today."

"Why not all of them?"

"Well, let's just say it's not their fault women are built differently than men. They didn't have the upper body strength or muscle mass to compete in some of the physical stuff."

"Sometimes I have trouble with—with physical stuff, too." Ciara paused. "Why can't you make the test easier, the way Finn does for me?"

"First of all, I don't have any control over what's on the exam. But even if I did, I wouldn't make it easier for women to pass it. That would only make it harder and more hazardous for them later, when they're on the job. Not to mention how dangerous it would be for people who might need someone to carry them out of a burning building."

"Oh. If the people get hurt, you mean. Or if they faint."

"Exactly."

"Is your student strong enough to carry a grown-up?"

"No, I'm afraid she isn't. Not because she's small, mind you, but because she hasn't been willing to work hard, like so many other women who've become firefighters."

Finn huffed, and Sam steeled himself. He hoped he hadn't offended her, but it would make it a whole lot easier to forget that kiss.

"I agree with you," she said, and he relaxed a fraction. "Women who *can* pass those tests have earned the right to do the job. If she expects preferential treatment, for any reason, well, that's beyond foolish...it's potentially dangerous!"

He wanted to stop the truck and kiss her again, right now. "Finn Leary, where have you been all my life?"

Her eyebrows rose slightly, and it took a concerted effort not to raise his own. What was it about her that made him blurt out stuff like that?

"What's her name?" Ciara asked.

"Jasmine."

"Finn bought me jasmine perfume once. It smelled real nice. It's a very pretty name."

"Y'know, you're right."

"Is your Jasmine pretty?"

"She's okay, I guess. But, thankfully, she isn't *my* Jasmine."

"I'm excited, so excited to see Garth!"

He couldn't help but appreciate how easily Ciara was distracted. But better than that, it was good to hear the familiar enthusiasm in her voice.

"And I'm excited to cut into a fat, juicy steak."

"How 'bout you, Finn? Are you more excited about Garth? Or about steak?"

"I read a restaurant review recently that raved about the restaurant's glazed chicken."

"Chicken!" Ciara groaned. "I bet—I bet you're just saying that because chicken is cheaper than steak. You're trying to save—to save Sam money, aren't you?"

Sam braked at the traffic light as Finn said, "Ciara, Ciara, Ciara…"

"What, what, what?"

Finn sighed and pointed at the windshield. "Light's green, Sam."

And so it was, as evidenced by the high-pitched *toot* from the sporty convertible behind him.

Ciara turned and yelled, "Aw, take it easy, bub!"

Finn's laughter started slow and soft, then escalated until the pickup's cab throbbed with the pleasant sound. Sam laughed, too.

"Hey. Are you guys laughing at me?"

"Not at you, Kee," Finn said. "With you."

"Oh. Well. In that case…" She cut loose with a gale of girlish giggles.

Was he seeing things, or had he spotted a shimmer of tears in Finn's eyes? He didn't know whether it was merely a side effect of sisterly affection, or something serious was going on with Ciara.

The former, Sam hoped, for her sake as well as Ciara's.

SAM THOUGHT IT was sweet, the way Finn and Ciara held hands as the maître d' led them to a table with a view of the atrium's waterfall.

"Is this satisfactory, Captain Marshall?"

"It's perfect." He traded cash for three huge brown-leather menus. "Thanks, Buck."

Buck lit the tiny brass lamp, adjusted its shade and tidied the heavy wood and brass-handled steak knives that formed a square around it. "I'll send the wine steward right over—" he flapped a linen napkin onto Finn's lap "—and check in with you later," he said, performing the same service for Ciara.

When he was out of earshot, Finn said, "You're on a first-name basis with the maître d'?"

"Former student. A lot of the guys moonlight to make ends meet." He lowered his voice. "How do you think I got us in here on such short notice?"

"He's cute," Ciara said. "How old is he?"

"Twenty-nine? Thirty?" He aimed a forefinger

at her. "Too old for you, young lady. Besides," he said as the busboy filled their water goblets, "he's married."

"Oh. I want to see the waterfall close up."

Finn shook her head. "Maybe later, sweetie."

"But it's right there." Ciara pointed. "You could watch me the whole way."

"I don't want you walking that far alone. What if you feel light-headed?"

"I won't—I won't get dizzy. And I haven't had a headache in a couple of days."

So, Sam thought, it *wasn't* a simple virus after all.

"I'm about to take a break," the busboy told Finn. "I could walk her down there, stay with her a couple minutes and bring her right back."

Finn smiled up at him. "Thank you, but—"

"I have an older brother who's on the spectrum, so…"

Sam could almost see the wheels of indecision turning in Finn's mind: explain that her sister's halting gait and faltering speech pattern weren't signs of autism, tell the kid to mind his own business or let him escort Ciara down the stairs.

"Can I, Finn? Can I, *please*?"

It was obvious that she hadn't made a habit of telling the girl no. And just as obvious that Ciara wasn't accustomed to hearing it. Finn might let him have it with both barrels later, but somebody had to say something.

"Five minutes," he told the kid, "and if she seems the least bit unsteady, whistle."

Ciara got up. "I already—already told you," she said, frowning at Finn, "I haven't been dizzy in a long time." She stood behind Sam's chair and wrapped her arms around his neck. "Thank you," she said, kissing his cheek. "I love you!"

And there it was again…that peculiar sensation that made him want to protect her from illness and accidents and boys who filled water goblets at restaurants. He could only shake his head as she walked away on the arm of the busboy. If this was how he'd feel watching his daughter leave the house with a beau, Sam didn't know if his heart could take it.

"I should have told you."

"Told me what?" he asked, eyes still on Ciara.

"That I had to take her to Vanderbilt. You probably wouldn't have sent her off with a stranger if you'd known."

That got his attention. "Vanderbilt? As in *hospital*?"

Finn nodded. "In addition to the headaches and dizzy spells, she's been seeing double. Her doctor ran a bunch of tests."

As if life hadn't already thrown enough at the poor kid! "And?"

"And we'll know more when the labs and films come back."

"Good grief, Finn."

He started to get up, with every intention of going after Ciara and her companion, when Finn said, "It's okay. He seems like a nice boy. And just look at her."

Sam followed her gaze to where Ciara and the boy stood, smiling and chatting as the frothy water cascaded down a minimountain of boulders.

"Yeah, she seems happy." He took a big gulp of water. "But I still wish I'd kept my nose out of your business."

"Ciara has taken a real liking to you, and I'd have to be blind not to see that you care about her, too. I suppose that makes her your business, a little bit." She sent him a slow, sad smile. "I'm touched that you *made* her your business."

There were tears in her eyes, and Sam wasn't sure what to make of them. But he was certain now that no matter how things turned out after his meeting with Epps, he couldn't leave Nashville. Couldn't leave *Finn*.

"Besides, it gave me time to fill you in. I didn't know when I'd get a chance, now that Connor has moved in."

"You mean, he doesn't know?"

"Not yet."

"Are you going to tell him?"

"Eventually. Probably. Maybe once we get the results."

He knew a thing or two about Connor Leary, but

from the sound of things, it was just the tip of the iceberg.

Brow furrowed and lips forming a taut line, Finn stared straight ahead. Thinking of all the *un*fatherly things Connor had done?

"Connor is, first and foremost, a showman," she said. "The minute he finds out something's wrong with Ciara, he'll give an Oscar-worthy performance—pacing, wringing his hands, crying… exactly what he did after the accident. Not out of concern for Ciara, mind you, but because he thinks that's how a concerned father would behave. His act didn't do her any good then, and it's the last thing she'll need if those tests reveal something…" She bit her lower lip. "If it isn't good news."

A hard knot burned in his gut at the mere thought of something bad happening to Ciara. How much more painful must it be for Finn?

A moment later, the kids returned to the table. "So was it everything you thought it would be?" Sam asked.

"It was noisy, wasn't it, Andy? And—and we could feel the mist bouncing off and hitting our faces."

Finn looked up at the boy. "Thank you so much. You made her day."

Sam opened his wallet, thinking to slip Andy a few dollars.

But he held up a hand. "No need for that, sir. It was a nice break. And Ciara is great."

"I gave Andy my cell phone number. He's going to call me to see what Dr. Peterson found out from all those—all those stupid tests." She was still smiling when a gold-vested waiter stepped up.

"Ready to order?"

"We haven't even looked at the menu," Sam admitted. "Can you give us a few minutes?"

"Of course. Take your time."

Andy held his hand up again, this time to wave goodbye to Ciara. Then, facing Finn, he said, "It's okay if I call her in a couple days, then?"

She smiled at her sister's wide, hopeful expression. "I don't see why not."

He'd better be as nice as he seems, Sam thought as that fatherly feeling rose up in him again, because he didn't know what he might be capable of if the kid broke his promise to call.

Since Pete's death, the Leary sisters had no one watching out for them. They hadn't asked for a protector. Might even have called him to task if he volunteered for the job. But it was a risk he needed to take.

Sam hid behind his menu, watching and listening as Finn and Ciara discussed entrée options. *You've already gone boots over Stetson for her*, Sophie had said. And he'd denied it.

Well, he couldn't deny it anymore.

Not even with Aggie's warning ringing in his ears.

CHAPTER NINETEEN

DURING THE TWENTY-MINUTE drive from Opryland to downtown, Ciara chattered nonstop. About Garth's guitar and headset microphone. His enormous hat. The long, upturned toes of his shiny boots.

"Hey, Sam? Why did Garth dress all in black?"

"Hmm. Maybe he's trying to walk in Johnny Cash's shoes."

"Johnny Cash?"

Finn turned slightly. "Connor claims to have worked with Johnny years ago," she explained to Ciara. "Apparently, he heard him tell a reporter that the black represented the poor and hopeless."

"I heard something like that, too," Sam said. "He wrote a song about it, one I've opened a couple of shows with."

"Can you sing it now, Sam?" Ciara asked.

Chuckling, he shook his head. "Maybe next time I come over, I'll bring my guitar. How's that sound, cupcake?"

Ciara giggled. "Cupcake! Why did you call me *that*?"

In truth, he had no idea. The word slid past his lips as naturally as her name or Finn's.

"Maybe," he said slowly, "because you're so sweet."

As the headlights of cars heading north on Highway 155 lit the truck's cab, he got a glimpse of Finn's face. *Man, she's gorgeous when she smiles that way!* It felt good, having a little something to do with her upbeat mood.

The closer they got to the apartment, the quieter Ciara became. He peered into the rearview mirror. "Fast asleep," he whispered.

Finn nodded. "Exciting day."

Moments later, when they pulled into The Right Note's parking lot, she turned to wake her sister, but Sam stopped her.

"If you'll get the door, I'll carry her upstairs."

The instant he lifted her from the backseat, Ciara wrapped her arms around his neck and, resting her head on his shoulder, exhaled a sleepy sigh. Sam didn't understand why she and Finn had made such an impact on him. Had his cousin Nate felt similar twinges of envy when Zach announced his intentions toward Summer?

Finn led the way inside, flipping on lights and opening doors as she went.

"Just put her here," she said, throwing back Ciara's bedcovers. "Make yourself comfortable, and if Connor gets home while I'm helping her into her PJs, ask him to keep his voice down, will you?"

Sam settled Ciara onto her pillow, and after pop-

ping a tender kiss on her forehead, he tiptoed out
of the room and eased the door shut behind him.

He wasn't the least bit hungry, but when Sam
spied a plate of chocolate-chip cookies on the
kitchen counter, he grabbed one. Grabbed a glass
from the drain board, too, and filled it with milk.
He sat at the table and propped his sore leg on Connor's chair. "Where are you tonight, Father of the
Year?" he wondered aloud. Maybe he'd found a job.
Sam hoped so, for Finn's benefit as much as Connor's. A working-full-time Connor would be good
for Sam, too. From all he'd seen of the relationship,
Finn would likely turn down his Thanksgiving invitation for no reason other than to keep Connor
from getting involved.

How did the man live with himself, knowing his
behavior was largely responsible for Ciara's condition, and that by shirking his responsibilities, he'd
transferred them onto Finn's shoulders? Maybe he
couldn't, and that was why he'd made a habit of hiding at the bottom of a bottle.

Well, Sam was more than happy to help Finn in
any way he could.

A crazy thought flitted through his mind: until
she'd come into his life, he hadn't given a whole lot
of consideration to having kids of his own…but he
sure was considering it now…

Finn breezed into the room and went straight to
the refrigerator. Sometime between now and when
he'd deposited Ciara on her bed, she'd kicked off her

high-heeled sandals. Why hadn't he noticed those bright pink toenails earlier? She stood, one perfectly shaped bare foot atop the other, inspecting the contents of the fridge.

"She's out like a light," Finn said, taking a seat across from him.

When they'd first met, Finn's mop of dark waves barely covered her earlobes. Now they curled and curved along her jawline, like beckoning fingers that reminded him how soft her skin had felt against his palm that night...

"It's late. I wonder where Connor is."

"Y'got me by the feet. But I'm relieved to have a few minutes alone with you."

The plastic bottle crackled as she unscrewed its cap. "Wondering what you'll do to Andy if he doesn't call Ciara, like he promised to?"

"Nah. He seemed like a good kid. He'll call. Besides, I think he's love struck."

Finn laughed. "Please. They were together all of ten minutes, if that."

In his opinion, her argument couldn't hold water; he'd wanted to know her better the instant she'd blinked up at him from the mess on The Right Note floor.

"Besides, he can't be more than seventeen, and Ciara will be twenty-three in a few weeks."

Yeah, but thanks to the head injury, they were closer to the same age mentally.

"So what's on your mind?"

Taking you in my arms and kissing the daylights out of you, that's what.

As a qualified first responder, Sam knew that a normal heart rate was about one beat per second. Researchers hadn't taken into account the effects a big-eyed brunette could have on a man's ticker, though.

"How soon do you expect to hear from Ciara's doctor?"

"Monday, probably, sooner if they find something serious."

"Well, let's hope you don't hear till Monday, then."

"Yeah," she whispered. "Let's hope."

Not liking how burdened she looked, he decided to change tack. "So, Finn…about this trip to Colorado… I'm hoping you and Ciara will come with me. If it's okay with Ciara's doctor, that is. And if Rowdy's available to run the diner for a few days."

She propped one foot on the seat of her chair, and, chin resting on her knee, Finn grinned at him. "You're just a little crazy, you know that?"

Crazy about you…

"I…have a confession to make."

His mouth went dry.

"It isn't easy for me to accept favors." She held up a hand, traffic cop style. "It's unfair and unreasonable, I know, but it's just, I can't always tell when there are strings attached."

"Guess that lets me off the hook, then, because I haven't given you anything."

"Oh, but you have." She ticked off everything he'd done, from rounding up help after the tree fell on the diner, to recommending contractors. The zoo. Tonight's dinner and show. "You've been nothing but generous, especially with Ciara."

Sam didn't see it that way, mostly because everything he'd done had given him a legitimate excuse to spend more time with her.

"And I haven't seen any evidence that you have ulterior motives." Her cell phone rang, and before she picked up, Finn shot him a peculiar, borderline-stern look. "So far."

So far? That stung, because he hadn't given a thought to strings or repayment or whatever she wanted to call it.

Her life hadn't been easy. He'd give her that. And considering who'd raised her, well, no wonder she had trouble putting her faith in people...men in particular. The way he saw it, he had two choices: admit that he'd never hurt her—and hope she'd believe it—or back off. *Way* off.

Finn lowered her voice. Got up and began pacing the kitchen. "I'm sorry, but I gave Connor my room, so that's where I'm sleeping."

It had to be her mother on the other end. First thing in the morning, Sam intended to call his folks, just to say hi. The more he learned about the Learys, the more grateful he was to have them.

"Sorry," Finn said again, free hand shading her eyes, "but he didn't exactly leave me much choice."

Couldn't be easy, he thought, keeping a civil tongue with a woman like that. And he admired Finn all the more for working at it.

"Yes," she said, "I can probably scrape up enough to reserve a room for you. For a couple of nights anyway."

Finn talked about the test results that would, hopefully, pinpoint the cause of Ciara's symptoms. Then, eyes closed, she tilted her face toward the ceiling, as if hoping to find a little extra patience up there somewhere.

"Yes, I do mind, Misty. I mind a lot, actually. Ciara isn't in any condition for something like that."

Sam heard it loud and clear: "Finnegan Ula Logan Leary, you are *not* her mother."

Through clenched teeth, Finn shot back, "I'm more of a mother to her than you've ever been!"

She'd spent years parenting her parents. Was it any wonder that she had trust issues?

CHAPTER TWENTY

THE INSTANT THE words passed her lips, she regretted them.

Sam sat up taller in the chair, one corner of his mouth turned down, eyes sparking with questions. Once the call with Misty ended, he stayed just long enough to find out where Misty had been when she'd called, when she might show up, how long she'd stay. Finn's vague, noncommittal answers only confused him more, but how could she explain things she didn't understand herself?

His goodbye had been cool and clumsy, and who could blame him? Finn watched him go down the stairs and across the parking lot, waiting, hoping he'd turn around, so she could wave him back upstairs and apologize.

But he didn't, and she couldn't blame him for that, either. So she stood at the top of the stairs and watched him drive away. Only a crazy man would come back and expose himself to the Leary family circus. Her eyes welled with tears; she hoped Sam was just a little bit crazy.

"What are you doing up there, honey?"

She squinted into the darkness below. "Connor? What in the world?"

"Forgot my key," he said, starting up the steps.

How many had he lost now? Five? Six? "I might just have to hang a bell around your neck."

"Didn't mean to scare you." He gave her a brief hello hug, then glanced at his watch. "Why are you out here all alone at this hour?"

Finn watched Sam's taillights get swallowed up by the night. "Oh, just catching a breath of fresh air."

He headed inside. "Did you girls have a good time tonight?"

She remembered the "overprotective dad" demeanor that had come over Sam when Ciara and Andy had walked off to watch the waterfall. How long since Connor had looked at her that way?

"It was a lovely evening." *Until you spoiled everything with that thoughtless* so far *crack*.

"You okay?" he asked as she locked up.

No, she wasn't. But admitting it would obliterate the last hint of her self-control.

"I'm going to make myself a cup of tea," she said. "Would you like one, too?"

"It's past midnight. Won't the caffeine keep you awake?"

"It's herbal. The wild-berry scent alone is calming."

"Thank God for the guy who invented the microwave, eh?" He pulled out a kitchen chair. "So much faster than waiting for water to boil."

Did he realize how much his simple observation revealed about his character? He'd taken the easy way in every important decision in his life. In her life and Ciara's, too.

"Where were you tonight?" she asked.

"I watched TV for a while, read the paper, got bored and took a walk." Hands folded on the table, he leaned forward and hung his head. "Almost gave in to the temptation to duck into a bar."

"Almost?" She dropped a tea bag into each mug and carried them to the table.

His hands were shaking as he spooned sugar into his. "You girls saved me," he said on a ragged sigh. "Thinking about you and Ciara and the promise I made helped me walk right on by. And you know? It was easier than I thought it'd be."

He hadn't shaved, and the shadowy stubble added to his haggard, troubled appearance.

"Did you eat anything today?"

"Just those pancakes you made for breakfast."

Finn got up and rummaged in the fridge for lunch meat, cheese and mayo. "Chips on the side?" She popped two slices of bread into the toaster. "Or apple slices?"

When he didn't respond, she faced him…

…and nearly dropped the mayo-loaded butter knife when she saw tears pooled in his dark eyes. He'd cried before—deep, grating sobs that prefaced promises to get clean and stay that way. Each time he fell off the wagon, her faith in him diminished a little more, until she had no faith in him at all. But there was something different about him now, something that gave her hope that maybe this time, she could trust him.

The toaster delivered two slices of golden bread in one metallic burst, and Finn went back to assembling the sandwich. She halved it from top to bottom because that was the way he preferred it. Peeled an apple and arranged the slices on the plate. Added a handful of barbecue-flavored chips…his favorite.

"How about some milk to wash that down?"

The clock above the stove ticked once, twice, three times before his eyes met hers. "Will you sit with me awhile?" Connor slid back the chair nearest hers. "Please?"

She wasn't the least bit sleepy. "Sure. What's up?"

He picked up half of the sandwich, put it down again and took her hands in his own.

"I know it sounds banal, because you've heard it all before, way too many times, but I'm really givin' it the old college try. Staying sober, I mean."

She'd heard that before, too.

"I don't blame you for not believing it." He inhaled and let the breath out slowly. "Heck. Even I don't believe half the stuff I say."

He turned her loose and bit into his sandwich. "That Sam… He seems like a decent sort."

Finn sipped her tea. If there had been any possibility of taking things to the next level with Sam, she'd blown it tonight. "Do I detect reservation in your voice?"

"Quite the contrary, actually." Connor popped an apple slice into his mouth, nodding thoughtfully as he crunched. Using another slice as a pointer, he said, "Gave it a lot of thought, walking around town tonight, and I've come to the conclusion that he's just the kind of man you need in your life."

Passing the buck already, are you, Dad? How long before she found one of his famous notes? *Love you, but you know me and my itchy feet.* If he bothered to write one at all.

"He's a firefighter, so he's gotta be brave, and from what I've seen, he's smart. Even-tempered, too. Patient with Ciara and respectful of you." He punctuated the list with a one-shouldered shrug.

"Sounds like you're describing a family dog," she said, smiling.

"A dog. There's something else you girls never had, thanks to your mom and me."

"Goes to show you how wrong a girl can be."

"Mmm?"

"All these years, I thought you and Misty were just being kind, saying no to pets because it would have been cruel to drag them from one fleabag motel to another."

"Sheesh." Connor winced. "Give me a heads-up next time you release a roundhouse punch to the gut, will ya, so I can at least tense up."

His reaction made her think of Sam's, and Finn cringed. *You're two for two,* she thought. *And if you're not careful, you'll end up like Aggie Jackson—old, angry at the world...and alone.* And she'd have no one to blame but herself.

And her parents.

"If you think that was harsh, you should hear some of the things I keep to myself."

His wounded expression reminded her why she so seldom spoke her mind.

"Sorry," she said. "That was uncalled-for."

Connor harrumphed. "I had it coming." He sipped his tea. "They say the truth hurts, and they're right." He polished off the chips. "So how do you feel about Handsome Sam?"

"I don't know where to begin," she said on a sigh.

"You like him, right?"

"Yes," she replied without even thinking.

"But..."

"But I haven't known him very long. All the good stuff could be a facade. I can't take that chance. I have Ciara to think about."

"Your mistrust, that's on Misty and me. It wasn't right, passing our responsibility for your sister to you." He slid the nearly empty plate to the center of the table. "Especially since it's our fault she can't take care of herself."

The fact that he hadn't been solely responsible for the accident had helped her tolerate her parents' brief, impromptu appearances. Yes, they'd been drunk that night, but if she hadn't distracted Connor...

"You'd probably be happily married with a house full of kids if your mother and I had been better parents."

"Oh, I'm not so sure about that." She'd just dealt him a low blow. In the interest of fairness, she said, "I'm not a very nice person."

Connor laughed. "That's nonsense. Everybody loves you." He recited a list: Rowdy and the rest of The Right Note staff, her regular customers, even a few tourists who returned to the diner every time they came to town because she'd made them feel welcome. Ciara's doctors and nurses, who took such good care of her because Finn held their feet to the fire.

"And then there's Sam. The man is crazy about you."

You wouldn't say that if you'd seen his quick getaway tonight.

"And you're crazy about him, too."

Connor hadn't been there to meet the boy who'd taken her to the homecoming dance, or to comfort her when the mean girls had laughed at her pathetic attempt to make her own prom dress. Where had he been when she'd cried herself to sleep every night for weeks, after Vince Williams had revoked his marriage proposal to tour with up-and-coming country star Millie Sanders?

Hurtful as all of that had been, it was history,

and she'd survived it. Dredging it up now served no useful purpose, so Finn hid a fake yawn behind one hand and put her mug into the sink. "Can I get you anything else before I turn in?"

"No, I'm good." He crossed the room in two long strides and stacked his plate and mug atop hers. "I hate seeing you so unhappy, honey," he said, kissing her cheek. "And it breaks my heart that I'm the reason."

Finn knew what he needed to hear: that she *was* happy, that she didn't blame him for mistakes of the past. She searched for a word or phrase to ease his conscience. Unfortunately, she'd grown tired of lying to protect him from himself.

Connor must have sensed it, because he sighed and said, "I think I'm going to turn in, too."

"See you in the morning."

She waited for his "you, too," or "sweet dreams." Instead, Connor said, "'Five little angels 'round your bed, one at the foot, one at the head…'"

Last time he'd recited the bedtime prayer with her, Finn had been three or four. She hadn't been able to tell him what he needed to hear a moment ago, but she could give him this:

"'One to sing and one to pray…'"

He stepped back and looked into her eyes as, together, they said, "'And one to take my fears away.'"

He kissed her forehead, then touched a fingertip to her nose. "Don't stay up too late."

"I won't."

"Love you, darlin'."

"Love you, too, Dad."

She felt him sigh as relief softened his features, and he left the room.

It was a heartwarming moment, one she'd cherish, and it brought to mind something he'd said earlier. *That man is crazy about you.* It gave her hope that maybe, just maybe, she could have that white-picket-fence life after all.

She thought about it as she changed into sweatpants and a T-shirt. As she made up the couch and slid between the cool, crisp sheets. Why had the possibility of a future with Sam made her heart pound and her stomach flutter?

"Because you want too much," she whispered. "You want it *all*."

What if she let down her guard, and an agent or producer offered him the chance to turn his dream into reality? Would he accept it? And if he did, would he leave like Connor and Misty had?

"You're being ridiculous," she muttered. He'd shown some interest in her, but not enough to inspire such thoughts or concerns.

Finn believed she knew why: if by some miracle something came of this...friendship with Sam, and he became a permanent part of her zany family, she'd never leave his side, no matter what sparkly temptation life dangled in front of her nose.

But she wasn't at all sure he'd do the same for her.

And until she was? Finn would keep right on doing what she'd been doing, and play it safe.

THE TRILL OF the phone roused her. Sitting up, Finn glanced at the clock. Only Misty would call at six on a Saturday morning. She answered with a gruff "Hello."

"Sorry to wake you, Finn."

"Dr. Peterson," she said, on her feet now.

"I hated calling so early, but I'm leaving for a medical conference in a couple of hours. Didn't want to keep you waiting until Monday to hear the results of Ciara's tests."

Shouldering the phone, she padded into the kitchen and filled the coffeepot's carafe. "It's good news, I hope." Though if it was, would he be calling at this hour?

"It's nothing critical."

She spooned grounds into a paper filter and hit the on switch. "But…"

"Relax. There's no *but*, either."

Finn sat at the table and held her breath—the only way to stop herself from hammering him with a dozen questions—and waited.

"We didn't find anything conclusive to explain Ciara's symptoms."

She heard the familiar rattle of the thin sheet of cellulose and pictured Peterson holding the image up to the light.

"There's some minor swelling in an artery near

the original impact site. If not for the sharp eye of a tech, I might not even have noticed it. But since it's there, I prefer to err on the side of caution."

"Exploratory surgery?"

"No, nothing that extreme. We'll try a ten-day round of DexPak first. It gave us good results following her last surgery."

True, the drug had reduced inflammation, but at a cost. "Headaches and dizziness were two of the main reasons I brought her to see you in the first place."

"If she experiences those side effects, or any other negatives, call me, and we'll try something else."

She isn't a human guinea pig, Finn thought.

"I have her chart right here in front of me, and she did fine last time. I'm reasonably certain the same will be true now."

"Reasonably certain? That isn't exactly comforting."

She heard the *click-click* of his ballpoint. "Do you have a pen and paper handy?"

Finn rummaged in a nearby kitchen drawer and produced both. "Yes, I do."

"You probably remember what to watch for, but just in case…" He recited the list, as if reading from a pharmaceutical handbook: headache, neck pain or stiffness, nausea or vomiting, dizziness, irregular breathing, vision or memory loss, difficulty speaking, loss of consciousness and seizures.

Finn made a habit of memorizing the contraindications listed on the brochures included in each prescription package, but she wrote them down anyway.

"And what's the plan if the DexPak doesn't reduce the inflammation?"

"We could try a ventriculostomy—we did detect a small amount of fluid near where we placed the shunt following the accident."

Finn had read all about that procedure. Peterson would have to drill a small hole in Ciara's skull, insert a thin tube and drain the fluids. If successful, placement of the shunt could put an end to all of her symptoms. But if the drain became blocked, everything he'd just listed could happen, and more. As if that wasn't enough, there was a risk of infection.

"How long would the shunt need to stay in?"

"How 'bout we cross that bridge when we get to it?"

"So you're saying it isn't likely that procedure will be necessary?"

"I'm saying that right now the DexPak is our best course of action. Are you still using the pharmacy on Twenty-First Street?"

Finn told him she was, and he offered to fax over the prescription right away. Finn thanked him.

"Happy to do it. You have my cell number, so don't be afraid to call me if anything seems off."

The call ended just as the coffeemaker hissed, signaling a full pot. Finn poured herself a cup and sat at the table, staring at the notes she'd written.

Ciara would take the news in stride. She always did. Connor, on the other hand, could spin a tornado from a light breeze. Was it possible to keep the news from him a little longer? It would mean doling out meds when he wasn't around. No, that wouldn't work; his comings and goings were too unpredictable. Honesty, presented in a calm yet academic way, seemed to be her only option.

He walked into the kitchen puffy eyed and rumpled and grabbed a mug from the drain board. "What kind of idiot makes phone calls at this hour on a Saturday?" he grumbled.

"Ciara's doctor. He's heading to the airport to attend a medical convention and didn't want us to wait until Monday to hear the test results." She brought him up to speed using only the least worrisome details, and surprisingly, he took the news well.

"I can pick up her prescription, save you the trouble of doing it."

"The pharmacy is only a few blocks away, and I have a few errands to run anyway." Remembering how she'd hurt his feelings last night, she added, "But it's nice of you to offer."

Connor helped himself to coffee and joined her at the table. "How 'bout when Ciara gets up, I make us a big country breakfast, like I used to. Everything I need for pancakes and sausage gravy is in the fridge. And I think I saw potatoes in the cupboard under the sink."

He liked to boast that he made the best home

fries this side of the Mississippi, and it drove Rowdy crazy, mostly because, despite dozens of attempts over the years, he'd failed to replicate Connor's recipe.

"I'm sure Ciara will love it."

"Ciara will—will love what?" She shuffled into the kitchen, yawning and rubbing her eyes.

"Conn... Dad offered to make us a big country breakfast."

She brightened. "Sausage gravy and—and pancakes?"

He winked. "My famous fried potatoes, too."

"Can I help like I did when I was little?"

"Wouldn't be a Leary breakfast if you didn't."

"Call me when it's ready," Finn said. "I'm gonna make up the beds and throw a load of towels into the washer."

"No need to make my bed."

"Mine, either," Ciara echoed.

"I heard the paper hit the top porch step. Why not put your feet up and relax, and let us take care of breakfast," Connor suggested.

"Even setting the table." Ciara looked up at Connor. "Right, Dad?"

He kissed the top of her head. "You betcha." He shooed Finn from the room. "We'll call you when it's ready."

She didn't know how to react. Connor, behaving like a dad? *Better enjoy it while you can, because it isn't likely to last long.*

CHAPTER TWENTY-ONE

SAM COULDN'T EXPLAIN his reaction to Finn's "so far" comment. He thought about it long past midnight on Friday. He came to the conclusion that all she needed was a little time to herself, and resisted calling or dropping by.

But that hadn't lasted long.

Early Monday morning, he'd received orders to report for a Thursday meeting in the chief's office, and Finn was the first person—the *only* person—he wanted to talk to about it. She'd said some pretty insightful things in response to the Jasmine Epps story, and he craved more of the same confidence boosting. When she didn't pick up, he used logic to fight off disappointment. She was busy monitoring Ciara's health, checking on construction at The Right Note, jumping through hoops to keep booze out of Connor's hands.

He also tried getting in touch that night, but the call went to voice mail yet again. As it had on Tuesday. By Wednesday, after Sam had sent three texts and left two messages, it dawned on him that her silence was a message to *him*.

He didn't like admitting that maybe Aggie had

been right, but what else was he to think, all things considered? Perfect timing, he told himself. He had classes to teach and a business to run. And if he hoped to come out of the meeting at headquarters with a job, he'd better show up with a clear head and a calm heart.

His cell phone pinged, alerting him to an incoming phone call.

"What's up, cousin?"

He hadn't heard from Zach in weeks. No surprise there. Nate and Sophie had told him that Summer was keeping the father-to-be busy. Sam grinned, picturing the big former marine painting pink-and-white stripes on the nursery walls or grappling with the elaborate car seat/stroller/infant carrier Sam had sent as a shower gift.

He propped his feet on the railing. "Calling to announce the addition of another Marshall to the family?"

"Aw, man. What a buzzkill."

Sam laughed. "Didn't mean to steal your thunder. Go ahead. I'll shut up while you give me all the statistics…except how many hours Summer was in lab—"

"So her water breaks, right, but she sleeps right through it. *I* don't, though. 'Hey, sweetie,' I say… and I'm shakin' her real gently, like, 'Hey, darlin', you wanna call your doctor while I throw your suitcase in the truck?'"

Sam pictured the scene and smiled. In his opinion, Zach had earned every bit of joy life had to offer. He'd never fully understood his cousin's decision to enlist, but supported his cousin's choice despite worry-inducing news reports that painted a very different picture of the Middle East than those drawn in Zach's upbeat letters. He'd come back to them in reasonably good shape…weeks before his sister Libby was attacked. Not long afterward, he'd met Summer, still battling ghosts that were eerily similar to Libby's. Now Zach was happy, finally, so yeah, it was good, real good, to hear proof of it in his voice.

"So she's still half asleep, see," he continued, "but she rolls over and goes, 'Zach, did you forget to put the cap on your bottled water again?' And I'm starting to panic, 'cause I read more of those 'when you're expecting' books than she did, and know *exactly* what's going on. Anyway, I jump into my pants and pull on my boots and clomp around to her side of the bed. Pick her up. Get her on her feet. And she opens those big beautiful eyes and smiles. 'Uh-oh,' she says, 'guess I'd better call the doctor while you throw my suitcase in the truck, huh?'"

Sam couldn't be sure if the sound he heard was Zach chuckling or Zach choking back a joyous sob.

"I drove like a speed demon the whole way to the hospital, flashers blinking, horn honking, gripping the steering wheel so tight I thought I'd bend it. And then?"

Sam was happy for Zach. And a little envious, too.

"And then just like that," Zach said, "I'm a husband *and* a dad." He exhaled a shaky sigh. "Didn't think I'd ever feel better than when Summer said, 'I do'…"

His voice trailed off. Had they been disconnected, or was Zach too overcome with emotion to speak?

"I was wrong," he said at last. "Dead wrong. They put that itty-bitty bundle in my arms, and… and you've heard that saying 'my legs buckled?'"

"Yeah…"

"Well, *that*. I sat in the nearest chair and started bawlin' even harder than she was."

"Summer, you mean?"

"No—I can't believe I'm about to say this—*my little girl*."

Envy smacked him yet again, and Sam decided he'd been away from the ranch too long. With no one but himself to worry about, he was in danger of turning into a self-centered jerk.

"Summer's okay, then?"

"Not just okay. Incredible. Beautiful. Magnificent. *Perfect*. I tell ya, Sam, life's good. Real, real good."

"You earned it. So did Summer. And I can't wait to meet little… What's the baby's name?"

"Cassidy Rose. Soon as we hang up, I'll send you a picture."

"Can't wait."

"You're gonna love her. So when *are* you visiting? Thanksgiving?"

Finn had almost said yes to his invitation to spend the holidays at the ranch, but then Friday and the "so far" comment had happened.

"I guess that'll depend on Nate and Eden." Not the whole truth, but not a lie, either. "Have they set a date yet?"

"Aw, who knows with those two. Every time I ask, all I get is 'soon.' Don't know which one is the holdout."

"Uh-oh. Trouble in paradise?"

"No, nothing like that."

Good, Sam thought. *Just because* you're *destined to grow old alone, doesn't mean they should.*

"They're trying to get their ducks in a row so they can legally adopt the boys after things are official. But you know what they say about red tape."

"Yeah, official paperwork can be a pain, all right. I hope they get it straightened out soon. Because Eden is good for Nate, and he's good for her."

"Weird, isn't it, that Nate will become a dad to a crowd of boys, days after he puts that ring on her finger?"

That "wish it were me" sensation kicked in again. "Those are some lucky kids."

"And they know it, too. Every one of them has cleaned up his act. So much that you probably won't recognize them."

Sam didn't know what to make of the emotions swirling in his head—and thumping in his heart. He'd been born into a huge, loving family, a family that was growing by the minute. Why couldn't he be satisfied with that? Why did he want what Zach had—and what Nate was about to get—so badly that he could taste it?

"So how're things in Music City?"

Should he tell Zach about the scheduled meeting with the department's high muck-a-mucks? Nah. He'd wait until afterward, when he had more concrete information.

"Downright harmonious," he said. "Get it? Music City…" And then he noticed someone pacing behind his pickup. Standing, Sam peered over the railing. *What in the world?*

Connor looked up, as if summoned by Sam's thoughts.

"Apartment eight, right?" he shouted, one hand shading his eyes.

Nodding, Sam waved him up. "I'll have to get back to you, Zach. I just got some unexpected company. Give my love to Summer, and kiss that baby for me."

"No way. You're gonna have to come home and do that yourself."

"Okay," he said, chuckling, "it's a deal."

Pocketing the phone, he wondered how Finn's dad had found out where he lived. To his knowledge, *she* didn't even know his address.

"Hey," he said, opening the door wide.

Connor stepped past him and, hands pocketed, said, "You're not an easy man to find."

"Really." Sam led him into the living room. "What's up?"

"I, ah, I want to talk about Finn."

"Well, that's a relief," he admitted. "I thought maybe something happened to Ciara."

"Kee? Nah. She's good. Fine." Connor worked the kinks out of his neck. "Doc prescribed some new meds. Seems to be helping." Nodding, he cleared his throat. "Don't think she's had a headache or a dizzy spell in days."

"That's good to hear." And he meant it. The poor kid already had enough to contend with.

"Yeah, it beats exploratory surgery."

The man had been in his house slightly more than a minute, and already Sam had tired of his small talk. "So…is Finn okay?"

"Yeah. Physically anyway."

"Not to be rude, but…" Sam glanced at his watch, a not-so-subtle hint that Connor might consider getting to the point. "Why'd you come looking for me?" Maybe, in addition to an explanation, Connor would tell him who'd directed him to the apartment.

"Oh. Right. So anyway, I just stopped by to apologize for my girl. She's got a lot on her shoulders, between taking care of Kee and running the diner and the renovations and all. I'm sure you understand if she sometimes seems a little short-tempered. If she said something to tick you off, well, put the blame where it belongs. On her mom and me."

"What makes you think she ticked me off?"

Connor grunted. "You guys were like this." He held up his forefinger, crossed the index finger over it. "And then?" He made a wide V of the digits. "Doesn't take a genius to figure out…" He lifted his chin. "Wait. You mean…you mean you ticked *her* off?"

In a way, Sam supposed he had. He didn't understand why, but at this point, what difference did it make?

"So what did you mean, she's all right…physically?"

Connor shook his head. "Aw, she's been moping around since Friday night. Hardly says a word, except to Kee. She'd wring my neck if she knew I was here, telling you any of this, but I've heard her crying. After lights-out. In the shower. Any time she thinks Ciara and I can't hear. The other day, I caught her standing at the sink blubbering like a baby."

"Did you ask her what the problem is?"

Eyes wide, Connor seemed stunned by the question. "Of course I did. I'm a sorry excuse for a father, but I'm not totally heartless."

Sam's patience was running out. "Never meant to imply you're either. But when I hear she's been crying—which is totally out of character for her—it's only natural to ask *why*."

"You know what they say…careful what you wish for? Well, in a word, the problem is *you*. At least, that's my opinion, and you know what they say about those? 'Opinions are like armpits—everybody has a couple, and mostly, they stink.'"

Sam grinned, even though it hurt like mad, hearing he might be the cause of Finn's misery.

"I'm not here to assign blame, Sam. God knows I'm in no position to do that! I just thought, what could it hurt to stop by, ask you to call her, see if you can mend fences or whatever."

"Already tried calling. Texted her, too. When she didn't answer…"

"You took it to mean she wants nothing more to do with you."

Sam winced, and Connor added, "Well, you're wrong. Finn would never admit it, but she needs you. That's why you have to talk with her. Face-to-face. The sooner, the better."

The thought that jumped into his head made him feel like a five-year-old: *he'd* made an effort. If she refused to meet him halfway, what more could he do?

"She'll be home alone tonight. I know that for a fact."

"Alone? But what about Ciara?"

"I'm taking her out for pizza. Finn has some unpacking to do at the diner, prepping for the re-opening." Connor inspected his fingernails. "The contractor made great progress this week. My guess is they'll finish up in a week, two at most, and she has some decisions to make about what to keep and what to toss."

"What time will you and Ciara leave tonight?"

"Five, six o'clock? Poor kid isn't real steady on

her feet—hasn't been since the accident, if you want the truth—but right now it's worse, because she's still adjusting to the new meds. I don't have my license back yet, so we'll need to walk. Slowly. Her favorite pizza parlor is always packed, so we could be gone for a good two, three hours." Standing, he walked to the door. "So will you stop by?"

"Yeah. I guess. Why not?"

Connor laughed, and just before stepping outside, he said, "When you get there, you might want to adjust your enthusiasm level."

On the way to his room, Sam remembered that day at the zoo, when the sunshine had turned Finn's cheeks pink and the humidity curled her waves into soft ringlets. He got a glimpse of himself in the foyer mirror. If the mental image of her could paint a goofy love-struck grin on his face, what would happen when he got an eyeful in person?

CHAPTER TWENTY-TWO

"WHERE'S DAD?"

Finn didn't even want to think of the possibilities. "I have no idea," she said without taking her eyes off the checkbook.

Ciara patted her shoulder. "Don't—don't worry, Finn. He isn't in a bar."

She didn't remind her sister that as long as he could wrap his fingers around the neck of a whiskey bottle, Connor could get drunk just about anywhere.

"He'll be—he'll be home soon." She crossed to the front door and, standing on tiptoe, peeked through the curtains. "Did he tell you? We're going to Luigi's tonight for pizza. To celebrate that I don't need surgery. And to stay out of your hair since you're so busy with diner stuff."

Dr. Peterson hadn't completely ruled out an operation. Ciara had the right to hear the truth in terms she could understand. And Finn intended to make Connor see that, first chance she got.

"Yes, he told me." But only because he'd needed money to pay for their father-daughter night out.

On Connor's first morning in town, Finn had given him three hundred—in cash—for new jeans, a decent shirt and tie, and taxi money in case she was working and couldn't drive him to interviews. He'd taken it on the condition that she accept his IOU. And right now, it was in the bottom of her jewelry box with all the others—each a tiny reminder that her father's promises weren't worth the paper they were written on.

Ciara sat on the arm of the couch, and Finn finally looked up from her accounting.

"We can—we can bring something home for you..."

Finn smiled. "That would be real nice. Thanks, sweetie."

Ciara went back to watching the window, and Finn focused on the electric bill. It wasn't easy paying attention, though, with her sister over there, chattering happily about pizza toppings and root beer and a walk to the ice-cream parlor afterward.

Oh, Connor, please don't let her down again.

If he did, Ciara would accept whatever lame excuse he came up with, forgive him and promptly forget about it. *Better that than become a bitter, untrusting grouch like you.*

"Need to change my shoes," Ciara said, heading for her room. "Might have to walk a lot. And Dad walks *fast*."

She'd loan Connor the car—if a judge in Florida hadn't taken away his license.

He walked in just then, looking...*guilty* was the only word that came to mind.

"Where's Ciara?"

"In her room, putting some finishing touches on her outfit." She didn't detect even a hint of alcohol when he kissed her cheek. Maybe he'd traded whiskey for vodka or gin, since they didn't leave a telltale scent, or opted to take pills instead. "She's really excited about your night on the town."

"So am I." He pointed at the paperwork scattered on the old desktop. "Don't suppose you can leave this for a few hours and join us."

It was tempting, but Finn shook her head. "I'd better not. The guys are wrapping up at The Right Note. And once I start putting things back where they go…"

He seemed relieved that she'd said no. She couldn't blame him. Since the accident, she hadn't exactly been the warmest, most loving daughter.

"If I know you, you won't want to stop until the job's done." Smiling, he shook his head. "No idea where you got your work ethic."

The comment reminded her of a loud, dishes-smashing battle between her parents. "This isn't the first time you've been with another man!" he'd bellowed, pointing at Finn. "She's got a do-the-right-thing gene as big as her head. She sure as heck didn't get that from either of *us*!" She'd only been six at the time, too young to fully comprehend what he'd insinuated. But one glance at Misty had cleared things up in less than a blink: Connor wasn't convinced Finn was his daughter.

She stared hard at the checkbook, but the numbers blurred. Finn rubbed her eyes, wondering why she kept buying tickets to ride this emotional roller coaster. Memories like that were counterproductive. Especially considering the fact that, after the accident, their shared rare blood type had made it pretty clear he was, indeed, her father.

"Dad," Ciara said, "I was beginning to think you forgot about—about our date. I'm so glad you're home!"

"Where else would I be?"

If Finn had blinked, she would have missed the uncertainty that flickered across Ciara's features. In that instant, her sister hadn't seemed quite so naive. Was it possible she *did* remember his broken promises?

Glancing at his watch, Connor said, "Ready to go?"

"I've been ready for *a whole hour.*"

"Had an errand to run," he said. "Took longer than I thought." He held out his arms, and she stepped into them. "But your old dad is here now, right?"

Ciara wrapped her arms around his waist. "Yes, you're here now."

Finn squeezed Ciara's hand. "You guys have fun, okay?"

"I will. Dad, can we bring Finn something to eat?"

"You bet." He kissed Finn's cheek, then lowered

his voice to say, "If she's not too tired, we might catch that movie she's been talking about. But don't worry. If she starts looking peaked, even a little, I'll bring her right home."

It wasn't easy, watching them walk away hand in hand. He'd been different this visit—more attentive, helpful, fun loving—and Ciara was lapping it up like a hungry pup. If he fell off the wagon and disappeared again, it would hurt more than the past three times combined.

Finn tidied the batch of now-paid bills. First thing tomorrow, she'd stop by the post office for stamps and get the whole stack into the mail.

"I hope you appreciate this, Pete," she mumbled. He'd raised a stink every time she suggested going the online route. It didn't make much sense that she kept doing things the old-fashioned way, but then, why should that make sense when so few other things about life did?

Right now, all that talk of pizza and ice cream was making her hungry, and unless Connor had raided the fridge, she could make a sandwich from that leftover meat loaf. Thankfully, the small plastic container still sat on a middle shelf. She popped bread into the toaster and put the meat loaf into the microwave. And while she tried to decide between catsup and mayo, someone knocked.

"Don't tell me," she called through the door, "you forgot your key again, didn't you?"

"No, but I almost forgot how pretty you look in yellow," Sam said when she opened it.

She glanced down at her oversize T-shirt. The sundress she'd worn to the zoo had been almost the same shade.

"Connor and Ciara just left." She stepped aside to let him in.

"I know. I stayed in the truck until I saw them round the corner."

She started to ask why, but he kept going before she could cut in. "Hope you don't mind me showing up unannounced. I tried to call and text a few times." He held up a white paper bag. "Figured you were swamped, getting the diner ready to reopen, so I took a chance that you hadn't had supper yet." He sniffed the air. "Something smells amazing."

"I was just heating up some of last night's meat loaf." She led the way into the kitchen. "There's plenty, unless you have your heart set on whatever's in that bag."

"Lunch-meat subs," he said, stuffing the sack into the fridge. "They'll keep."

"Paper plates are in there." She pointed at the pantry's narrow door. "So are the napkins."

While Sam set the table, Finn poured iced tea. "It's decaf," she said. "Fresh brewed and guaranteed not to keep you awake."

She did her best to ignore his arresting smile and focused on the questions churning in her mind: Was his arrival a coincidence? Or did the timing have something to do with Connor's peculiar, almost guilty expression earlier? *Only one way to find out...*

"Have you talked with Connor lately?"

"Guess that depends on your definition of the word *lately.*"

Clever.

"Why do you ask?"

"Because he was acting suspicious earlier, sort of the way you were just now."

"Didn't realize I looked suspicious."

Did he realize he had the power to make her every nerve jangle just by aiming those long-lashed blue eyes in her direction?

Finn had a feeling Connor had paid him a visit, but for now she'd sidestep the issue. For now. She put the meat loaf plate in the middle of the table and jabbed a fork into it. "Dig in," she told him. "Nuked food tends to cool faster than stuff heated in a pan on the stovetop."

Providing useless information, Pete once told her, makes others aware you're not on solid ground. "If you don't know what to say, keep your mouth shut," he'd always insisted.

Sam put a slice of meat loaf on her plate, then opened the fridge and withdrew the catsup before serving himself.

"So how are things coming downstairs?"

Finn topped off her wedge with a red squiggle. "Really well. Hopefully, I'll still be able to say that a week from now, so I can schedule the grand re-opening celebration."

He raised an eyebrow, exactly as he had right before recommending the shortlist of contractors.

"Don't tell me you know someone who can help with publicity, too?"

Sam laughed quietly. "Matter of fact, I do. Young reporter who interviewed me for an article in *Nashville Lifestyles*. She's always looking for lifestyle story ideas."

"I subscribe and leave copies of the magazine near the cash register, in case people need something to read while they're eating alone. Now I wish I had time to read more than the cover." She sipped her tea. "Which issue were you in?"

"I think it was called something like 'Most Eligible.' Hit the stands a couple years back."

Yes, Finn had seen that one but decided not to spend even one minute reading about musicians flaunting their "I'm so hot!" attitudes.

"Did you get any fan mail after it was released?"

He laughed again. "No, thank God." Sam sobered slightly to add, "It's probably tough for someone like you to believe, but not every musician spends his life seeking out opportunities to score."

Someone like me?

He muttered something unintelligible, then said, "What's left to do? To get the place ready to open, I mean."

"There are dozens of boxes in the storeroom, full

of dinnerware, flatware, utensils… I was in too big a rush when I packed them up to separate the good stuff from things with cracks, chips or dents. I need to go through all of it, wash up the useful stuff and get rid of the rest."

He carried the now-empty paper plate to the trash can and stepped on the pedal. "More iced tea?"

"No, but thanks."

"How 'bout when we finish up here, you give me the nickel tour of the diner?"

"It's not all that different than it was." She'd hoped to open for business without anyone but the staff knowing about the changes she'd made.

"Yeah, right."

"You've…you've seen it?"

"Yes and no." He dumped his ice cubes into the sink and put the tumbler in the dishwasher. "Don't look so surprised. It isn't my fault you're barely bigger than a minute."

"I'm… *What?*"

"When you hung that butcher's paper to hide what was going on inside, you didn't take it all the way to the top of the windows. I didn't even have to stand on my toes to peek over the top of it."

Why did the image of him peering into the window make her smile?

She got up, disposed of her own plate and said, "Since you won't be surprised on opening day, I might as well let you see what a great job your contractor pal has done."

FIVE MINUTES LATER, standing in the space between the snack bar and the service counter, Sam said, "Wow. This is amazing. People are gonna love it."

"I hope so. I didn't have a lot of time to choose fixtures and whatnot. Your guy is *fast*."

"They call him Speedy down at the station house." He walked to the other side of the counter. "It doesn't even look like the same place."

"Which is part of the problem. There isn't much Pete left."

"Well, from everything I've heard about him, I'm pretty sure he'd approve."

"I hope so," she said again. "What have you heard?"

"That he saw you and Ciara as the kids he never had, and that during the last years of his life, he put things in motion to ensure you guys were well taken care of when he wasn't around to do it anymore."

A wistful smile lifted one corner of her mouth.

"So it's a safe bet he'd approve of the changes," he concluded.

"I hope you're right, because what's done is done." She laughed softly. "Almost done anyway."

"There's one way you can find out for sure," he said, following her to the storeroom. "Have everyone who comes in that first week fill out a survey to let you know who's been here before and which menu item they like best. Then you have a draw, and the winner gets, oh, I dunno, twenty bucks off their next meal or something."

Her brow furrowed slightly, and Sam didn't know whether to blame it on his idea or the stubborn packing tape that refused to break when she tried to open a box.

"You know, that's not a half-bad idea." She met his eyes. "Were you a publicist in a former life?"

He popped the tape securing the carton's lid, then did his best cowboy impersonation. "There y'go, li'l missy."

She topped it with a less-than-perfect thank-you. "No way…you saw that old Western, too?"

"Only ten or twelve times! John Wayne is one of my favorite actors."

Yet another thing they had in common. Sam pressed a palm to his chest. "I've said it before, but it bears repeating—where have you been all my life, Finn Leary?"

He hoped her shy smile meant they were okay again. He rolled a low stool closer to the carton he'd opened and watched as Finn inspected a heavy ceramic mug for chips and cracks.

"So, Finn. Tell me. How are things?"

"Good. This one's a keeper," she said, putting it aside.

"No, not the mug, you nut. What's going on with Connor? And how's Ciara? She looked a bit off when she left earlier."

She picked up another mug. "The drugs are helping, but she has a ways to go yet."

Sam already knew that, thanks to Connor's surprise visit. But he couldn't admit it to Finn. Not without upending what little progress the man had made, working his way back into his daughters' lives. For Finn's sake and Ciara's, Sam hoped Connor wasn't faking it just to keep a roof over his head and food in his belly.

"Good to hear Ciara is holding her own."

She tossed two cups and three soup bowls into the trash bin.

"And how about you?"

She glanced up from a fluted sundae glass. "I'm fine. Why, do I look peaked, too?"

"As a matter of fact, you do. I've pulled enough all-nighters to recognize the signs."

"Ah. I think I get it now."

He was almost afraid to ask, "Get what?"

"You're letting me off easy." Finn sat back on her heels. "That's really nice of you, but there's no excusing what I said the other night. So let's say I'm sorry for aiming my misplaced hostility in your direction and move forward."

"Not to steal your thunder, but I came over here to apologize. My reaction was uncalled-for."

Finn examined a sandwich platter and added it to the "keep" stack. "Well, well, well. Aren't we a pair?"

"A pair of what?"

"Do-the-right-thing, my-fault-not-yours, mea culpa types, that's what."

Sam smirked. "Yeah. I guess that sounds like us."

"Sounds like? It *is* us."

"At least we have sincerity going for us."

She believed him, and it was such a relief that he blurted out, "Maybe we should get married, 'cause who else would have us?"

Sam tensed and held his breath, watching as she calmly put the next platter into the "toss" pile and picked up another. The calm before the storm?

When he couldn't stand the silence anymore, he asked, "So what are your plans for announcing the reopening?"

"Beyond making a few signs to hang in the windows? None."

"Signs are a good start. But what about posters to paste on telephone poles? Three-by-five cards for bulletin boards in libraries and grocery stores? Press releases to get the media interested in covering the grand reopening? The Right Note has been around for years. It's become an icon. Who knows? Maybe WSNV or WKRN will send out a film crew. And there's no telling how many people the videos might bring in."

She stopped working long enough to make eye contact. "Okay. 'Fess up. You were a publicist in a former life, weren't you?"

"No," he said, laughing, "but I've worked on a few fire department fund-raisers and a couple for other charities."

"Fund-raising."

"Yeah…"

"But the difference is my reopening will be blatant advertising. The only one who'll profit from it is me."

"True, but it's not as apples and oranges as you'd think. I'm no expert, but I'm happy to share what little I know. And I work free. If you're interested in a few pointers, that is."

She thought about it for a moment, then buried her face in the crook of her arm. "Good grief," she said, voice muffled by her sleeve. "How will it all get done by opening day?"

Rolling the stool closer, he leaned forward. "Finn," he said, relieving her of a small metal milk pitcher. "I know you've been on your own for a long time and that it isn't easy for you to accept help from someone you barely know..."

Taking her hands in his, he studied three work-induced blisters on her right palm. If she'd let him, he'd help carry her load, so they'd heal and never return.

"But you can count on me."

Finn turned his hands, traced his heart line and life line and the burn scars that zigzagged across his palms.

"Did it hurt much," she asked, her voice a near whisper, "when you first started playing guitar? Before the strings caused these calluses?"

"I've been playing so long that if it hurt, I've forgotten about it."

She nodded slowly. "Symbolic, isn't it?"

He rolled the stool forward an inch. "That the past toughens us up, to protect us from future hurts, you mean."

Turning his hands again, she inspected his fingernails and cuticles, then gently stroked each knuckle and slightly raised vein.

"You should write a song," she said, eyes twinkling. "'There Are Calluses on My Heart.'"

Sam slid his arms around her. "In junior high, I broke my left arm and—"

"How?"

"Fell off a horse," he said, grinning. "Anyway, by the time the cast came off—"

"How long was it on?"

"Six, eight weeks?"

"Wrist?"

"Forearm. Both bones."

Her nose wrinkled in sympathy, and tenderness welled up inside him. "*Anyway*, by the time the cast came off, my fingertips had gone all soft on me, and I pretty much had to start over, rebuilding the calluses."

"Bet that took a really long ti—"

Sam placed a finger over her lips and chuckled. "Hush. Let a guy get to the point, will ya?"

She was so close to him that when she giggled, he felt her warm breath on his cheek.

"If we're patient," he continued, "if we take our time, all the damage life has done to your heart will heal. And maybe," he said, touching his forehead to hers, "just maybe, that wall you built around it will come down, too."

"Hmm…"

"What?"

"I've been told my heart is as big as my head."

"Oh, yeah? By who?"

"By a lot of people."

"But my point is, your great big heart will heal, if we give it time."

"You said *we*."

"Yeah, so?"

"So I thought you came here to apologize."

"I did." Sam frowned. "You mean I didn't?"

Her soft laughter rumbled against his chest, and he pulled her tighter still.

"Not in so many words. But then, neither did I."

Heart thumping with affection, Sam combed his fingers through her hair, stopping just above her ears.

"I don't mind admitting that I'm a little distracted here. Remind me exactly what I'm apologizing *for*?"

"For coming over here looking contrite, promising to help, saying I can trust you…"

She got to her feet, and Sam had a feeling she was about to deliver a painful *but*.

Finn bent at the waist until they were eye to eye. "But you haven't proved it."

"No, I haven't. But, Finn, I *can't* prove it. Yet."

"Oh, that's right. I nearly forgot. We have to be

patient, don't we, and give my poor broken little heart time to heal."

Was she being cynical? Sarcastic? Sam searched her face. Her beautiful brown eyes glowed with affection. For *him*.

And that put him on his feet. "That's right. We."

Standing on tiptoe, Finn pressed a tiny kiss to the corner of his mouth, and it warmed him from scalp to soles. What would Sophie say if she could see him now, caving to every emotion he'd tried so hard to smother?

She'd say "What're you waiting for? Kiss her, you big idiot!"

And so he did.

CHAPTER TWENTY-THREE

SAM HAD STAYED with Finn until every carton had been unpacked and every plate, glass and fork found its way into the "keep" or "toss" bins. He'd talked about the ranch and his family, and reminded her that the invitation to share in the big Marshall Thanksgiving feast was still open.

Finn wanted to go, partially because the trip would let her see how he interacted with his parents, siblings and the cousins he'd grown up with. "You'll learn everything you need to know about a man," Pete had said, "by watching the way he treats his mother." If she'd heeded the warning, there'd be two fewer scars on her heart.

Her ex-boyfriend's face flashed in her mind, but she blinked it away and concentrated on the task at hand: filling Ciara's weekly pills container. "Too bad there isn't a pill to make people reveal themselves as cheating liars." And because she didn't like the way that made her sound, she added, "And one to cure self-pity."

On the way to the coffeemaker, Connor kissed her cheek. "Sorry, I didn't catch that. What were you saying?"

"Oh, nothing. Just counting out loud," she said, adding a multivitamin to each cube.

"So how'd it go last night?"

"How'd what go?"

He faced the other direction and filled his mug. "Whatever you did last night. It isn't often you get a night to yourself…" Turning, he winked.

Hearing that, Finn was more convinced than before that Sam's surprise visit had only been a surprise to *her*.

"So is Sam's house nice?"

He opened a box of cornflakes. "I, ah, I guess."

Finn placed Ciara's meds beside her cereal bowl.

"What do you think of it?" he asked.

"I've never been there."

"Never been where?" Ciara wanted to know.

"To Sam's house." Finn looked at Connor. "Or is it a condo?"

"It's a fourth-floor apart…" He stopped talking so suddenly that he sloshed milk on to the back of his hand. "I, ah, I'm just guessing it's an apartment. Because he's a bachelor."

"Fourth floor, eh?" Finn ripped a few paper towels from the roller and sopped up his mess. "That's pretty specific…for a guess."

He sent her an awkward smile and sat beside Ciara. "So what're you having for breakfast this morning? Crispy rice? Sugar flakes? Oatmeal?"

"Can I fix myself some cinna-cinnamon toast?"

Finn kissed the top of her head. "You can if you

want to, but I'm happy to make it for you." Not the most nutritious way to start the day, but she'd see to it her sister ate a hearty, healthy lunch to make up for it.

"It's okay." Ciara crossed to the other side of the kitchen. "You—you do so much." She popped two slices of bread into the toaster.

"Did you get lots done last night?"

"As a matter of fact, I finished going through all the serving pieces, and even some of the pots and pans. I only need to run them through the dishwasher and they'll be ready for Rowdy's rib-stickin' recipes."

"Want me to help you put things where they go?"

Finn gave her sister a sideways hug. "What would I do without you?"

Connor topped off his coffee and added a splash to Finn's mug, too. "What are your plans for the stuff you can't use anymore?"

"All the ceramic pieces are already in the dumpster. It's decades old, and I'm worried that the clay or paint might contain low levels of lead."

"Ah, good point. I hadn't thought of that. That's too bad, though, because I was thinking it'd make a great donation for the homeless shelter off Seventh Avenue." He scooped up a spoonful of cereal. "*All* of those places are lifesavers, literally and figuratively."

"I'm sure we can still find a few things to donate." She handed Ciara a butter knife, got the sugar bowl out of the cupboard and put it near the toaster. Had Connor picked up that opinion of shelters from a news story or personal experience? And why hadn't it occurred to her before now that he might have been desperate enough for a hot meal and a place to sleep that he'd gone to one for help?

"I've known people who cooked or served meals over there," she said, "but never met anyone on the other side of the counter."

Connor started to say something, then glanced at Ciara, humming quietly as she sprinkled cinnamon and sugar on her buttered toast. His eyes welled up—if Finn had blinked, she would have missed it—just before he lowered his head. He had a story to tell, all right, but did Finn want to hear it?

"So what are your plans for the day?" he asked.

"Ciara and I are going shopping for new curtains for the diner."

"Finn wants red-and-white checkers, because the floor is—is black-and-white checkers."

He smiled, but clearly his heart wasn't in it. "It's gonna look great."

Connor had too much time on his hands. If he had a job, he'd be too busy during working hours to dwell in the past. Staying busy had kept her own dark memories at bay, and she blamed the waiting around with next to nothing to do for the negative thoughts that crept into her head.

"Would you like to tag along? We could have lunch at Puckett's."

For a minute there, it appeared he might say yes. "I'd better not. I have an audition tonight, and I should probably tune up the old git-fiddle and croon a tune or two."

She sat beside him. "An audition?"

"Yeah. Lead guitarist for a house band."

"That's great news!"

"Long time coming, too. Once I start pulling in a regular paycheck, I'm going to contribute more around here. But only until I save enough for a place of my own."

"Why can't you stay here, Dad?"

"Aw, honey, you know why. I can't stay in Finn's room forever. She pays the bills, and she shouldn't have to sleep on that lumpy ol' couch every night."

"It isn't lumpy. I slept there before. It's comfortable." She glanced at Finn for corroboration. "Right, Finn?"

"It's perfectly fine."

"Hey! I have—I have a great idea! Why don't we just get another bed and put it, put it in my room, and you and me could be roommates, and Dad could have your room. That way, nobody has to sleep on the couch, and Dad can *stay*!"

"That would be fine, except there isn't a spare inch of available floor space in your room."

"Bunk beds, then!"

"Sweetie," Connor said, grasping her hand, "we can't do that. That slanted ceiling is too low, and poor Finn would conk her head every time she sat up in bed."

"Oh. Yeah." Ciara sighed. "I forgot about that."

"Quit worrying, okay? When I do move out, I promise to get a place nearby. And anyway, I don't have the job yet."

"Where's the audition?" Finn asked. There were probably a hundred bars and pubs in Nashville. What were the chances he'd say—

"The Meetinghouse. It's close enough that if I get the gig, I can walk to work."

Unless he'd been putting on one terrific show for her benefit, Connor had been clean and sober for a week now. But was he strong enough to put himself in such close proximity to an unlimited supply of alcohol?

"I didn't realize they needed a guitarist. I mean, since Sam signed on as a partner, I naturally assumed he'd take the stage every chance he got."

How had he found out about that?

"According to Mark, Sam's too busy writing up lesson plans and putting future firefighters through their paces to take the stage."

Too busy? But what about the all-important meeting that had him worrying about the problem with Jasmine? Had she really grown so self-involved that it had never crossed her mind to ask him how things had gone? No wonder he'd taken her "so far" comment so much to heart!

Finn licked her lips, remembering the sweet,

eager kiss that had had her up half the night thinking that maybe, just maybe, time and patience *were* what the doctor ordered.

"Can I ask you a huge favor, Finn?"

Hopefully, he wouldn't ask for cash, because until The Right Note reopened, every penny was spoken for.

"I thought I'd wear that shirt you got me for Christmas last year. You know, the white one with the pearl snap buttons? But it's been stuffed in my duffel so long that it's one big wrinkle."

She'd hadn't seen him in it, but if he looked half as fit and professional as the magazine model had, Connor would get the job.

"I'll set the ironing board up in the living room and press it for you before we leave for town." She made her way to the hall. "What time is the audition anyway?"

"Nine. I'm opening tonight."

Surrounded by booze and under real pressure for the first time in ages. Could he pass the test?

He could…with a solid support system nearby…

"Ciara and I will be back well before that. Why don't we come with you for moral support?"

A slow smile slanted his lips. "You'd do that?"

"Of course—of course we would, Dad!"

"It's been ages since we've heard you perform," Finn said. "Plus, it'll give us a good excuse to get all dolled up and…"

Connor put his mug and bowl into the sink. "And what?"

She stopped herself from saying, "and to see Sam." What about him anyway? Would he stay home writing up lesson plans or join Connor onstage? She couldn't voice the question without admitting how much she'd come to care for him, mostly because she hadn't fully accepted the idea, herself.

"Are you planning to wear jeans and boots?" she asked Connor.

"Yup."

"Then I'll give your boots a going-over, too."

"Don't know what I ever did in my miserable life to deserve a kid like you, but if I ever figure it out…"

I promise to do it again and again and again, she finished silently.

An hour later, Finn slid the steam iron along his shirtsleeves, trying to remember the first time he'd delivered the now-familiar line. Had she been four? Six? The dreamy-eyed girl she'd been all those years ago wanted to believe every word of his promise, but that girl was long gone. Taking care of herself and Ciara had taught her—

Finn stood the iron on its end, heart pounding and eyes stinging as she remembered something Sam had said last night. "I know you've been on your own a long time, and it isn't easy for you to accept help…but you can count on me."

Was *that* why she'd started falling for him? Because he said and did all the right things and made her feel protected...the way Connor should have? Was she so hungry for affection and so desperate to feel safe that she'd gone in search of...*of a father figure?*

Poor Sam. Poor kind, unsuspecting Sam!

Finn slumped on to the arm of the sofa and held her head in her hands. "You need a shrink, not a—"

"Here y'go, sweetie." Connor stood the boots beside the couch and draped the jeans over its back cushion. "Thanks again, and if you need me," he said, kissing her forehead, "I'll be in my room, practicing."

His room? An hour after telling Ciara that he felt guilty about her sleeping on the lumpy old couch?

"Some things need to change around here..." Finn murmured.

She caught a distorted glimpse of herself in the iron's curved, mirrorlike base.

"...starting with *you.*"

CHAPTER TWENTY-FOUR

LAST TIME SAM reported to headquarters, the chief's secretary had issued a courteous apology, then sent him packing with a vague promise to call and reschedule. Since then, Epps's attendance in class had been spotty. He'd hoped it meant she'd decided against becoming a firefighter.

No such luck, as it turned out.

Now, alone in the chief's reception area, Sam waited for the command to enter the big guy's office. Waited, too, for the jitters to attack, the way they had on his last visit here. The calm before the storm?

The big wooden door opened, and the receptionist closed it quietly behind her. "They're ready for you," she said, sitting at her L-shaped desk. Carla Buck said the nameplate on its corner.

"They?"

She sent him a sympathetic smile.

"How many?"

"Nine."

"Whew," he said, and got to his feet. "Water might come in handy."

She withdrew a blue bottle from the fridge under her desk and handed it to him. "Good luck in there."

"Thanks, Ms. Buck. Let's hope I won't need it."

"Please. Call me Carla." Lowering her voice, she whispered from the corner of her mouth, "We underlings have to stick together."

He paused with one hand on the doorknob. "What's the mood in there?"

"If I had any idea how to read their moods, I'd know when to ask for a raise."

Grinning, he rapped quietly on the door and took a deep breath when a raspy voice on the other side said, "C'mon in, Marshall."

They weren't in uniform, and Sam didn't know what to make of that. One by one, they tabled soft drinks and coffee mugs to shake his hand and introduce themselves—Epps's older brothers, father, grandfather, uncle and four others in the chain of command—including Sam's captain.

Chief Carlson gestured toward the only available chair, curiously positioned beside the big mahogany desk. As he sat, Sam empathized with every witness who'd ever faced a jury.

Carlson pointed out a two-tiered serving dish on the credenza behind him and said, "Help yourself to a doughnut, son."

Sam held up the water bottle. "I'm good, but thanks."

Epps's brother, also a lieutenant, spoke first. "I guess you know why we called you in here."

To accept my walking papers?

"Jasmine has been driving us crazy for the past few weeks. Crying. Pouting. Ranting."

So she'd told them about their meeting at The Frothy Monkey, had she? He hoped she'd left out the part about her running out of the place in tears.

"We're at our wit's end," her father said. "All she can talk about is you…"

"…and the fact that you've flat-out refused to tutor her," the other brother tacked on.

The chief leaned back in his big leather chair. "To say she's unhappy with you is an understatement." He tapped a half-inch thick stack of message slips. "Every one of us has a pile just like this one. And in every case, you are the subject."

The others grumbled their agreement.

"In the interest of fairness," her grandfather said, "we want to hear your side of things."

When they'd scheduled this meeting, Sam had decided he wouldn't sacrifice his principles, not even to save his job.

"I'm sure you can appreciate where Jasmine is coming from," he began. "She's young. Inexperienced. And has some mighty big shoes to fill." He met her relatives' eyes, one at a time. "Everyone in this room felt that way to one degree or another when we entered the academy."

"Spare us the preamble, Marshall," Jasmine's uncle said. "She asked for help and you sent her packing. We just want to hear *why*."

Her father agreed.

"No need to sugarcoat things, either," said the brother.

So they wanted the truth, did they?

"Is that my file on your desk?" he asked the chief.

"Yours and Cadet Epps's."

"So you know exactly how many of my students—men and women alike—went on to become firefighters. A healthy percentage of them women."

The man nodded. "It's an impressive number."

"And know the total number of graduates versus dropouts."

Carlson said, "We do."

"Where are you going with all this, Marshall?"

Sam faced her uncle. "Just establishing my credibility, Captain. I know firefighter material when I see it."

Her father frowned. "And you don't see it in my girl."

"In my opinion, sir, tutoring Jasmine is unfair to the rest of the class, and it's unfair for her." He could have pointed out that, based on attendance, attention span and borderline insubordination, he would have been within his rights to dismiss her at the conclusion of the second class. Instead, Sam said, "In my opinion, she'd be a detriment to herself and any man assigned to the same truck."

"Why?"

A simple question. Too bad he couldn't give her dad a simple answer.

"First of all, Jasmine doesn't have the strength or dexterity to pass the physical parts of the exam. Not without dedicating herself to an exercise regimen designed to build muscle and stamina. And I'm sure it's no surprise to you that she has problems focusing enough to memorize necessary material."

"Meaning she'd fail the written exam, too."

"Yes, sir, without a serious attitude adjustment, I believe she would."

Her father didn't look or sound surprised, and neither did anyone else in the room. He hoped they hadn't called him in here to suggest he'd dole out passing scores that she hadn't earned...

"Bottom line," Sam said, "I don't think she's cut out to be a firefighter. At least, not at this stage." He could have added that she didn't *want* to be a firefighter, but why add insult to injury? Besides, she had to face these men at family dinners and backyard barbecues; driving a wedge between her and her family seemed cruel and pointless.

His judge and jury scooted their chairs closer to the chief's desk, effectively shutting Sam out of their whispered discussion. A moment passed, then two, as they muttered, grunted and nodded. If they intended to fire him for not fudging Jasmine's test scores, so be it. What excuse would they use to legitimize their decision?

He stood. "If you gentlemen would like me to leave..."

"Sit still, son," the chief said, waving Sam back

into his chair. The others returned to their original positions. "Now it's your turn to listen."

He wondered what flimsy charge they'd cook up to justify giving him the ax, but whatever it was, he wouldn't fight their decision. He'd miss every element of his job, from sizing up recruits to watching them on graduation day, fidgeting during a high school band's off-key version of "God Bless America," speeches by the mayor and the chief, the applause of friends and family as finally, they accepted their shiny badges. Without the job, he had time, and options: head home to the ranch. Pitch in more often at The Meetinghouse. Help Finn reopen The Right Note.

Finn...

If she made a stink about Jasmine asking for special favors, what would she do when he told her the girl's complaints caused his dismissal? He bit back a grin, picturing her defensive tirade.

It meant she cared about him, right?

Epps's grandfather cleared his throat. "Your honesty may well have saved that stubborn girl's hide."

"We tried to talk her out of enrolling," her father cut in. "But that daughter of mine is spoiled and pampered, obstinate and rebellious."

"Definitely not firefighter material," the uncle concurred.

The chief stood, planted both meaty palms flat on his desk. "We appreciate your candor."

"We're aware this wasn't easy for you," Carlson

said, "what with all the rumors about nepotism floating around the department."

The men got to their feet, each shaking Sam's hand as they filed from the room. All but Epps's father and the chief.

"We'll handle Jasmine from here on out," the chief said, leading Sam to the door.

Her father added, "Her mother and I hope that being dismissed from the academy will take her down a peg or two, help her grow up a little." He squeezed Sam's shoulder. "Thank you hardly seems sufficient."

So. He still had a job with the department. He wasn't looking forward to taking Epps aside to explain why she'd been discharged, but saving her from an unhappy, disappointing—even dangerous—future would make it easier.

"If it's all the same to you, I want to break the news to her, give her the option to stay or leave. She's an adult, after all, so shouldn't we treat her like one?"

The men exchanged a wary glance.

"All right," her father said. "And you'll report her decision to us?"

"I will not. As I said, Jasmine is an adult. What she tells you—if anything—is up to her."

The chief nodded. "Have it your way, then, Marshall. And just so you know? I half expected things to turn out just this way."

Sam headed for the elevator, smiling to himself. He couldn't wait to share the good news with Finn.

"DOESN'T DAD LOOK—doesn't Dad look handsome when he smiles that way?"

"Yes, he's in his element, all right." Finn squeezed Ciara's hand.

Since Connor announced he'd passed the audition at the club, Finn had been ambivalent. Should she thank Sam for giving her dad a chance to get back to work? Or take him to task for providing the venue that might break his newfound sobriety?

Time would tell, she decided. For now, Finn did her best to concentrate on the long-awaited reopening of the diner.

Sam and Ciara joined her at The Right Note's service counter and listened as Connor talked with a reporter. His rough-and-rowdy lifestyle had tinged his collar-length brown hair with bright streaks of silver and etched deep lines on his forehead and beside his mouth. But he still stood straight and tall, and retained the bulging arm muscles that had once constructed a swing set and held on to the seat of her two-wheeler until she'd learned to ride on her own.

"Do you think Finn will apply for a liquor license," the food critic asked Connor, "so she can add cocktails to her menu? I'm sure she's aware that would easily double her profits…"

Connor's smile dissolved into a thin, grim line as he glanced at her. He crossed both arms over his chest and faced the reporter. "My daughter spent her life in the shadow of a drunk," he said. "That drunk would be me. So as long as I'm in the picture, no, I don't think she will." Lifting his chin a notch, he grinned slightly. "The old 'lead him not into temptation' rule, y'know?" He caught her eye, and winked.

"That was a brave thing he just did," Sam whispered. "Real brave."

And Finn agreed. What did the experts say—the first step in solving a problem was admitting you had one? She closed her eyes and sent a little prayer heavenward. *Let it mean he's on the road to recovery...*really *on it this time...*

"Why so quiet?" Sam asked.

"Just…just nothing to say." It was the truth.

"You're not upset with me for bringing this circus into the diner?" Sam nodded toward the reporters and cameramen, jockeying for position near Connor.

"No, it'll be good for business. Might have been nice, though, if you'd run the idea past me first."

Sam winced. "You're right, of course." He faced her. "But in my defense, I called a couple of times when this opportunity presented itself. When I didn't hear from you, I decided to take a chance."

It was Finn's turn to wince. She'd seen three missed calls from Sam earlier, but had decided to follow up with him later, when Connor was performing at The Meetinghouse.

"Reminds me of something Pete used to say—

getting forgiveness is sometimes easier than asking permission."

The Right Note teemed with diners, and a line of people waited outside for tables to free up. All thanks to Sam's savvy marketing, from notices in the local papers, to press releases to media outlets, and full-color posters he'd designed, then tacked to every bulletin board and sign post on Broadway. She had no idea how much time and money he'd invested, or how many favors he'd pulled in to get so many reporters to show up for the opening, but as soon as things quieted a bit, she intended to find out. And thank him, of course.

"A good adage," Sam said. "But you're right. Sorry I didn't try harder to run it by you."

"Don't be sorry! I'm glad—and grateful for everything you did. Just look at this place!"

It was the right thing to say. His proud little-boy smile proved it—and made her heart beat a tick faster.

"And I'm sure we'll reap the benefits of everything you did for a long time to come."

"The joint is jumping now. I hope it lasts!"

"If it does, I'll need to hire a couple of extra people."

"Good idea," Rowdy said, sliding two steaming plates of steak and eggs onto the counter. "For the kitchen *and* the floor."

His not-so-subtle comment reminded her of his response when she'd announced The Right Note's reopening date. "I'm not gettin' any younger," the lifelong bachelor had said.

Finn suspected the request had more to do with the cop who'd interviewed him after the tree fell into the diner. Prior to that night, Rowdy's visits to Red's Barber Shop had been spotty, at best. Since then, he shaved daily and sported a stylish razor cut. And unless she was mistaken, he'd dropped a few pounds, too.

"I've been interviewing cooks," she told him. "I've whittled the list down to two. They'll both be here today, one to help with the lunch rush, the other to work the supper shift. I'm leaving it up to you to decide which is most qualified for the job."

"No kiddin'?"

"Why do you sound so surprised? You're my right-hand man."

Bean stepped up to grab the plates. "Hey," the waitress said, "no fair. I wouldn't mind putting in fewer hours, either."

"Don't worry," Finn told her. "The new gal should be here any minute now, and I know I can count on you to show her the ropes."

"Glad to!" she said, hurrying off to deliver the food.

The Right Note crew had become more like family than employees. Their contributions were many and their demands few, and ever since Finn had taken the reins, she'd done her best to keep them just as happy as Pete had.

"I've been wondering…" Sam mused. "Is Bean her last name?"

"It says Paula MacAllister on her driver's license. Pete dubbed her Bean."

"Because she's tall and thin, like a string bean."

"Pete had a special handle for everybody. Angel for Ciara, Houdini for me. Rowdy's given name is Tyler Holmes, but it's said that he was quite the wild man in his youth."

"Wait…Houdini?"

Finn rolled her eyes. "Well, once upon a time, I got locked in the walk-in cooler. After hours. On a night when I was closing up shop, meaning I was here alone. But I got that door open in less than an hour."

"Didn't even know that was possible."

"Lucky for me, I had followed a repairman in there one day to put something away, and let the door slam behind me. He taught me some very colorful language…and that giving the push lever a good kick would pop the latch. I didn't have his height or girth, so it took a couple tries, but eventually it worked."

"In that case, it fits." Sam began counting on his fingers. "You're a dynamite businesswoman, a great cook, a loving sister and daughter, a loyal friend, super easy on the eyes and an escape artist." He shook his head. "Is there anything you *can't* do?"

"I can't handle compliments very well, so knock it off, will ya?"

"If you want less praise, you'll have to quit being so darned near perfect."

Ciara leaned over to ask if Finn planned to give a speech welcoming everyone to the reopening.

"Not a chance."

Sam hmphed quietly.

"What?" she said, elbowing him playfully. "You think I should?"

"Couldn't hurt." Nodding toward the reporters and cameras, he added, "They'll eat it up."

"I wouldn't have a clue what to say. And I barely passed public speaking in high school."

Turning, Sam gently gripped her shoulders. "Just be yourself and speak from your heart, and they'll love you."

She caught sight of the crowd in her peripheral vision. "And if they don't?"

"I'll eat my hat."

"You aren't wearing a hat," she said, grinning up at him.

Sam helped himself to one of Rowdy's chef's caps and put it on. "Want me to get their attention for you?"

She stared out at the crowd, one of the biggest in The Right Note's history, and laughed softly. "And just how would you do that? Jumping jacks? Tap dancing? Both?"

He patted his injured thigh. "Jumping and dancing? I dunno… But I'd do it for you."

Finn believed him.

"I've mastered a whistle that's guaranteed to quiet 'em down, at least long enough to make a proper introduction."

She surveyed the packed diner again. "Oh, I don't know, Sam…"

Before she had a chance to stop him, he brought his fingers to his lips. The shrill blast caused an instant hush in the room.

"Just a few words from your generous hostess, ladies and gentlemen," he said in a loud, clear voice, "I give you Finn Leary, The Right Note's owner."

"You can do this, kiddo," Rowdy said.

"Go get 'em, boss!" Bean added.

Connor and Ciara stood near the old-fashioned brass cash register, nodding and giving the thumbs-up sign. She could almost hear Pete saying, "Well, what're you waitin' for, Houdini…Christmas?"

"I just want to say how grateful all of us are that you joined us. It means so much that you're spending part of your day here, helping kick off the new and improved Right Note. I think those of you who knew Pete can probably hear him saying, 'Yer the best, all o' yas!'"

"Atta boy, Pete!" said a man near the door.

"We'll never forget you, Petey!" yelled a woman at the end of the snack bar.

Surrounded by friends—and Pete's loving memory—Finn continued, "To show our appreciation for your support, dessert is on us today."

She concluded with another thank-you and, moved by the hearty applause, headed for the kitchen.

Sam stepped up behind her. "See there? You did great." He turned her to face him. "And *they* loved you, too."

Why the emphasis on *they*?

"I don't think I could have done it if you hadn't been here to break the ice and introduce me…" *And offer moral support.*

"'Course you could have." His fingertip traced the contour of her jaw. "You can do anything, remember?"

Finn held her breath; the last time he'd looked at her this way, he had kissed her. Or had she kissed him? Not that it made any difference. Standing in the circle of his strong arms, she'd felt vulnerable and safe and more womanly than she ever had before…all at the same time. And because it scared her, she'd tried putting some distance between them to figure out if she could trust him. Until this moment, looking into eyes that glowed with kindness and caring—for *her*—she hadn't considered the possibility that he might be battling the same fears.

"Thanks, Sam," she said, taking a half step closer.

"For what?"

Finn shrugged, wrapped her arms around him and rested her head on his chest, and hoped the gesture would be answer enough. She wasn't ready to say the words out loud.

At least, not yet.

CHAPTER TWENTY-FIVE

"You feeling okay, sweetie?"

Ciara groaned. "Why do you keep—keep asking me that?"

Finn smoothed her sister's silky hair. "Because you've been a little peaked the past day or so. Are you sleeping okay?"

"I'm—I'm sleeping fine." She rummaged through her closet and withdrew a knee-length skirt and long-sleeved turtleneck. "Do you think this will be okay for tonight?"

"The spotlights might make things hot if we're sitting close to the stage. Maybe a lighter shirt will be more comfortable."

"Good idea." After returning the turtleneck to its shelf, she held up a white top. "This one?"

"Perfect."

"And I could wear my cowboy boots?"

"You'll look like a real cowgirl."

"What time are we getting there?"

The earlier, the better, Finn thought. Get a seat up front, watch Connor play the first set and quietly leave during the break. She glanced at the black-and-white guitar clock Misty had sent Ciara for her last birthday. "If we leave here at eight, we can take our time walking over and still sit near the stage." *And get you home early enough for a good night's sleep.*

"It's seven now, so I have a whole hour to get ready." She smiled at Finn. "What are you going to wear tonight?"

"Oh, I don't know. Jeans and my pink blouse, maybe."

"With your white sandals? It'll be cold outside soon, and, and you won't be able to show off your pink toenails."

"Maybe. Call the diner office when you're finished in the shower, okay? I have a few bills to pay." *Thanks again, Pete...* The job would have taken half the time if she hadn't been so stubborn about doing everything his way. Someday—

Ciara surprised her with a huge hug. "Thank you, Finn."

"For what?" The exact words Sam had said...

"For being the best sister, ever." Another hug, and then, "I'm so excited to see Connor sing and play. And Sam! Are you excited, too?"

Afraid was more like it. But instead, she said, "You bet I am."

Finn sat at her desk and set a timer for twenty minutes, but even before filling out the first check, Connor barged in, shouting angrily into his phone. Normally, she detested using the speakerphone, but in this case...

Finn heard Misty insisting that it was her turn to take advantage of the extra sleeping space in Finn's apartment.

"You shouldn't be there in the first place," she said. "Your addictions destroyed Ciara's entire future."

Finn wanted to shout that thanks to hard work, determination and a team of caring doctors, Ciara enjoyed a very happy, productive life. If Misty had bothered to stay in touch, she'd know it, too.

"You have no right to be there!"

"And you do? If your nagging hadn't distracted me..." Connor's voice trailed off. "No, no... I promised myself I'd never go down that road again."

"What road?" Misty demanded.

"Blaming others for my mistakes. I was driving that night, so when all's said and done, you're right. It's my fault that Ciara has had to work harder than other girls her age. I'll spend the rest of my days regretting what I did—and the things I didn't do—and making up for it."

Misty's shrill, mean-spirited laughter punctuated his confession.

"You haven't changed a bit, have you? Still saying whatever it takes to make yourself look good. Smartest thing I ever did was to divorce you."

"Need I remind you who filed the papers?"

Finn had to give him credit for holding his temper in check—not an easy feat when dealing with

Misty—and for cleaning up his act. Suddenly Finn felt protective of him.

"What's going on here?" she asked, standing beside him.

Her mother's voice rang with sarcasm. "Well, well, well. It's good to hear your voice, too, Finn."

"Where are you, Misty? Chicago? New York? Seattle?"

"Miami, but I can be in Nashville tomorrow…if you still want to see me."

Based on Connor's expression, he was fighting the urge to hit the end-call button.

"If you're definitely arriving tomorrow, I'll make you a reservation at Embassy Suites. You'll have all the space and privacy your heart desires over there, and it's right up the road from the diner, so we can visit whenever you—"

"I'd rather stay with you girls." Her whimper changed to a growl when she added, "But thanks to your *father*, I guess a cold and impersonal hotel will have to do."

In the silence that followed, Finn and Connor exchanged an exasperated glance.

"Just so we're clear…I can't afford a hotel."

"I figured as much. Don't worry, I'll take care of you, as usual."

"Better reserve a room for two, then. I'd hate to see you get into trouble if the hotel staff sees Carl going in and out."

Carl? Connor and Finn mouthed together.

"We're…we're engaged."

Connor chuckled. "Another engagement? So soon after Lester?"

"You have no right to pass judgment on me, Connor Leary, and I'll thank you to keep your opinions to yourself."

"Hit the mute button," Finn whispered as Misty ranted on. He looked uncertain, but did as she asked. "This is a big night for you, so give me that phone and let me take it from here."

"Are you sure, honey? She's a handful…"

As if I didn't know! "I pressed your favorite shirt, and it's hanging on my closet doorknob. I gave your boots a going-over, too. You don't want to be late."

Connor's uncertainty morphed into wariness as he held on to the phone.

Finn held out her hand. "Tell Ciara I'll be up in a few minutes, but *don't* tell her that Misty called. She's really looking forward to seeing you open the show tonight. We can't let Misty spoil the excitement for either of you."

She didn't wait for him to agree. Instead, Finn took the phone and made a flicking motion with her fingers, signaling him to head for the stairs. She waited until the apartment door closed to unmute the call.

"…and furthermore," Misty was saying, "I resent—"

"It's just you and me now, Misty. I sent Connor upstairs to check on Ciara. Do you have any idea what time you might arrive? So I can make sure your room is ready?"

"I'm not sure."

"How will you get here?"

"Carl is driving, but he's at work right now, and I don't know when he'll want to hit the road."

In other words, if *Carl* decided he'd rather not make the trip, Misty wouldn't, either.

"Are you calling on your cell phone now?"

"Yes…"

"Then, this is what we're going to do—you're going to call me from the road. When you reach, say, Atlanta. That'll give me plenty of time to call the hotel and book you a room."

Misty exhaled a heavy sigh. "All right."

Finn didn't give her an opportunity to nix the idea. "Talk to you tomorrow, then. Have a safe trip!"

Connor was ready and waiting when she entered the apartment.

"You sure got the short end when it came to parents, didn't you?"

"Oh, you're not all bad," she said with a wink. "And you look very…musiciany tonight."

He grinned. "Guess I'd better get a move on. Sam might change his mind about letting me open if I show up late."

"We'll be along shortly. Save us a seat near the stage!"

"Will do." He gave her shoulder a gentle squeeze. "I have a few dollars saved up…"

He'd been taking odd jobs—emptying trash, sweeping up, doing dishes—for a couple of restaurants along Broadway.

"It isn't right that you have to pay extra for Misty's, ahem, fiancé. Let me help you pay for the room."

Finn kissed his cheek. "Thanks, but you worked hard for that money. I can afford a couple nights at the hotel…if she even shows up."

"Good point. There's at least a fifty-fifty chance she won't. But it doesn't seem fair for you to be saddled with two deadbeat parents at the same time. I don't mind helping out."

"You're not a deadbeat. You're working now, remember?" She gave him a gentle shove. "Now go, so you can get first dibs on the best mic."

He picked up his guitar case but dawdled at the door.

"There's absolutely no reason for you to be nervous," Finn told him. "I remember how you wowed the audiences everywhere you played. And this time, you're working with at least one friend. And you'll have Ciara and me, front and center, cheering you on."

"Yeah, but this'll be the first time in I can't remember when that I've performed sober. Well, except for the audition, of course."

"Of course. And I have a feeling that's just going

to mean you'll be better than ever." Finn blew him a kiss. "I believe in you…Dad."

He laid a hand over his heart, telling her without words how much her faith in him meant.

CHAPTER TWENTY-SIX

TORRY GREETED THEM at the door and made his usual
fuss about how adorable Ciara looked.

"We need to find an excuse to get you onstage,"
he said, offering her his elbow, "so everybody can
see how pretty you are." He led her to a table close
to the stage. "Your dad told me to save this one for
you two." He pulled out a chair, and once Ciara sat
down, he turned to Finn. "What can I get you ladies to drink?"

"Anything cold. And decaffeinated."

Ciara said, "Who's that—who's that man? He
looks familiar."

Finn and Torry followed Ciara's gaze to where a
middle-aged gentleman sat alone, alternately typ-
ing on his tablet and checking his phone.

"His name escapes me at the moment, but I know
he's a big-shot producer." Torry rapped his knuck-
les on the table. "I'll be right back with two ginger
ales and a bowl of beer nuts."

Everyone in Nashville knew that scouts some-
times visited the pubs, searching out new talent.
Had this one stopped by to check out Mark and the
Marks Brothers? Or Sam?

As if thinking his name had conjured him, Sam stepped out from behind the sparkly black backdrop, completely engrossed in the music sheets he held. The producer called his name, captured his attention and waved him over. The men sat nearly head to head for a full five minutes, and might have talked longer if Mark and the rest of the band hadn't appeared at the end of the hall, one carrying drumsticks, one adjusting the shoulder strap of a bass. Mark was wiggling a pick under his guitar's strings. As they took their places onstage, the producer shook Sam's hand, then sat back, arms crossed.

Her heart sank. Finn didn't know how to feel, because she liked Sam and wanted what was best for him. And yet...

Sam stood center stage and adjusted his mic stand. Eyes closed, he concentrated on tuning his guitar, oblivious to the din of the quickly growing audience.

"Sam!" Ciara hollered. "Hey, Sam, down here! Me and—me and Finn came to see you and Dad!"

Instantly, his intense expression vanished, replaced by a genuine happy-to-see-you smile. "Hey, yourself! I'm glad you made it. Your dad and I can use your support." He met Finn's eyes and winked. "Yours, too."

"Mic check," Mark said.

Ciara's eyes widened as the guys flipped switches and twisted dials on the amps, tapped the silver globes of their microphones. She and Finn faced the back of the room in time to see the sound engineer give a thumbs-up to the band. Mark nodded, his signal to dim the club's lights and throw the stage into absolute darkness.

The stage went pitch-black, then a spotlight beam puddled in a slowly growing oval, center stage. The music started soft and slow, building second by second until Connor leaped from the darkness and sang the first rib-racking notes of the opening number. The band's tight five-part harmony equaled anything Finn had heard on the radio. Any one—or all of them—deserved a recording contract. So why did the idea make her heart ache?

The group slid from song to song, each highlighting one of the Marks Brothers, and when the set ended, Connor and Sam headed straight for Finn and Ciara's table. Halfway there, the long-haired producer pulled Sam aside.

Connor's sympathetic smile told her that he'd read her heart and understood exactly why tears stung her eyes.

"You sounded—you sounded so good, Dad!" Ciara said as he reached them.

He scribbled something on a cocktail napkin and tucked it into her hand. "Take this to Benny behind the bar," Connor said.

"What is it?"

"You'll find out when you give him the note." He winked—more than enough to encourage her cooperation.

"What is it?" Finn echoed.

"An order for a root beer float." He chuckled. "I figured it would take just long enough to give us time to discuss—" he nodded toward Sam and the producer "—that. Don't worry about it, honey. It's probably nothing."

"I'm such an idiot," she said. "I knew better than to fall for a musician. I fought it, but seeing that… It makes me realize I lost the fight. I don't want him to leave!"

"Don't jump to conclusions. If every one of my tête-à-têtes with guys like that had panned out, your old dad would be a rich and famous recovering alcoholic."

"This is the first I've heard about anyone offering you a contract."

"Because the minute they got a whiff of my breath, they changed their minds."

But why single him out, when every third performer had some sort of addiction issue? She couldn't pose the question, though. Not without hurting his feelings.

"Besides," he continued, "those guys are all cut from the same cloth. They promise the moon but rarely deliver. Sometimes it's because the singer just doesn't have sticking power. But more often than not, it's because the guy offering the deal doesn't know the meaning of the word *loyalty*."

"What about the guy with Sam? Is he one of those?"

Connor shrugged. "No, Bernie has a pretty good reputation."

It didn't come as welcome news, and Finn's heart rate doubled. "Do you think he's offering Sam a contract right now?"

Connor glanced at the guy, too. "Who knows?" He held her hands in his. "Now ask me if I think Sam will sign."

Finn swallowed. Hard. "Do you think Sam will sign?"

"Not if it means leaving Nashville."

"Really? Why?"

"He's a smart guy. He knows you're one in a million."

Ciara returned to the table with her root beer float, and before taking her seat, she kissed Connor's cheek.

"You remembered that these are my favorite."

"You bet I did."

One by one, the Marks Brothers climbed back onstage. "And I remember what it looks like when the next set is about to start, too."

"How's it going?" Finn asked. "Are you enjoying yourself?"

His shoulders lifted in a nonchalant shrug. "If that's your way of asking if Mark intends to make this a permanent thing, yeah, I think so."

He nodded toward Ciara. "She's fading fast. No need to hang around until the last set. I'll see you at home." He kissed the top of her head.

So this is what it feels like to have a dad who cares. How ironic that just when she admitted she wanted a life with Sam, he'd probably leave…and the father who'd made a habit of letting her down had decided to stay.

"I'll wait up," she said, "so you can tell me… everything."

"Sounds good." He blew her a kiss. "Love you, honey."

He'd barely strapped on his guitar when Ciara frowned. "You should have—should have said it back. And you should have called him Dad, too."

"You're probably right."

"Probably?" Ciara snorted. "Definitely."

Smiling, Finn turned to watch Connor. He seemed so comfortable, so happy up there, and made it look easy, keeping the audience in the palm of his hand. She knew better than most that it had come at a price. If anyone deserved a contract, it was Connor.

"Finn?"

"Hmm?" She shifted her attention to Sam, who'd perfected the same stage presence at half the age, in half the time. He was every bit as talented and deserving as Connor. A decent human being would be happy that he might get a chance to make his musical dreams come true. So why wasn't she?

Because you want too much, she thought again. *You want it—*

"Finn," Ciara said again…

…and fainted dead away.

CHAPTER TWENTY-SEVEN

SAM LEFT THE club's office and closed the door behind him. Halfway to the stage when he saw the flashing lights of an emergency vehicle.

"Hey, Sue, what's going on?" he asked a waitress.

"Those two girls who were sitting there," she said, pointing at Finn and Ciara's table, "well, the younger one fainted, so the other one called 911."

Sam shouldered his way through the crowd of curious onlookers gathered in the club's vestibule in time to see the ambulance pull away from the curb...and Finn's worried, frightened face in the vehicle's rear window.

If he hadn't left his keys and wallet in the dressing room, he would have followed immediately. Sam ran back inside, where that same waitress said, "Do you know those girls?"

Know them? he thought. *I* love *them!*

"Where's Mark?"

"Onstage, I guess. No. Wait. I think I saw him go into the storeroom."

Instead, he found Mark in the dressing room.

"Good grief," his friend said. "What did Bernie

say to put that look of doom and gloom on your face?"

Sam didn't have time to go into Bernie's offer: studio time to record Sam's original songs, along with several written by another client, tour dates with megastar Carly Overton and appearances on all the major morning talk shows.

He palmed his keys, and on the way to the door, Sam added, "They just took Ciara away in an ambulance."

"Finn's kid sister?" Mark shook his head and exhaled a heavy breath. "Which hospital?"

Sam realized he'd forgotten to ask. "Where's Connor?" he asked, pecking a dispatcher friend's number into his phone.

"Onstage, last time I saw him. The guy's good, Sam. Real good. If it's okay with you, I'm giving him the job. He'll be backup for the nights you can't work."

"You can deliver the good news tomorrow. Right now, I need to find him and get him to the hospital, so he can be with his daughters."

Mark frowned as Sam talked to his dispatcher friend.

"Vanderbilt," he said. "Got it. Thanks, Tom, I owe you one." He pocketed the phone and glanced around, looking for Connor.

"There he is." Sam gestured for him to come closer.

"He's Ciara's dad," Mark said, "so I get why he

needs to get over there. But you're making noises like you're going, too." He nodded toward a table of rowdy young women seated near the stage. "But you can't. See the gal in red? That's the maid of honor. She booked this place for her friend's bachelorette party...specifically because of *you*." He handed Sam a twenty-dollar bill. "Put Connor in a cab, on me, and get back onstage before one of 'em busts a lung screamin' your name."

Until that instant, Sam hadn't noticed the party. They caught sight of him just then and began waving excitedly. He forced a smile and waved back, then turned to Mark.

"I hate leaving you in the lurch, man." He tucked the twenty into Mark's shirt pocket. "I can't explain it right now, but I need to be there, too."

Connor joined them. "Hey, why the long faces?"

"Because Finn and Ciara are on their way to Vanderbilt," Sam said.

"Vanderbilt? Why? What happened?"

"Only way to find out is to get over there." Sam met Mark's eyes. "Sorry, dude, but I'll make it up to you."

He led Connor to the door.

"Is that why an ambulance was here?" He thumped himself in the forehead. "I had a feeling I oughta check things out..."

"No way you could have known." He opened the door. "My truck is out back."

Neither man spoke as they made their way to the

hospital. Sam frowned, noticing Connor's labored breathing. They'd raced out of the club and across the parking lot, but not at a pace fast enough to make him pant. The temperature gauge in the rearview read fifty-five, too cool to explain the sheen of perspiration on his upper lip and forehead.

"Hey, man, you doing okay?"

Connor laid a hand on his chest. "My heart's beating like a parade drum, and I can't catch my breath. Aside from that," he said on a whispery chuckle, "I'm good."

Sam's training kicked in. "Any numbness in your fingers?"

"No, but they're tingling."

It could mean anything from a panic attack to a full-blown heart episode.

"There's a good reason Vanderbilt made the best-hospitals list, so don't worry. Ciara is in good hands."

"Easy for you to say. She isn't your kid."

"Let's not jump to conclusions—women faint for all sorts of reasons."

"Not women with Ciara's history. What do you really think is going on?"

The man was in no condition to hear his best guess, so Sam said, "Hospital is just ahead. No sense speculating when we can get the facts directly from her doctor."

"Man." Connor slumped lower in the passenger

seat. "Times like these, I sure could use a good, stiff drink."

Sam pulled into the lot. "Look at it this way—getting through this without booze or pills will be proof you can get through anything."

He got Connor situated on a bench across from the sign-in counter. "Stay put while I find out where Finn and Ciara are."

The man seemed only too happy to comply.

Somewhere in this ER, Finn and Ciara were in good hands. Sam wanted to put their father in good hands, too. So he made a call and hoped his pal in the radiology department was on duty.

"Williamson," she answered.

"Melody." Sam put his back to Connor and lowered his voice. "Thank God you're working tonight."

"Sam? Sam *Marshall*?"

They'd dated a time or two, but he'd quit asking her out when she'd offered him a key to her place and started talking commitment.

"Hate to bother you, but I'm hoping I can call in a favor."

"Oh, so that's how it is, huh?" she said, laughing. "You carry an old lady out of her burning house and the family is indebted to you for life."

Sam grimaced slightly because it had been Melody's grandmother he'd saved the night the ceiling caved in on him. The next day, Melody had taken one look at his mangled thigh and asked how she'd ever repay him. He'd told her that one day he'd call in a favor and left it at that. Now that day was here.

Sam explained why he'd called, and Melody agreed with his assessment of the situation. She promised to meet him in the ER, and after putting Connor into her care, Sam began a search for Ciara and Finn. He saw an ambulance parked outside the ER doors, and the twenty-eight painted on its side identified it as the same vehicle that had delivered Ciara to Vanderbilt. He noticed the paramedics heading toward the exit and hurried to catch up with them.

Sam had worked with the guy, and the woman had been in one of his first classes. Their radios squawked with another assignment, so they told him where he could find the Leary sisters and got on their way.

Ciara was barely visible behind half a dozen nurses and aides, and yet she smiled when she saw him. "Where's—where's my dad?"

"Oh, he got a little dizzy, so I asked a friend to take a look at him. Wouldn't want him infecting you if he picked up the flu or something."

Finn grabbed his forearm. "Dizzy?" She lowered her voice. "I *knew* it was a bad idea for him to spend time at the club. One night, *one night*, and already he's—"

"He wasn't drinking."

Her weary, worried expression relaxed a bit. "Then, what caused the dizzy spell?"

He shrugged. "Could be any one of a hundred things. He's had a crazy couple of days. Auditioning, rehearsal, getting onstage after who knows how many weeks, then finding out his baby girl was carted off in an ambulance." He winked at Ciara and forced lightheartedness into his voice. "That's enough to make even a superhero shaky."

Finn tightened her grip on his arm. "Where is he?"

"My pal did a quick once-over on him, then sent him up to Radiology. Near as we can figure, he's having a mild panic attack."

"You're sure it's nothing more than that?"

"Well, as sure as I can be for now." He gave her hand a squeeze. "Don't worry. These people are the best. We'll hear something soon. Worst-case scenario, they'll prescribe an antianxiety medication. Best case, he'll calm down when the doc tells him Ciara's all right."

"Antianxiety meds? Oh, I hope not."

Sam understood perfectly: a few weeks without pills and booze didn't change the fact that Connor was still an addict.

"Remember, they know what they're doing. I gave Mel a brief rundown of your dad's history. She won't put him on anything that'll cause a setback."

He glanced at Ciara, still encircled by hospital personnel. "Has her doctor been in yet?"

"No, but he's on his way. He already made arrangements for new scans." She nodded toward the

bed. "They're doing what tests they can now, too."
She heaved a big sigh.

Sam moved, forcing Finn to put her back to Ciara.
"So tell me what happened."

"She's been…*off* lately. Pale. Dark circles under
her eyes. Sleepy. No appetite…" She shrugged. "I
kept pestering her—are you sleeping all right, does
your head hurt, is your stomach queasy—but she
said no to everything."

"No fever?"

"No fever."

Something he'd read during his academy days
niggled at him: Ciara's traumatic brain injury made
her a prime candidate for a transient ischemic attack. Were her recent dizzy spells, double vision
and headaches evidence that she'd already suffered
a ministroke—maybe more than one? If a TIA had
put Ciara in the hospital tonight, the doctor had time
to get her on the right medication to prevent a bigger, more damaging stroke down the road.

Finn glanced over her shoulder. "She looks so
tiny and vulnerable, doesn't she?"

"But they're taking good care of her here. So
don't worry."

She studied his face, and he didn't know what to
make of the almost angry spark in her eyes. "I'm
fine. Really."

The wind had rumpled her hair, worry had lined
her brow and sadness dulled the usually bright

gleam in her dark eyes, yet she was as beautiful as ever.

Sam held out his arms, expecting her to step into them. Instead, she hesitated, then moved to the left. The depth of his disappointment came as a surprise. Fortunately, she filled the silence by repeating how bad she felt for Connor.

"I'm sure when he gets here, he'll tell you there's no place he'd rather be," Sam assured her.

"How long do you think it'll be before your friend lets us know what's wrong with him?"

"Could be an hour or a few minutes. Tell you what. There's a vending machine right down the hall. What can I get you?"

"Bottled water if they have it."

Sam withdrew a few rumpled dollar bills from the pocket where he kept loose change…and Bernie's business card fluttered to the floor.

She picked it up, frowning as she handed it to him.

The look of disapproval told him Finn had seen him talking with the producer. But if "this isn't the time or place to talk about it" sounded defensive and argumentative in his head, how much worse would it sound to Finn?

A doctor entered the room, and Finn hurried to his side.

"Dr. Peterson, I'm so glad you're here!"

They stepped up to Ciara's bed. Between them, Sam saw the ashen-faced young woman who, despite the chaos all around her, seemed calm and unafraid, thanks to her sister's loving, reassuring words.

Two orderlies rolled a gurney into the room and told Peterson they'd been summoned to deliver Ciara to Radiology. "Meet you there," the doctor told Finn, white coat flapping as he exited the room.

The IV drugs were working, as evidenced by Ciara's droopy eyelids and soft murmurs. Finn pressed a kiss to her forehead. "I'm right here, Kee."

As the men wheeled her into the hallway, Ciara reached for Sam's hand.

"Where—where's Dad?"

A little white lie at a time like this wouldn't hurt anyone, right? "He told me to let you know he'll see you soon, and that he loves you."

She smiled, exhaled a relieved sigh. "I'm—I'm glad you're here," she slurred, "so Finn won't be alone."

He glanced at her, and Sam chose to blame fear, worry and exhaustion for the indifferent expression Finn aimed his way.

One of the orderlies punched the elevator's up button, and they all stared at the glowing green numbers above the doors. "This could take a while," Finn told Sam.

"I know."

"Maybe long into the night."

"I know."

The doors opened, and she followed the gurney inside. "You don't have to stay."

"I know."

There wasn't much space inside, what with the bed, the two big guys and Finn already in there. But Sam squeezed in anyway.

The nearest orderly shot him a sympathetic grin.

"You want to hear what *I* know?"

She answered with a slight shrug.

"I know that it's dangerous to jump to conclusions, because you can't predict where you're going to land."

Her brow furrowed slightly as she tried to figure out what his comment had to do with anything. Then, in one blink, a wily grin grew on her lips. In another, she said, "And *I* know that the explanation requiring the fewest assumptions is most likely to be correct."

Leave it to Finn, he thought, to put him in his place without a hint of melodrama.

CHAPTER TWENTY-EIGHT

QUIET SQUEAKS AND the scent of honeysuckle floated by, both gone as quickly as they'd materialized.

"Mornin', sleepyhead."

Sam...

Oh, how she loved waking up in his arms!

Eyes shut tight against the early-morning glare, Finn hid her face in the crook of his neck. "Forgot to draw the blinds last night, did you?"

"I, ah...what?"

Fully awake now, Finn opened one eye, saw the glare of fluorescent ceiling lights and heard the thick triple-ping that signaled an upcoming announcement from the hospital PA system: "Dr. Radajii," said a velvet-voiced nurse, "Dr. Radajii, pick up line two-oh-two. Dr. Radajii, a call on two-oh-two..."

Later, she'd dig out her old psych textbook, see what the experts had to say about her dream of being Mrs. Sam Marshall. Right now, she needed to unravel the confusion swirling in her head. Things had happened fast: a trip upstairs for scans and X-rays, then straight to the OR. Last she heard, Connor was resting in a semiprivate room, but she needed to find out about his condition, too.

She sat up and worked the kinks out of her neck, instantly aware of the chill left behind now that his strong, warm body had separated from hers. But... how had she ended up sound asleep and entangled in his arms in the first place!

"How long was I out?"

"Couple of minutes."

There were creases on his handsome face, put there by the headband she'd donned to keep her bangs out of her eyes. Things like that didn't happen in a couple of minutes. And neither did achy shoulders and stiff muscles. Sam sat up, too, and did his best not to wince when he stretched his injured leg.

"I'm sorry," she said.

"For what?"

"For turning you into a human pretzel for...for God only knows how long." She got to her feet. "Did you get any sleep?"

"No, but—"

Mark interrupted with "That's only because you were doing the best chain saw imitation I ever heard. How's a li'l pip-squeak like you make that much noise?"

Ciara was the only person who'd ever heard her snore. Until now. But what was *Mark* doing here?

"Plus," he continued, "this guy was too busy watching you sleep to catch any z's himself."

Sam shot him a dirty look, and he added, "Good thing we're in a hospital, 'cause if looks could kill..."

Sam's cell phone buzzed, and he stood to answer it.

"It's about time you called. What's going on up there?"

He paced between Finn's chair and Mark's, then moved farther down the hall. It didn't take a mastermind to figure out that he was talking to his friend in Radiology. "He'd better not keep any details from me," she mumbled.

Mark glanced up from his magazine. "What's that?"

"Oh, nothing." She walked toward Sam. "Just talking to myself."

He winked and tossed the dog-eared issue of *Time* on to the side table. "Talking to yourself. My mom used to say that's one way to make sure somebody's listening."

She stopped just short of his chair. "I'm sure there are a thousand things waiting for you back at the club, so if you need to leave…"

He feigned confusion, then nodded. "Oh. I get it. You think I'm here to support *you.*"

Finn felt like a self-centered brat. The man barely knew her and Ciara. Of course he'd come to support his friend and business partner. Would Sam remain a partner once he went on tour?

"Truth is," Mark whispered, "I'm here hiding out from those things, so if anybody asks where I am…" He gave the zipped-lip signal and grabbed a tattered issue of *Sports Illustrated.*

Finn caught up with Sam just as he was ending the call. One hand on the back of his neck, he shook his head and frowned at the floor. Maybe she didn't want the whole, unvarnished truth after all...

"Is Connor all right? Can I see him yet?"

"Mel says he's holding his own. She wants to keep an eye on him for another couple hours. Soon as we get word that Ciara is okay, we'll head up to Radiology and check on things for ourselves."

She looked in the direction of the surgical suite, too. "I wonder how often the staff has to deal with worried family members barging in there, demanding updates."

"I'm sure they understand." He scrolled through his phone's contacts. "Let me see what I can find out about what's going on in the OR."

"I had no idea firefighters had so many hospital connections."

He put the phone to his ear. "Connections?"

"Radiology, the OR... One phone call here, another there... You're like Information Central."

"You'd be surprised how many interesting individuals you meet when you put broken, battered, burned patients into their hands...and check in later to see how they're doing."

Finn had no trouble believing he'd followed up with the people he'd helped.

"I thought there was some kind of rule that said first responders had to keep a safe emotional distance from—"

He held up a finger and gave her an apologetic smile, indicating the person he'd called had picked up. Finn tidied a stack of magazines on a nearby table while Sam and his contact engaged in a short catch-up conversation. Then he chuckled and said, "Yeah, yeah, but the phone works both ways, y'know."

Why hadn't she thought to grab her purse before following him over here? At least then she could use her cell phone to check email or play a game of solitaire to distract her from his side of the call.

"Sounds good," she heard him say. "You're right. It's been too long. Shoot me a text with your new address, and we'll work something out." He cleared his throat. "So, anyway, the reason I called… Think you could check your computer real quick, see if you can get me an update on a patient? Name's Leary. Ciara Leary. Dr. Peterson's patient. She's been in the OR for a couple of hours, and…"

Finn watched as he drove his big hand through his hair, then scrubbed it across his bristled chin. She'd known him long enough to recognize it as a "stay calm, be patient" tactic, and hoped he wouldn't have too hard a time prying some information from his friend.

"Right. Yes, that's the one." He exhaled a relieved breath. "Great. Excellent. We'll get right back over there. Thanks, Bob. I owe you one."

He began making his way to the surgical suite.

"Catch you back at the club," he said to Mark. "Thanks for being here."

"Yes, we appreciate it," Finn agreed.

Mark's left eyebrow rose. "You'll be onstage tonight, then?"

"Probably."

The club owner snapped off a jaunty salute and headed for the elevators as Sam and Finn went in the opposite direction.

"It was nice of him to keep you company. But really, you didn't have to stay," Finn said.

"Yes. I did." He frowned over at her and shook his head. "They're moving her to Recovery."

"How do *you* know? I thought there were rules about sharing patient information."

"There are. Unless you have friends in the know." He looked around to ensure no one was listening. "Happens all the time among first responders and hospital staff."

"Because…"

"Because despite popular belief, we *do* get emotionally involved sometimes." Sam shrugged. "Mostly, people are helpful because they know it relieves the stress of wondering how the folks we deliver here are doing."

She had to half run to keep up, and she wondered how much faster he'd walk on *two* healthy legs.

"Did your friend say how things went?"

"No, but he did say that Peterson is getting cleaned up, so he can bring you up to speed."

"All that information is from Bob's computer?"

Sam laughed quietly. "No, took him a few quick phone calls, too."

"What'll this favor cost you?"

"Dinner at his house. He wants me to see his new house, meet the wife and kids. And a dog named Boo."

"How long has it been since you talked to him?"

"A year. Three." He shrugged.

Finn had no idea what to say next. She'd never been any good at small talk, but "What's going on with Ciara?" was beginning to sound like a mantra, and it beat repeating "When will we know something about Connor?"

But as it turned out, she didn't need conversation material because the doors to the OR suite opened and Dr. Peterson stepped out.

"Let's talk over here," he said, leading her to the chairs against the wall.

Finn's knees nearly buckled. Was the news really so bad that he thought she needed to hear it sitting down?

"Don't look so worried," the doctor said. "She's doing fine."

"Then, why did the operation take so long?"

"There was a blood clot, and it caused a small stroke."

Finn hugged herself. "A stroke?"

"Hard to believe, I know, but even little kids have 'em…if they've suffered severe head injury, like

Ciara has." He took her hands. "Her vitals are strong, and thanks to your pampering, she's healthy."

If I did such a great job, why did she have a stroke?

The doctor pulled back as if she'd shouted the question.

"Her vital organs are strong," he repeated.

"Why do I sense you're about to say *but…?*"

"But the area of her brain that sustained the impact of that crash isn't."

"Wasn't, you mean." She withdrew her hands.

Peterson looked confused, but *Sam* understood her perfectly. "You had her on the table for what, five hours? Six?" he said, sitting in the chair beside hers. "Enough time to fix whatever was wrong, right?"

Peterson's glance flicked from Finn's face to Sam's and back again, as if questioning this stranger's right to involve himself in private medical matters.

Finn said, "Sam is…a friend."

A nurse hurried past, crepe-soled shoes squeaking on the linoleum, and Finn recognized it as the sound that had ended her beautiful dream. "A very dear and trusted friend."

The comment must have pleased Sam, if his smile was any indicator.

The surgeon winked. "High time you allowed yourself a…*friend.*"

Mark, Torry, Connor and now Dr. Peterson. It

seemed everyone but Sam knew how she felt about him. *Felt*, past tense. How long, she wondered, before he'd leave Nashville to pursue his dream?

"Let me explain what we found and what we did." Peterson removed his blue surgical cap. "Ciara experienced a cerebral hemorrhage—a small blood clot hidden behind a clump of residual scar tissue."

"All these years after the accident?" she asked.

He nodded. "It isn't all that unusual. Things built up, created just enough pressure to cause the TIA."

Finn heard herself gasp and felt Sam's hand on her shoulder.

"That's the downside. The upside is that it moved enough to enable us to see it."

The only thing preventing her from climbing into Sam's lap and bawling like a baby was the arm of the chair. That, and concern about Ciara's condition, and maybe a tinge of stubborn pride.

"So you're saying the clot is still there?"

"We drilled a dime-size hole in her skull directly above it," he explained. "Then we inserted a catheter and gave it a shot of tPA—a clot-busting drug—and watched its size reduce significantly."

"So…is the clot gone, or isn't it?"

"It's shrinking. We've left the catheter in place, so we can dose her with more tPA until it reduces to the point that it's no longer a threat."

But Ciara hated being in the hospital. "How long before I can take her home?"

"No way to predict that for sure, but since we

were able to get this far without the injurious side effects normally associated with craniotomy, there's every reason to expect positive results in a couple of days."

Injurious side effects. Craniotomy. tPA. Finn's mind buzzed with information. And questions.

"And then?" Sam wanted to know. "More scans to ensure the clot is gone?"

Peterson frowned. "Yes."

"I know you guys hate hearing stuff like this, but I was a firefighter."

"You're still a firefighter," Finn corrected. She met the doctor's eyes. "He was injured on the job and teaches at the academy now."

Peterson still appeared dubious, but he nodded. "I see."

"So what should we look for," Sam continued, "once she's home again? Paralysis of facial muscles? Changes in vision? Memory problems? Dizziness?"

"Again, no way to know for sure, but I don't anticipate any of that. Like I said, she's young and strong, so I expect a full recovery."

Finn pressed fingertips to her temples, hoping it might ease her light-headedness. "When can I see her?"

"Right now."

She was on her feet in an instant. "Sam, too?"

Peterson smiled again. "Ciara mentioned him a couple of times, so, yeah, I think it'll be all right."

As the surgeon led the way to the recovery room,

Sam leaned near Finn's ear to whisper, "I realize I overstepped my bounds back there. You know, asking questions, making statements about something that really isn't any of my business. It's just, well, you seemed a little overwhelmed. I thought maybe if I tossed a few things out there—"

She stopped walking and faced him. "Maybe I'm still dreaming."

Sam raised his eyebrows. "Come again?"

"Are you apologizing?"

"Yeah, I guess so."

He looked nervous—not "how is Ciara" concerned, but "what's Finn going to say now" worried.

"You guys coming, or not?" Dr. Peterson asked.

Knees bent slightly, Sam kissed the tip of her nose, then turned her around and gave her a gentle shove.

"We're right behind you," Finn said.

They entered the recovery room, and as they approached Ciara's bed, Peterson studied Sam. "Looks like you have something to say."

"Yeah, but it'll keep."

"Okay, well, I have rounds. You know how to reach me."

"I *don't* know how to thank you," Finn said.

He winked. "Just pay the bill on time, and we'll call it even."

The minute he disappeared around the corner, Sam said, "Doctor humor, a true oxymoron."

She was more interested in something he'd said a moment ago.

"What'll keep?"

In place of an answer, Sam pointed. "Ciara's awake…"

Finn squeezed her sister's hand.

"You doin' okay, sweetie?"

"Yes, I'm fine. I had a dream…"

Funny, Finn thought, *so did I*. Leaning over the side rail, she fought tears of relief. "A happy one, I hope."

Ciara looked across the room to where Sam leaned in the doorway, hands pocketed and one boot crossed over the other.

"Oh, a *very* happy dream." She glanced at Sam, then met Finn's eyes again. "I dreamed you two got married, and Mark and the Marks Brothers played the music when Dad walked you down the aisle, and Torry was the preacher, and even Mom was there, and you looked *beautiful*."

Finn didn't know what made her heart start to pound…her reaction to Ciara's description of the wedding, or the fact that her sister hadn't repeated a single word.

From the other side of the bed, Sam said, "That was some dream!"

But that's all it is, Finn told herself. And the proof was printed on a business card in his pocket.

Sam cared for her. Every look, every action, everything he said to her proved it. If it meant that he loved her, she wouldn't ask him to turn down what might be a once-in-a-lifetime opportunity, simply to quell her fears of coming in second to his Nashville dreams.

Ciara's drowsy giggle broke the moment of intense eye contact.

"Can my maid of honor dress be yellow?"

Finn had dedicated herself to delivering anything and everything that would make her sister happy. But this?

"And white daisies in our bouquets?" She turned toward Sam. "Daisies are Finn's favorite flowers."

"Easy to see why," he said. "They're simple and sturdy, yet beautiful and graceful."

"Just like Finn."

He nodded. "Just like Finn."

"So can I, Finn? Can I wear a yellow dress and carry a daisy bouquet?"

The poor kid had just endured an hours-long operation, and had a long, long way to go before fully recovering. What could it hurt to humor her, since the requests centered on a girlish dream?

Girlish dream, indeed. It was Finn's dream, too.

"I've seen you in yellow," Sam said, "and—"

"Because I wore a yellow dress to the zoo," Ciara interrupted, her voice still gruff from the ventilator tube.

"Yup. And you looked real pretty that day."

"Finn, too?"

"She sure did." He met Finn's eyes as a sexy

smirk exposed the dimple in his cheek. "But Finn looks pretty every day."

Finn tensed, wondering how Ciara would respond to *that*. She needn't have worried, because her sister had drifted off to sleep and hadn't heard a word.

"Did you notice that she isn't repeating herself?" he asked.

Finn nodded. "I hope it's not just some quirk, like the result of swelling or something."

"Time will tell, but I have a feeling she's gonna be better than new."

"I guess it's safe to check on Connor now that she's asleep…"

"How about if I stay with her? If she wakes up before you get back, I can send you a text or whatever…and she won't be alone."

Leave it to Sam to know exactly what she—and Ciara—needed.

"That'd be nice. Thanks, Sam."

"I'm happy to help out."

She believed him. Which only made it harder to think of a time when he wouldn't be around to help out.

"You'd better get movin' before I change my mind. I hate these hideous things," he said, settling into the ugly pink chair beside the bed.

"I wish you'd change your mind about…"

Finn couldn't believe she'd said the words aloud and ducked out of the room before he had a chance to respond.

And before she had time to wonder which emotion had caused that wide-eyed expression on his handsome face…relief? Or dread?

CHAPTER TWENTY-NINE

FINN WOULD HAVE recognized that shrill, gravelly voice anywhere. Years of smoking and drinking had taken a toll on her body...and her throat.

"Misty," Finn said. "I didn't expect to see you here." She stepped up to Connor's bedside. "You called her?"

"Well, yeah. I figured she'd want to know. She *is* Ciara's mother."

Finn wondered if Misty, too, had picked up on his unspoken, *like it or not*. Probably not, based on the way she was studying her newly manicured talons.

But wait. If Misty knew that her youngest daughter had just undergone brain surgery, why was she here, pestering Connor, instead of checking on Ciara?

"Have you checked into your room?"

"Yes, and I don't know how you found time to book it, with all that's been going on."

"It gave me something to do to keep my mind off everything," Finn admitted.

Misty fluffed her overprocessed curls and batted heavily mascaraed eyelashes. "Oh, it'll do, I suppose."

Finn read between the lines. If she'd been so distracted that she'd forgotten to call in the reservation, it would have provided Misty with the perfect excuse to move herself—and Carl—into the apartment. Connor must have sensed it, too; he huffed and shook his head. "Sheesh, Misty. Least you could do is *pretend* to be grateful. This kid works hard for every dime, thanks to the two of us. God only knows what she's giving up so you'll have a clean, safe place to sleep."

"I could stay with the girls free if *you* weren't—"

"So what did your doctor say?" Finn asked Connor.

He frowned and shot a sideways glance at his ex. "I don't want to talk about it right now."

Finn could hardly blame him. No matter how serious or simple his condition, Misty would find a way to make herself the center of attention...while belittling Connor in the process.

"Did he say when you can go home?"

"She. And let me tell you, if I was twenty years younger..."

"And twenty IQ points smarter," Misty snapped. "You'll never change, will you? I bet you'll die at the ripe old age of ninety-eight...chasing some floozy."

Connor continued as if Misty hadn't spoken. "She's putting the paperwork through right now, so I reckon I'll be out of here within the hour."

"You reckon right," said a pretty young woman. She scribbled something on Connor's chart, then faced Finn. "Dr. Daugherty," she said, extending her right hand. "You must be his daughter."

"Finn," she said, shaking her hand.

"And this is?" the doctor asked, turning to Misty.

"The wicked witch of the world," Connor ground out.

Daugherty ignored his sarcasm and said to Misty, "I take it you're here to visit your younger daughter."

"A person would think a hospital as big as Vanderbilt would have more than one doctor. What do *you* know about Ciara?"

"Only what Connor told me. Would you mind waiting in the hall for a few minutes? I need to give him a last once-over before I cut him loose."

"You're joking, right? We were married. For what seems like an *eternity*." She snickered. "I've seen it all before."

"Be that as it may," the doctor said, nodding toward the door, "it's hospital policy."

"Fine." Misty grabbed her purse and faux leopard jacket, spike heels click-clacking across the tile as she stormed toward the exit. Just shy of the door, she paused. "Are you coming with me?" she asked Finn.

"Not yet."

"Fine. Then just tell me what room Ciara's in."

"She isn't in a room yet. If you can wait a few minutes until I've had a chance to talk to Dr. Daugherty, I'll walk to Recovery with you."

Misty glared at the doctor. "You mean *she* gets to stay?"

"I'm going to close the curtain, of course, but unless Connor has a problem with it, yes, she gets to stay."

"Well?" she said, aiming that steely gaze at him.

"You'll be all right for a few minutes."

"Fine," she said, pointing at the hall again. "I'll just be out there. Alone. Waiting by the restrooms."

Daugherty closed the door. "Wow. If she's a regular part of your life, no wonder you had a panic attack."

Finn said, "You're sure it wasn't anything more serious?"

"Positive. Despite his history, he's as healthy as the proverbial horse." She pulled the screen around the bed, leaving Finn on the outside.

Despite his history? It meant that Connor had been honest with the doctor. Finn saw it as a sign that maybe, this time, he really was on the road to recovery.

"I didn't want to ask in front of Misty," he said through the curtain, "but how's Ciara, honey?"

"She was talking and joking when I left her." *And dreaming about yellow dresses and daisy-themed bridal bouquets.* "Still groggy from the anesthesia, but that's to be expected." Knowing that stress had been responsible for the panic attack, she decided against going into detail about the catheter still delivering clot-busting drugs into Ciara's brain. "Dr. Peterson assured us she'll be fine."

"Us?"

"Oh. Well, Sam came and found me after he dropped you off. He sat with me all night. When Ciara fell asleep just now, he offered to stay with her so she'd have someone she knows nearby if she wakes up while I'm here with you."

"Now, why doesn't that surprise me? I really like that boy. He's good people. You could do worse. So, if he pops the question…"

"If he does, I might demand a psych evaluation."

"What's that supposed to mean?"

"What sane, rational man would attach himself to the loony Leary family? Besides, why would he stay here when that big-shot producer is going to line him up with tours and albums?"

"Did he tell you that?"

"No, but he's a walking, talking, singing bundle of talent. He deserves to see his dreams come true."

The doctor threw open the privacy divider and announced, "All finished. Soon as you're dressed, you're free to go."

"Just like that?" He buttoned his right shirt cuff. "No bed rest? No meds? No follow-up exam?"

Grinning, she handed him a business card. "Now that you can recognize the symptoms—you remember we talked about that—give me a call if they crop up again. Otherwise, I'd say keep away from angry ex-wives, and you'll be fine."

He buttoned the other cuff and shook the doctor's hand. "Thanks, Doc. You're the best."

The minute she was gone, Connor closed the

door again. "All right," he said, sitting to pull on his boots, "give it to me straight. What should I expect when I walk into Ciara's room?"

Finn relayed an abbreviated version of the information Peterson had provided. "One really great surprise that came out of all this is that even though Ciara talked a blue streak once she came to, she didn't repeat herself."

He got up and grabbed her shoulders, giving her a little shake. "Seriously?"

"Seriously."

Connor buried his face in the crook of her neck, and for what seemed like a full minute, he wept like a small boy.

"It's another sign," he said, plucking a stiff tissue from the dispenser on his nightstand.

"A sign?"

He blotted his eyes. "That if I play my cards right, I might get a start on making amends with you girls."

Tears stung Finn's eyes, too. "Cards?" she teased. "Don't tell me you've traded gambling for drinking!"

He hugged her. Tight. "Don't worry. I don't have a lucky bone in my body. And you know as well as I do that I don't have a poker face."

Finn counted her blessings: Ciara would be fine, and from the looks of things, she had her dad back.

With any luck, things would work out between her and Sam, too…

If she could figure out how to send him off to reach his musical goals while holding him close enough to secure their future together.

CHAPTER THIRTY

AGGIE JACKSON BLOCKED Misty's path. "Saw that frizzy blond head from all the way down the hall," she said, jerking a thumb over one shoulder, "and said to myself, 'What's *she* doing in town?'"

"I'm here to see Ciara, of course."

Neither woman seemed to notice Finn's and Connor's approach.

"Oh, please. Spare me. You know what they say about fooling some of the people some of the time. I heard all about how Finn had to put you and your new boyfriend up in a hotel."

"You didn't get that from her. Finn isn't a gossip."

"Matter of fact, you're right—for a change. Friend of mine runs the Embassy. Said you and some long-haired freak checked in with a bunch of ragtag suitcases. Now out with it—what are you *really* doing here?"

Misty tried to maneuver around her, but didn't succeed. "Listen, old woman, I don't owe you any explanations. Now step aside, because I'm not above moving you forcibly."

Connor walked up and assumed a referee's pose. "Hey, now, what's the hubbub all about? This place is full of sick people. You oughta be ashamed of yourselves."

Both women took in the dozen or so onlookers who had gathered.

Misty put her back to them. "I'm on my way to Ciara's room."

Aggie hugged Connor. "You're lookin' pretty good, Leary. Clean livin' agrees with you."

"Thanks, and ditto. So what brings you to Vanderbilt today?"

"Why, that sweet girl of yours, of course. When I stopped at The Right Note and Rowdy told me what happened, I just had to stop by." She held up a small pink bag. "And bring a little something to cheer her up." She turned to Finn. "How's she doing?"

"Her doctor says she's doing great. Hopefully we can take her home soon."

"Wait. What's this about a test? I didn't hear anything about a test." Misty stamped a high-heeled foot. "Why doesn't anyone ever tell me anything?"

"Maybe," Aggie said, "because you don't ask. And maybe because they don't want to encourage you to hang around."

Connor pinched the bridge of his nose. "Times like these, I could use a good, stiff drink."

Misty snickered and showed him the cap of a silver flask. "Say pretty please, and I might share."

He held up a hand. "No, thanks. I'm done with that stuff."

"Hmph. Where have I heard *that* before?"

"Come back in a year and ask your question again. On second thought, don't."

"I'll be in LA a year from now." She inspected her fingernails. "It just so happens that I have an audition with a major Hollywood producer…thanks to Carl."

"When will those big shots in Hollywood learn you can only produce so many witch movies and make a profit?"

"Aggie…"

"Sorry, Finn." She shrugged and, facing Misty, said, "I'll make you a deal. Give me fifteen minutes to say hi and deliver the present, and I'll skedaddle. Seeing the two of us go at it is liable to set off a massive relapse."

"I don't want to wait for Finn to walk me down there. I'll go alone. It'll give me a chance to touch up my makeup."

Aggie leaned close to Connor. "She needs a make*over*. And it'll take a whole lot longer than a few minutes." She patted his arm and darted off to the elevators. "See you around, kiddo. And stick to your guns. You look better than you have in years." The doors opened, and she stepped into the car. "Hey, Misty," she hollered. "Do those sweet girls of yours a favor and leave town without making a spectacle of yourself."

The doors slid shut, and Connor chuckled.

"What's so funny?" Misty demanded.

He looked at her, long and hard. "Nothing. Absolutely nothing."

With that, he made his way to the stairs, pausing in the doorway to say, "Fifteen minutes. You gave your word."

"But…but what *room* is she in?"

"Room?" He chuckled. "If you're here for the right reasons," he said as the door swung closed behind him, "you'll figure it out."

"THAT'S TERRIFIC, SAM! I'm so proud of you! I knew you could do it!"

Sophie had a knack for lifting his spirits. Today, however, it wasn't her contagious enthusiasm that prompted his call.

"Yeah, it's an honor, just to be considered. Bernie doesn't approach just anybody."

"So when do you hit the road? Will the tour bring you to Denver? You won't have to miss Nate's wedding, I hope, because he's really counting on you as best man. I'll be disappointed, too, because it seems like forever since I've seen you! Oh! And what happens to your partnership at The Meetinghouse? And your students… Who will replace you at the academy?"

Laughing, Sam said, "Whoa. Slow down, girl. I can only answer one question at a time." The fact was, he couldn't tell her anything…yet.

"I need some sisterly advice."

"Oh, cool…you know how much I love telling you what to do."

"Did I tell you that Finn's sister had a minor stroke?"

"No. But good grief. Is there such a thing as a minor stroke?"

"They're called TIAs. Ciara was involved in a near-fatal car crash years ago, and it left her with permanent brain damage. Seems a blood clot was lurking, got loose and caused the stroke."

"Poor Finn. She must be beside herself."

"Things were touch and go for a while there, but Ciara's doing great. Home from the hospital. Almost back to normal. In fact, better than before." He explained how she no longer repeated words. Told her that Misty had shown up, then disappeared again without a word, how hard their dad was working to stay away from drugs and booze.

"Oh, Sam, what a mess! You want my advice? Stay away from the Learys. Get far, far away, as fast as you can."

"I told myself the same thing. But then I got to know them. Ciara is amazing, and Connor is turning out to be a pretty good dad. And…" It should be simple, telling her he was in love with Finn. That he'd endure just about anything to keep her in his life. Why, then, couldn't he find the words?

"Uh-oh."

"Uh-oh, what?"

"You didn't tell her, did you?"

Last time they'd discussed Finn, Sophie's advice had been simple and straightforward: "Tell her how you feel."

"No, I didn't. Because I barely knew her then." Allowing himself to fixate on Aggie's warning hadn't helped move things forward, either.

"So?"

"So what?"

Sophie groaned. "Sam, Sam, Sam...unless I'm seriously mistaken, you're in love with her. So what's stopping you from telling her *now*?"

"Bernie."

"Wait. What?" She snickered. "Help me out here. What does a record producer have to do with..." Sophie paused, then said, "Oh, wait just a minute here. I think I get it... Didn't you tell me that Finn has a bad attitude toward musicians?"

"With good reason, but, yeah."

"Am I to assume, then, that you haven't told her about Bernie's offer, either?"

"I had every intention of telling her. The very night he made the offer, in fact. But then her sister had the stroke, and her dad had a panic attack— I thought it was his heart, to be honest—and her mom got all wigged out because Aggie insulted her, and..."

Did this all sound as ridiculous to his sister as it sounded to him?

"Anyway, now that things are settling down, I thought I'd take her to dinner. Someplace nice.

Alone for a change. Lay my cards on the table. See how she reacts." *And hope for the best.*

"Let me ask you something, big brother."

Sam waited.

"How much do you want this? The contract and everything that goes with it, I mean."

"More than just about anything. It's all I've thought about since, well, since I left Colorado and settled here in Nashville."

"You won't miss teaching?"

"Maybe a little."

"Helping run the club?"

"Nah. The guys were doing fine before they brought me in as a partner. I don't do much more than plug in the amps and test the mics anyway. They probably won't even notice I'm not there."

"Until they want to sing some dynamite three-part harmony, or need somebody to play some wild and crazy guitar licks like only Sam Marshall can."

"This is Nashville, Soph. Guitarists and singers are a dime a dozen."

"Yeah? Then, why did this Bernie guy single *you* out?"

"Because I'm a tall, blond, blue-eyed cowboy?"

"Oh, right. Like *those* aren't a dime a dozen in Nashville."

They shared a moment of companionable laughter before Sophie said, "Okay, let's cut to the chase—what about Finn?"

What about Finn? It's all about Finn!

"You'd hate her if she made you choose," Sophie said before he could answer. "Not at first, maybe, but eventually."

"Maybe she won't ask me to choose."

"Sam…"

The doubt in her voice swirled in his head and settled deep in his heart.

"Classic catch-22 scenario, if ever there was one," he said. "Choose the road, and miss her enough to mess up my performance. Stay in Nashville and end up resenting her."

"What if she sold the diner, and you brought her out here? She'd have so much family around, there wouldn't be time to miss you while you're on the road. We'd make sure of it!"

Now, there was something he hadn't considered.

"Or…you could always learn to miss her less, through phone calls, texts, FaceTime chats."

"Which philosopher said, 'that's a poor imitation, at best?'"

"You're asking me? I barely squeaked a C out of my English lit class." Sophie laughed but got serious to add, "You're pretty sure, then, that she'll make you choose…her or the record deal."

"When it comes to Finn Leary, the only thing I *am* sure of is that I'm crazy about her."

"Sounds to me like you just solved your own problem."

"I did?"

"I know *talking* isn't exactly a strong suit among

the Marshall men, but talking to her is the only way you're going to find out for sure."

"Gee. I knew that much when I called you. Fat lotta help you've been."

"You're welcome."

He heard the smile in her voice. "I didn't say thank you. Yet."

"Oh, but you will."

"Oh, I will, will I?"

"Think about it—Finn might be scared to death of making a lifelong commitment to a musician, but if she loves you, really loves you, she'll move heaven and earth to make things work."

Sam nodded as understanding dawned. "Because she moves heaven and earth to take care of Ciara. And her dad. And every employee at The Right Note. Even her mother, who isn't exactly easy to love."

"And *that's* the stuff you need to concentrate on while you're pitching your idea."

"My idea?"

"What would you call it?"

Sam wasn't sure, exactly. He smiled as that idea began to take shape in his mind. If he laid down those cards in the right order, it might just be the right thing...for everyone.

Either that, or he'd have to go to Aggie, hat in hand, and admit she was right.

Because if he asked Finn to put her trust in him

while he was on the road, and she said no, it would mean she didn't love him.

And that would break his heart.

CHAPTER THIRTY-ONE

"I wish you'd come with me."

"Much as I'd like to meet your family and see the Double M, I just can't. Dr. Peterson says it's too soon for Ciara to fly, for one thing. Air pressure, you know?"

And, Sam guessed, Finn was no doubt concerned about what might happen if she left Connor and the diner unattended for a long weekend.

"I understand. Believe me, if I could get out of this shindig…"

"Don't even think about it. Your cousin is counting on you. And I'm sure the whole Marshall family is looking forward to seeing you. How long has it been?"

When she smiled up at him that way, it was all Sam could do to concentrate. "Couple months, give or take."

"Well, speaking as someone who doesn't have much family, I'll think you're certifiable if you don't go. Because if they're half as sweet and caring as you…"

Fingers to her lips, she made an oops face, as if she regretted saying even that much. Seemed to Sam they were both certifiable, since neither of them could ratchet up the courage to say what was on their minds.

"Call me when you get there, so I'll know you made it safely."

"I'll call every day."

They'd shared some pretty hot kisses—a few initiated by Finn—so her shy smile puzzled him.

"But I'll wait until you've closed up shop, and the kids are tucked in for the night. So you won't have to watch every word. You know?"

She laughed. "Wonder how Connor and Ciara would feel about being called kids."

"They'd agree...if they're honest."

And if *he* was honest, he'd tell her every detail of Bernie's offer, and that he loved her so much he was giving serious thought to walking away from the deal.

"You know," she said softly, "I think I'm going to miss you."

"You know, I might just miss you a little bit, too."

He wanted to hug her, wanted to kiss the stuffing out of her. So his hesitation didn't make a lick of sense. He'd said the words to other women. Shouldn't it be easier to say it now that he was older and wiser...and meant it?

"Heard from Misty?" *Coward*, he chided himself, *hiding behind her absent mother.*

"No, not a peep. But that's Misty for you. Here today, gone tomorrow. I'll hear from her when she needs something, or she'll turn up when she gets into trouble. And as usual, I'll help any way I can." She frowned, then added, "Bet you think I'm crazy, or stupid—or both!—bailing her out all the time."

"No, I think you're Finn Leary." Sam cupped her chin in his palm. "And Finn Leary doesn't know any other way to *be*."

She stood on tiptoe and kissed his cheek. Too bad she hadn't aimed a bit left, Sam thought, to kiss his lips instead.

Tapping his temple with her fingertip, she said, "You're sweet. A tad tetched, but with a heart as big as your head."

"Thanks. I think." He ran a hand through his hair. "Well, my flight leaves in a couple of hours, so I'd better hit the road."

"I'll say a little prayer that you'll have a safe flight."

Sophie said stuff like that all the time, and so did his mom. But Finn was the first non–family member who'd prayed for his safety, and he had no idea how to respond to that.

Just as he grasped the doorknob, she said, "Have a good time, and send pictures if you can. You know how Ciara loves weddings!"

Yeah, he sure did. Half a dozen times, he'd caught himself grinning dopily, picturing the way she'd blushed and fidgeted when Ciara described her dream about the yellow dress and white daisies.

"I don't want to say goodbye. Is that silly, or what?"

No woman had ever gotten teary eyed when he left her, not even family members.

"It's just four days."

She lifted one shoulder daintily, and a lone tear tracked down her cheek.

Sam put the bag down and took her in his arms, and this time, he kissed her like he meant business. If he missed his plane, well, he'd just have to catch another.

He took a half step back and pressed forefinger to her lips. "These are mine," he whispered. "Just thought you oughta know."

Lashes fluttering, her mouth formed a tiny O, and she hid it behind one hardworking hand and nodded.

Be a man. Be a man and say it, for cryin' out loud!

Rowdy burst through the door and muscled a big box into the storeroom. "Hey, you two. What's up?"

"I'm leaving for Denver," Sam said. "Doing the best man thing at my cousin's wedding."

"Oh, yeah? Enjoy," the big guy said. "Didn't realize they'd finally set a date."

"Yeah…"

"Guess that means you'll stay out there for a couple of weeks? Do the whole 'Thanksgiving with family' thing instead of going back and forth?"

"Nah. I'll be back," he said, looking at Finn. Sam met Rowdy's eyes again. "Do me a favor?"

"If I can…"

"Watch over this one for me, will ya?"

Not exactly the proclamation of love she deserved, Sam thought, hurrying to the parking lot, but it was a start.

While Sam sat at the gate waiting to board the plane, his cell phone buzzed.

"Sam. It's Bernie. Got a minute?"

"I'm at the airport, and they're about to start boarding the plane…"

"Then, I'll cut to the chase. Have you had enough thinking-about-it time yet?"

"You didn't get my messages? I'll be out of town. In Denver. I'm best man at my cousin's wedding."

"When do you get back?"

"Monday afternoon."

"Then, let's meet for coffee on Tuesday morning. My office. Ten o'clock. Oh. And here's a little something to mull over while you're way out West—you're not the only cowboy in the rodeo, y'know?"

Yeah, he knew. Funny, but that didn't sting nearly as much as he'd expected it to.

Maybe because, unlike so many other desperate-to-sign performers, Sam had a fulfilling job to fall back on. A place to perform—and get paid for it—any time he pleased. And that parting moment at The Right Note, when Finn's big eyes had flashed "I love you" so loudly he could almost hear it.

Why, with all that in mind, it hardly stung at all.

"OH, WOW, ISN'T that the most beautiful gown ever?"

The sisters huddled on the couch, scrolling through the wedding pictures Sam had texted Finn. The dress wasn't Finn's style, but Eden certainly made a lovely bride in the drop-waist ball gown.

"Sam says it's the same dress her mother wore," she told Ciara.

"The veil, too?"

"He didn't say. But you know how guys are."

Connor, standing behind them in the foyer, harrumphed. "Yeah, we don't pay attention to ruffles and lace. And all that pomp and circumstance for a three-hour party seems like a big, fat waste of money to me."

"But, Dad," Ciara said, "a girl only gets married once."

"Unless her name is Misty."

She exhaled a long, soft sigh and leaned her head on Finn's shoulder. "Do you think a girl like me could ever get married?"

Finn glanced at Connor, and he mouthed, *You take this one…*

"What do you mean…a girl like you?"

"You know, with all my brain issues. I'm not very smart. And I'm kinda clumsy. And then there's *this* thing." She traced the ropelike scar that followed her hairline. "Not exactly the sexiest package a guy could buy."

She punctuated the statement with a quiet giggle, but Finn heard no humor in it.

"Not a word of what you just said is true. You *are* smart. And pretty. Sweet as pumpkin pie. And who tripped over her own feet and nearly did a header in the diner this morning?"

"You did."

"And who cuts corners too sharp," Connor put in, "*all* the time, and rams his shoulders into door frames?"

"You do."

"See there? You're no clumsier than most people."

"Either that," Finn countered, "or clumsy runs in the Leary family."

They all had a good laugh, and then Connor sat on the other side of Ciara. "Any man worth his salt will see what a gem you are, and he'll snap you up in a heartbeat."

"Yeah, well, I don't hear any snapping going on."

"Why this sudden interest in finding a husband?" Finn asked.

"Because one of these days, Sam is going to work up the courage to ask you to marry him."

A loud, strange giggle popped from her mouth. "Marry him! We've never even been out on an official date!"

"Only because you can't go anywhere without dragging your dumb, klutzy sister along…"

Connor slid an arm across her shoulders. "First of all, Finn is right—you're not dumb, and you're not klutzy. And second, I'm sure the reason she takes you everywhere is because she enjoys your company."

Finn nodded. "That's one hundred percent true."

"So, then, when you and Sam get married, will you move into a real house?"

"Probably not. I like living here above the diner." Finn counted on her fingers. "No rush-hour traffic getting to and from work, no worrying about finding a parking space, no lunches to pack…"

"Finn, stop! You just don't get it! I want a place of my own, and a boyfriend who'll want to become my husband. I want to be a mom someday, too—not like Misty, but a *good* mom, who loves her kids and takes care of them, even when it isn't easy, the way you've always taken care of me." She looked at Connor, then back at Finn. "And I want to know if you guys think I'll ever have *any* of that…or if I'm going to become a grumpy, lonely old lady like Aggie."

Connor drew her into a fatherly hug. "Aw, sweetie, I wish you could see yourself the way I see you. Because if you could, you'd know what a treasure you are." He kissed her temple. "You're just a kid. Don't be in such a hurry to grow up."

"I'm not a kid, Dad. I'll be twenty-three in a few weeks. *Twenty-three* and I've never even been on a date with a guy!"

"When you get my age—"

"See? You don't get it." She leaped up and ran to her room. "You just don't get it!"

The door banged shut, and Connor winced. "Think I should go in there?"

"No, let's give her a few minutes alone."

"I've never seen her get mad before, have you?"

"No, at least not to that degree." She patted his hand. "Maybe it's a good thing."

"That she's stomping around, slamming doors, fussing and fuming? How's that a good thing?"

"This fascination with weddings and gowns and veils... That's totally new. So maybe her tantrum is a sign that she's catching up with her life in other ways, too. Getting angry once in a while is perfectly normal."

"She wouldn't have to catch up if I hadn't gotten plastered that night." He held up a hand. "Sorry, didn't mean to go all Misty on you." He grinned a bit at his little joke. "Seriously, this isn't about me. Or your mother. It's about Ciara." He sighed. "Maybe you're right, and all she needs is time and patience."

"And a dad who loves her so much that he'll never leave her again?"

"That, too." He scooted closer and drew Finn into a hug. "*You* deserve that, too, you know."

"Yeah, because if Ciara is right about Sam, I'm going to want you to walk me down the aisle."

"You won't make me wear a top hat and tails, will you?"

"No way."

"Or a cummerbund and one of those ruffled shirts?"

"Absolutely not."

"I can wear my boots?"

"I'd be disappointed if you didn't."

He leaned his head on hers. "It's a shame Misty isn't here. These are the kinds of things a girl should talk about with her mom, not her crusty old dad."

"Oh, don't be so hard on yourself. You're not crusty."

"I'm not all that old, either, but I digress. I haven't been there for you girls in a long, long time. But I'm here now. Here to stay, for good." He chuckled. "Don't worry, not *here*, because in a couple weeks, I'll have enough in the bank to get a place of my own. There's a place for rent in walking distance from here, did you see?"

"No, I didn't."

"Top floor of the coffee shop. It isn't real big, but it's clean and furnished."

"You're just fifty-five. Don't be in such a hurry to get out on your own."

"You're hilarious." He held up one finger. "Say, something just occurred to me… Torry's leaving for California in a few days to audition for some movie role. He'll be gone a couple weeks, and the club won't have a comic to fill in between sets…"

"It appears that clumsy *and* funny runs in the Leary family."

Her cell phone buzzed.

"*Another* message from Sam? How many does that make today?"

"I'm not sure." Finn intended to read the text later, in private. "Ten or twelve. But some of them were pictures of the wedding, don't forget, so they don't count, since they were more for Ciara than me."

"Three. Three were pictures."

Finn smiled and held the phone to her chest, remembering Sam's running commentary on Nate and Eden's wedding vows. The silly joke his uncle had shared. The art of dancing with a tiny niece balanced on the toes of his cowboy boots. How his sister, Sophie, had nearly given her cousin a concussion, jumping up to catch the bride's bouquet… and how he'd caught the garter. Uh-oh, he'd typed. You know what that means…

Connor snapped his fingers. "Earth to Finn…"

"Sorry. Guess my mind wandered a bit."

"A bit? More like it wandered all the way out to Denver."

"I should probably check on Ciara."

"Yeah, but first tell your old dad the truth. Do you love him?"

She nodded and felt a little like the fuzzy brown dachshund statue that rode in the back window of Pete's Oldsmobile. What was it about Sam that made her feel like a goofy, mush-brained girl?

"Well, do you?" Connor pressed.

"Yeah, I do."

"Then, you need to tell him."

Finn only shrugged.

"So you're not going to tell him."

Another shrug.

"What are you afraid of?"

"Nothing. Everything." She turned to face him. "What if I've been misreading his cues, and every sweet gesture was nothing but the by-product of his thoughtful personality? And what if I make a commitment, and he leaves me to tour the country?"

"You want to know what I think?"

Finn waited for him to continue.

"I think he'll pay me a visit after he gets home to ask for your hand in marriage."

"I'm not so sure. I'm not even sure I want that."

"You can't fool an old fool." Connor winked. "Of course you want that. And when he asks, I'll say yes…on one condition."

"What condition?"

"He has to guarantee that even if he signs with Bernie and goes on the road for a time, he'll make Nashville home base, and he'll always come home to you."

"That's a lot to ask."

"Why?"

"Because he's a musician, and we both know—"

If she could take back the words, Finn would do it in a heartbeat.

"That didn't come out right," she began. "What I meant was—"

He held up a hand. "No, after all the years I put music ahead of you and your sister, I had that coming. But Sam is a better man than I am."

"You're a good man." At least, she thought, he'd become a good man.

"That boy is good to the bone. And trust me, I know good when I see it."

"But you've heard him sing and play that guitar of his—he's wonderful. It's only a matter of time before someone like Bernie makes him an offer he can't refuse."

"We don't need the details to know that Bernie already made him an offer."

"And if he signs? What then?"

"So what if he does?"

"He'll go on tour and get all caught up in the lights and the autographs and the groupies and—"

"He's better than that. Give him a chance to prove it. And stop making him pay for my mistakes."

Finn nodded. "I'd better check on Ciara." She got to her feet, then said, "You've given me a lot to think about. Thanks, Dad."

"No, thank *you*."

"For what? You're the one who doled out all the great advice."

"Thanks for not calling me Connor. Don't get me wrong, my mama chose a fine, strong name." He got to his feet, too, and gave her a fatherly squeeze. "But I like Dad a whole lot better."

Finn would have said, "Me, too," if not for the happy, relieved sob pulsing in her throat.

Only one thing could make life more perfect, and if Connor was right, it would happen in about a week.

CHAPTER THIRTY-TWO

HALFWAY THROUGH THE two-hour, twenty-six-minute flight between Denver and Nashville's Berry Field, Sam wrote the last lines of a new song. Whether or not he performed it onstage, the lyrics would likely remain the most meaningful—and personal—of any he'd written to date. And with a notebook that bulged with nearly three hundred Sam Marshall tunes, that was saying something. But the biggest challenge still remained: finding the right notes to accentuate each word.

The right notes...

He laughed to himself, because even *that* reminded him of Finn, looking sweet and sad as he left her at The Right Note.

She'd been front and center in his mind since he'd headed to the Nashville airport. And while the Marshall family and friends had gathered to celebrate a successful dry run at Nate and Eden's ceremony, a hundred little things had made him think of Finn. In his childhood bedroom after the rehearsal dinner, while drafting his fun-yet-moving best man speech, Sam had caught himself doodling Finn in the margins. Lady Luck must have been smiling on him, because if Sophie had walked in a tick sooner and caught sight of it, she'd never have let him live it down. Why, he wouldn't put it past her to volunteer to write his eulogy, just so she could rub it in one last time…payback for the times he'd razzed her for drawing various boys' names in colorful bubble letters all over her high school textbooks.

He couldn't wait to see Finn's reaction when he told her he'd stepped on his new sister-in-law's white satin shoes…because visions of *her* in a flowing white gown and gauzy veil had distracted him. She'd probably blush and giggle when she heard that he'd mindlessly written Sam and Finn Marshall in the guest book, then made up a flimsy "need to use the men's room" excuse rather than tell his aunt Maeve why a squiggly black tornado had appeared above his signature, hiding his mistake.

His seatmate leaned forward slightly, tapped a many-ringed finger on his tray table.

"I can't help but notice that you aren't wearing a wedding ring."

Instinct made him cover his left hand with the right, which prompted her to snicker.

She extended the hand. "I'm Ada."

He shook it, and returned her smile. "Sam."

"Do you live in Nashville?"

"Yes, ma'am. Just heading home after a quick trip to Denver."

"And I was out there visiting my sister." She

glanced at his hand again. "So, Sam, are you allergic to gold?"

"No…"

"I ask because I don't see evidence that you've *ever* worn a wedding ring."

"That's because I've never been married." Sam would happily don a gold band for the right woman. For *Finn*.

"A man as handsome as yourself? Please. Surely there's a fiancée…"

"Not yet." Because he needed to put music to those lyrics.

"Not yet?"

"Well, I have someone in mind…"

She waved the comment away. "I believe this is your lucky day, and mine, too. I'm the proud *ima* of four unmarried daughters, you see." She handed him a business card that said Ada Abraham, Master Matchmaker. "You can see right there in black-and-white why their marital status is bad for business." Laughing, Ada rested fingertips on his forearm. "I have a good feeling about you, Sam, so I'll tell you what I'm going to do. I'm going to give you your pick of my girls, which will spare you the trauma of memorizing and delivering a proposal, one hundred percent *free*!"

Sam patted the pocket that held his song lyrics. "Much as I appreciate the offer—and I'm sure they're all as lovely as their *ima*—my heart belongs to another."

"Ah, and you've just broken mine." Ada thumped her ample chest.

Their flight attendant walked down the aisle. "Seat backs and tray tables up, please," he said, pointing at the "fasten seat belt" light above their heads. A quiet *ding* punctuated his demand.

Saved by the bell, Sam thought, grinning to himself.

"Good afternoon, ladies and gents, this is your captain speaking." The garbled voice recited altitude, approximate arrival time and the current temperature in Nashville. "We trust you've enjoyed your flight and hope you'll fly with us again."

"Why do pilots bother with all that nonsense?" She stuffed snacks, a water bottle and her paperback into a tote nearly as large as his carry-on. "Do they realize that most passengers can only decipher every other word?" She zipped the big red bag and held out her hand, palm up this time. "Since you won't be using the business card..."

Laughing, Sam gave it back.

"I paid extra for the raised print, you see. Waste not, want not."

"A Ben Franklin quote. One of my favorites."

"Ah, he's smart and well read, too—yet another reason to mourn what could have been." She smiled at him, then quickly turned to the man across the aisle. "A two-and-a-half-hour flight, and I just now noticed that you're not wearing a wedding ring," she said, holding out the card.

Oh, he could hardly wait to share this story with Finn! Chuckling and shaking his head, Sam leaned back and, eyes closed, pictured Finn.

Finn, who'd stolen his heart and turned him into a scared-to-say-*love* bonehead. Whose capacity to love and talent for nurturing made him yearn to be one of the people on the receiving end of her TLC. Who'd hidden behind a hand when he'd said her lips belonged to him, and said with nothing more than a *look* that she felt the same way.

When he'd first moved to Nashville, staying busy had been the only thing that had kept him from heading straight back to Denver. Vacation planners claimed New York was "the city that never sleeps," but in Sam's opinion, *Music* City was just as much an insomniac. It took a while to adjust to nonstop commotion, blaring sirens, blinking lights…and tourists who followed anyone carrying a guitar case in hopes of running into someone worthy of signing anything that could hold ink. Every now and then, he still yearned for the peaceful beauty of the Double M's mountain vistas. But these few days without Finn proved without question that *people*, not places, had the power to lure him from his dream: he missed Finn more than he'd thought it possible for one person to miss another, and he couldn't wait to get back to her.

He'd tucked the handout given to all of Nate and Eden's wedding guests into his jacket pocket. Opening it, he saw the list of people who'd participated in the ceremony, song lyrics, scripture verses, then came to his favorite part…when the bride and groom joined hands and recited together:

I promise to be your constant friend, your faithful partner in sickness and health, in joy and sorrow, to honor and respect you, laugh with you and cry with you, and to love you from this moment to my last on earth.

He'd heard similar vows in the past, but none had put a lump in his throat or moved him to tears. It wasn't until he'd heard Nate and Eden's special twist on the traditional pledge that Sam realized he wanted to *live* those words…with Finn.

IN SAM'S ABSENCE, the guys had made great progress on a project that had grown out of Connor's idea to donate The Right Note's old furnishings and utensils to a homeless shelter. They'd decided to open their own shelter instead.

Rowdy had surprised them all by announcing that he owned three rental properties, and intended to donate one to house those in need.

When the contractor who'd renovated the diner heard about it, he'd volunteered materials and manhours to bring the place up to code.

Connor's visits to local and regional media outlets promised prime-time coverage before, during and after the fund-raiser they were planning. He'd met with the mayor, too, who'd put him in touch with local agencies that would provide trained staff.

Torry's connections had encouraged the involvement of some of recognizable names—groups, duos and solo artists who'd agreed to appear in person or via live video feed.

Even Bernie had gotten involved by promising to orchestrate a recording of the fund-raiser. Once packaged and sold online, he was sure it would bring in income now and far into the future.

It didn't surprise him to hear that Finn would cater the after-party, or that she'd written to-do lists for everyone.

"I can't believe you got so much done while I was gone. Did you leave anything for me to do?"

"Finn cracks a mean whip," Mark said, handing Sam a copy of the itinerary she'd designed and doled out. "And don't worry. You're the guy in charge of making sure everybody can get here at the same time, on the same day. And that the fund-raiser doesn't conflict with anything else on that date."

Sam chuckled. "Gee. Is that all?"

"Actually, no. She wants you to think up a catchy title for the fund-raiser. And a name for the shelter."

"No way." He looked at Mark's list. "Where does it say that?"

Torry stepped up, pointed over Sam's shoulder. "See? Right there. 'Sam—date, ASAP.' And here, 'Event title, ASAP.' Trust me…she means every syllable of that acronym, so I'd get right on it I were you." He pretended to shiver. "That Finn is a force to be reckoned with."

"That's m'girl," Connor said.

It had been her father's offhanded comment, weeks ago, about the need for more homeless facilities and rehab centers that had inspired the idea in the first place. The changes in the man had been remarkable, and he deserved a lot of credit for making—and sticking to—the decision to turn over a new leaf. Would he have been as successful without Finn's open-armed welcome? Sam didn't think so, and the answer stirred his imagination, sparking possible names for the organization.

"By the way," Mark said, handing him an envelope, "Bernie left this for you."

"What is it?" Sam turned it over a few times.

"How should I know? Do I look like the type of guy who reads other people's mail?"

Sam copied his smirk. "Well…"

"Aw, just open it, smart guy, so we can all get back to work."

Sam could tell from the size and heft of the package that it contained a contract. He could feel a paper clip, too, which meant Bernie had attached a note, something along the lines of *Sign this agreement, or walk away from what could be a once-in-a-lifetime opportunity.*

He folded it in half and tucked it into his back pocket. "I'll look at it later."

"If you don't sign," Mark said, "you're out of your ever-lovin' mind."

Torry agreed. "The man has connections everywhere, meaning if you have any talent at all, he can hook you up with movers and shakers in all areas of the entertainment industry. Think of it, Sam. Movies. TV. *And* albums."

Bernie had definitely helped boost Torry's career, which now included major motion pictures and guest spots on sitcoms in addition to performances on some of the most sought-after stages.

"I'll read it after I've checked on Ciara and Finn."

"When you see Ciara, you won't believe your eyes," Connor said. "Tell those girls of mine that I'll be home in an hour or two."

"Speaking of home," Mark said, "if you sign that thing, what are the chances you'll sell your share of the partnership and make Colorado home base?"

"Nah. I need to stick around at least long enough to figure out how a guy who claims he never reads other people's mail knows what's in this envelope."

"He didn't have to read it," Torry said. "He read the writing on the wall."

"All right, give a guy a break, will ya?" Mark said.

Sam made his way to the double entry doors and lifted a hand. "I'll be at The Right Note if anybody needs me."

He stepped outside, hands pocketed and shoulders hunched, and plowed into the biting early-November wind. In the distance, rays of the setting sun sparked from the "Batman" building's iconic radio towers.

The sight caught him off guard, and he stopped walking, enraptured by the beauty of the scene.

Poor Finn, he thought, rounding the corner, because she had no idea that by saying yes, she would be in for a lifetime of stuff like that.

The Right Note's slow-blinking welcome sign came into sight just then. *Truth in advertising*, he thought. She greeted everyone with genuine warmth, but he liked to think that she reserved that sweet, one-of-a-kind smile for *him*. Would he see that smile when he admitted that he didn't just want her lips all to himself, he wanted all of her, for the rest of his days?

She was bent over a tour map when he walked in, showing the couple at the checkout counter how to get to Riverfront Station. "Here's the Ryman." She pointed at a dot on Fifth Avenue, then slid her finger farther up Broadway to Third Avenue. "And the Johnny Cash Museum. You'll be able to see the station from there. This time of year, you shouldn't have any trouble grabbing a couple of seats on the Hop-On Hop-Off Trolley. The driver will usually stop so you can get pictures of the Parthenon and the Capitol building. The Nashville skyline is gorgeous at night!"

The couple thanked her and made their way to the door. She was right: the Nashville skyline *did* look gorgeous at night, but it couldn't compare to the way her face lit up when she spotted him. Should he wait until they were alone to tell her what he'd decided, or do it right here, right now?

"How was the flight? And traffic from the airport? When was the last time you ate anything? I know they don't feed passengers on airplanes anymore..."

"The flight was fine." Later, he'd tell her about Ada's offer to hook him up with one of her unmarried daughters...without the usual matchmaker fee. "And so was traffic. I grabbed a burger at the airport, so thanks, but I don't have an appetite." He paused and took a deep breath. "I have something to tell you, though. And something to ask you."

A short line had gathered at the counter.

"Let me take care of these customers," she said, "and then..."

He'd give her all the time she needed. If she said no, he'd need the rest of his life to get over it.

"So what's in the envelope?" she asked.

He'd almost forgotten it was in his back pocket. "To be honest, I'm not sure. Mark handed it to me as I left the club to come over here." Sam didn't want to talk about Bernie. Or the deal. "You guys made some serious headway on the shelter project while I was gone. I'm impressed."

"It didn't *all* happen while you were gone, you know. Writing up lesson plans and teaching is important work. Demanding, distracting work. I'd be surprised if a few things *didn't* escape your notice."

She turned to greet another customer, and Sam used the time to collect his thoughts. Should he explain everything now, or wait until later, when they could be alone?

"The envelope," she said. "It's from that man, isn't it?"

"What man?"

"The one with the ponytail and goatee you were talking to the night Ciara and Connor went to the hospital. What is he? Agent? Manager?"

"Producer."

She raised her chin a notch and stood up straighter. "So what did he offer you?"

Another customer approached, and as she rang up the tab, Sam said, "I don't want to talk about this now. Or here."

"Okay. So when?"

"That's up to you."

She didn't know it yet, but their entire future was up to her.

Finn made change and, smiling, invited the diner to come back soon.

"Can we talk after closing?" she asked.

"Your apartment?"

"No. Connor and Ciara will be there."

He'd give anything to get into that pretty head of hers and find out what inspired that almost suspicious expression.

"Here, then?"

She nodded. "I'll call you when everyone has left
for the day."

"Sounds like a plan. Can't wait."

Why did he get the feeling she didn't mean it?

CHAPTER THIRTY-THREE

HE'D WAITED UNTIL nearly midnight for her call. Thinking maybe she'd forgotten, he tried her cell phone at twelve thirty…and got her voice mail.

Any number of things could explain that, he'd told himself. Running a diner wasn't a fine science after all. Maybe an appliance malfunctioned, or a few stragglers decided to hang around long past closing time.

So Sam had driven over there and parked out back. And it surprised him to find The Right Note was dark and locked up tight.

He went up to the apartment and knocked gently, so as not to wake Connor or Ciara. But there were no lights on inside, and no answer to his knock, either.

First thing next morning, he called again…and left another message.

He walked into the diner at the height of the breakfast rush and saw her duck into the back. Tried again at lunch, and she was nowhere to be seen.

Rowdy wasn't talking, and when he asked Bean what was up, the girl looked like the kid caught with her hand in the proverbial cookie jar.

Connor had avoided him, too. When he'd finally gotten a moment alone with him, Sam said, "What's going on?"

"I promised to stay out of it," Connor had said. "She believes in me again, and I won't let anything jeopardize that."

If Sam closed his eyes, he could still see the discomfort etched on the man's face.

On day ten, he accepted it: Finn had written him off without so much as an explanation.

That's what you get for putting things off for so long.

Sam threw himself into his work, hoping it would distract him from feeling confused and hurt.

Tonight, he'd instructed his class to meet him at the warehouse. Sam lined them up and said, "Every one of you excelled at in-station tasks."

Sam reminded them what they'd accomplished: bench-press a ninety-five-pound barbell five times, pick up a sixty-pound ventilation fan and hang it overhead, carry the eighty-pound hose—while wearing their twenty-five-pound air masks—to the seventh floor of the training tower in one minute and thirty seconds, maneuver the tunnel maze, scale a six-foot wall without a ladder, drag a hundred-and-sixty-pound dummy seventy-five feet in a minute, connect and disconnect hose couplings also in a minute or less and force open a door.

"But today, you're going to do all of that in conditions that you that you might experience under fire—pardon the pun."

They laughed, but that would end in a minute, when he let them know exactly *what* he aimed to put them through. Sure enough, the big space fell silent when he said, "You may have noticed that I turned off the heat."

"Yeah, we did," a cadet said.

"Feels like a meat locker in here!" another added.

"Enjoy it while you can, because next I'm gonna turn on the sprinklers." He pointed. "And fire that up."

"A jet engine?"

The guy beside him moaned as another said, "Can you say *hypothermia*?"

More laughter echoed in the corrugated metal building, but it was nowhere near as hearty as before.

"Things are getting real," Sam said. "This last run at the physical segment of the final exam might reduce the number by another one or two."

They stood at attention, looking somber and scared. Sam remembered feeling the same way, years earlier, on a night very much like this one.

"Before we begin, I want you to know that whether or not you move to the next phase—the personal interviews—you have every right to be proud of yourselves. Making it this far hasn't been easy, but you'll leave here better men—and woman," he said, looking at Jasmine, "and better prepared to meet whatever life throws at you with strength and dignity."

For some reason, the words brought Finn to mind.

Sam whistled to get their attention. "Are we ready?"

They said they were, so he pushed them, hard. Bellowed advice to help improve their time. Shouted suggestions that, if implemented, would increase their chances of graduating.

And not one fell behind. Not even Jasmine.

Afterward, as his exhausted students huffed and puffed and peeled off their gear, realization dawned: they'd done well tonight, and it meant they'd cross that stage *together*. They responded with the enthusiasm of children, laughing, hugging, shouting, high-fiving.

"I predict you'll probably outscore every class to date," he told them. "I'm proud of you."

They stood at attention and saluted him, then gathered their equipment and filed from the warehouse, stopping to shake his hand.

"Couldn't have done it without you," the first man said.

"Those learned-the-hard-way anecdotes made a big difference," said another.

"He's right," a third agreed. "Everything you told us that *wasn't* in the book? That's what put us over the top."

Pride lit up Jasmine's face as she said, "If you hadn't been tough on me, I wouldn't be here."

She extended a hand, and Sam shook it.

"Thanks, Captain, for believing in me even when I didn't."

It felt good, hearing that his teaching strategies had helped them, felt gratifying to think that maybe in the middle of a crisis, some small tip or tactic he'd shared during their weeks together would come to mind and perhaps save a life—theirs or a citizen's. If only Finn had half as much confidence in him...

He shook off the thought and focused instead on the fact that he'd taken them as far as an instructor could. As they shuffled from the warehouse, tired and worn, he reminded himself that from here on out, their successes and failures were up to them.

He'd miss the job. There was something gratifying about turning ordinary civilians into capable firefighters. He would have stayed, if he thought he had a ghost of a chance with Finn. But how could he fix things if she refused to talk with him?

There wasn't anything for him in Nashville, so why not sign with Bernie and hit the road?

Alone in his truck, Sam dialed his captain's office number. "Call me first chance you get, sir," he told the recorder, "and let me know when we can get together." On the heels of a ragged sigh, he closed with "We need to talk, as soon as possible."

The message allowed him to cross one thing off his mental to-do list. Next stop, The Meetinghouse to talk with Torry and Mark about dissolving the partnership. And then?

And then Finn…

Thanksgiving was right around the corner, and it seemed to Sam that he had less than usual to give thanks for this year. It hadn't been easy, explaining to his mom that he'd be home for Christmas instead, but he was determined to do whatever it took to end things the right way with Finn, whether she liked it or not.

FINN'S CONCERNS THAT Ciara wouldn't handle Misty's latest disappearance well were laid to rest as they planned Thanksgiving dinner at The Right Note.

"Mom is old enough to make her own choices, and she keeps choosing other things and other people over us. So I guess as long as she's happy, we have something to be thankful for, right?"

Just a few months ago, Ciara never could have expressed her feelings with such wisdom and clarity. Yet another thing to be thankful for.

"I used to think it was my fault that she kept leaving," Ciara continued. "Because I was slow and weak and a lot of work. But she left after my operation, even when she saw that I *wasn't* slow and weak and a lot of work anymore." She gave a thoughtful nod. "That means it wasn't my fault, not ever. I miss her, but I feel a whole lot better about her staying away. I still don't understand it, though."

"You're absolutely right, Kee."

"Misty is a wonderful person—when she puts

her mind to it—but for some reason, she never believed it."

Without realizing it, Ciara had effectively summed up Finn's reasons for calling things off with Sam. He deserved better, so much better, than to link himself with someone so self-involved that she wouldn't share him, not even if doing so made him happy.

"It's so sad," Ciara continued, "that she never realized how much we loved her just for herself and no matter what, and that wherever we were *was* home."

Give him a chance, Connor had said. If she had, Sam would have tried to convince her there was room in his life for her and music, too, and she couldn't let that happen. Far better for him to see her as shallow and superficial than allow him to make a sacrifice like that.

Ciara's smile turned thoughtful. "You know what was most frustrating before this last operation?"

"What?"

"I had thousands of thoughts jumbled up in my head, but no matter how hard I tried, I couldn't *say* them." Reaching across the kitchen table, she squeezed Finn's hand. "You were the only one who understood that there was more to Ciara Leary than what came out of my stuttering mouth."

"We have lots to be thankful for this year, then, don't we?"

"Yes, and that's why I'm not sad about not seeing Mom. I'll miss her, but I have a feeling that wherever she is, she's taking care of Misty!" Ciara giggled. "And resting, I hope. Because she always works so hard."

"Works hard? *Misty?* She is one of the laziest people I've ever met!"

The woman was dishonest and heartless, too. The mess she'd made, stealing Finn's credit card, charging it to the max, then crashing a rental car. It would take years to dig out of that financial hole. If she thought it possible to tell Ciara about the lawsuit without resorting to spiteful name-calling…

"Well, it's true that she doesn't like chores. And as much as she loves music, she doesn't practice, either. But it must be hard work, trying to avoid doing things, don't you think?"

Finn agreed. Last week, avoiding Sam's repeated efforts to reach out had been exhausting. But the thought of facing him, seeing those blue eyes flash with disappointment when she admitted what a selfish woman she'd become…

"Being Misty Leary must be like being a hummingbird," Finn said. "Constantly in motion, always looking for the next sweet thing to feed her insatiable appetite. And you know what they say about those little birds…"

It reminded her of the hummingbird feeder Ciara had once hung from a shepherd's crook on the side porch.

"According to my hummingbird book," Ciara said, "their wings beat nine hundred times a minute, and their little hearts beat almost thirteen hundred times a minute."

Finn sat in awe of her little sister.

"Next spring, I'm going to hang another feeder. And the first bird that comes along? I'm going to call it Misty," Finn said.

Ciara studied her sister's face. "Can I ask you a question?"

"Of course you can, sweetie."

"Where's Sam?"

"Working, I imagine. It's getting close to the end of his session, so I'm sure he's busy, preparing tests and—"

"That isn't what I mean. I saw you hiding from him last week. And I heard you tell Rowdy and Dad not to explain things to him." Eyes narrowed, she added, "*What* things?"

"You know how I feel about musicians."

"And you know that Sam isn't just a musician. Why are you avoiding him? Did you two have a fight?"

"No." If only it were that simple.

"Is it because of me? You think I need to be taken care of, *still*?"

"Of course not!"

"Because I'd feel awful if I came between you and Sam."

"There's nothing to come between, Ciara."

"That isn't true. You love each other. I've always

known it." She tilted her head. "But if it isn't me, then what is it?"

She might as well get it out into the open and put an end to this line of questioning.

"Sam is a wonderful man. If I asked him to give up his music for me, he would. I'd hate myself if he did that, and eventually, he'd hate me, too."

Nodding slowly, Ciara studied her fingernails. "Finn…"

It was the same tone of voice she'd used when Ciara spouted self-deprecating things about herself.

"Someday you'll come to your senses. I hope it won't be too late."

It's already too late.

"Do you think you'll ever get married?"

Finn shrugged. *Only if I can find someone to match my selfishness…*

"If you have kids, will you teach them to call Misty Grandma?"

"I—I never gave it a thought."

"Remember what Pete used to say?"

That her face was easier to read than the morning paper.

"For what it's worth, big sister, I think you're being very silly. Life is short. I know what I'd do in your shoes."

Finn smiled. "What would you do?"

"I *am* going to get married, you know. I don't know who, and I don't know when…yet, but if we have a misunderstanding, no matter what it takes, I'll make things right."

It was hard to believe that weeks ago, Ciara had flown into a minirage, worrying if she'd ever experience love herself.

"My turn to ask *you* a question, little sister."

"You can ask—" she winked "—but I can't promise to answer!"

It would take time to adjust to Ciara cracking jokes and spouting all-in-good-fun sarcasm.

"*If* I ever get married—"

"To Sam," Ciara interrupted.

"If I ever get married," Finn continued, "I hope you'll stay with me."

"That isn't a question." She grinned. "But yes, I will...until I save enough money for my own apartment. Because once I get a *guy* of my own," she said, wiggling her eyebrows, "I'll want a *place* of my own, so you won't stick your nose in my business and cramp my style."

"Just listen to you!" Finn laughed. "Oh, I'll definitely have something to be thankful for on Thursday! And so will you!"

"Such as...?"

"Such as..."

Finn couldn't speak past the grateful sob in her throat.

Connor had been right. It had been unfair to assume Sam would make the same mistakes. Ciara had been right, too. Life was too short to waste another moment wondering what Sam might or might not do.

She needed to find him and tell him the truth.

And hope he was more forgiving and less judgmental than herself.

CHAPTER THIRTY-FOUR

"SHE'S TOO PROUD for her own good," Ciara said, "so she'll never admit that she needs help." She told Rowdy and Sam how Misty had raided Finn's hidden stash of cash, and that she'd rented a car using one of the stolen credit cards. She hadn't purchased insurance, so when she'd crashed the car, the rental company had filed suit against Finn.

"They want to put a lien on The Right Note," she added. "I'm not exactly sure what that is, but I know Finn is scared of losing everything." She looked at the two men in turn. "Do you guys have any ideas?"

Sam felt bad for her, but it did his heart good to have an explanation for her sudden cold behavior. He'd gradually reduced the demands on his time and financial resources in preparation for a move back to Colorado.

"Don't worry, Ciara. I think between us, we can come up with a solution to her problems…one that won't make her feel beholden to anyone."

"That'd *have* to be a prerequisite," Rowdy said. "That girl would sooner jump off the Empire State Building than take a handout—or a helping hand—from anyone."

"Yeah, I figured as much. But it'll all work out."

"From your lips to God's ear," the big man said.

"Things are already in motion. My recruits graduate in a few weeks, and I'm not signing up to teach any more classes."

"That's hard to believe. You love that job."

"True, but going home for my cousin's wedding made me realize I love the Double M more. I miss the space and the quiet. And then there's Bernie's offer…"

"I've seen pictures of the Rockies," Ciara said, her voice soft and dreamy, "and they *look* peaceful and calm."

He showed her his phone, scrolling to photos of the ranch he'd taken while home for Nate's wedding. She oohed and aahed, just as he'd expected her to. And her reaction went perfectly with his plot.

Rowdy peered over her shoulder. "They're okay, but we're just a hop and a skip away from the Great Smoky Mountains, y'know."

"But, Rowdy," Ciara said, pointing at a photograph, "the Double M Ranch sits right at the edge of the Front Range. We can see the Smokys if the weather is just right, but we have to drive hours to *be* there."

Rowdy gave her a quick once-over and grinned. "Who are you and what have you done with Ciara Leary?"

"She's right here, right where she's always been.

Only now she isn't hiding behind a traumatic brain injury."

For a minute there, Sam thought Rowdy might burst into tears. But he quickly collected himself. "So let's hear this big plan of yours, Sam."

Although he made it up as he went along, it was easy to see that they liked the idea. All he needed now was a big boost from Lady Luck to make it all come together.

"So it's agreed, then? We'll run it past Finn after dinner on Thanksgiving?"

"Oh, I can hardly wait!" Ciara said. "Finn will be distracted, baking my birthday cake and getting things ready for the big dinner. She'll never see it coming!"

Sam agreed. "Do you think she'll say yes?"

Rowdy looked worried, and Ciara said, "I'm going to tell her I invited you. She has never been able to say no to me."

Rowdy's robust laughter echoed in the stainless-steel-and-tile kitchen. "Oh, this will be a Thanksgiving to remember!"

"Yes, yes it will."

Ciara looked so pleased with herself that Sam didn't have the heart to point out that Finn might consider his appearance at dinner an intrusion.

And that it was just as likely she'd hate his idea.

"THAT WAS PROBABLY the best meal I've had in years," Torry said, shoving back from the table.

Mark patted his belly. "I won't need to eat for a week."

"You can't quit yet. You haven't had a slice of my birthday cake," Ciara protested.

Finn propped a fist on her hip. "Hey…how did you know I baked you a cake? I sneaked down here in the middle of the night so you wouldn't find out!"

Ciara feigned a bored look. "You have never forgotten my birthday. Ever." She looked at Sam. "Mom was a terrible cook, and I didn't like store-bought cakes. Finn learned to bake, just for me."

Laughing softly, Finn said, "Those first couple weren't exactly prizewinners, were they?"

"Oh, they were a little lopsided, but they tasted good. I would have eaten them even if they were awful, because you went to all that trouble just for me."

Finn dabbed a napkin to the corners of her eyes. "Don't you know it's bad luck to make a person cry on Thanksgiving?"

"Speaking of Thanksgiving," Sam said, "I wonder if you guys would mind indulging me. It's a Marshall family tradition to take turns sharing what we're thankful for, so…"

"What a great idea!" Ciara said. "But can I go first? I have so much to say!"

He understood the "can't say no to Ciara" thing. "'Course you can."

She took a sip of water. "I'm thankful for Dr. Peterson and the surgery that fixed…everything that was wrong inside my head. And to Finn, for…" She sighed. "If I made a list of everything I'm grateful to her for, we'd be here until Christmas." She locked eyes with Sam across the table. "And I'm thankful for Sam…"

She wouldn't give away his surprise, would she?

"…and that's all I can say about that for now." Turning to Mark, seated beside her, she said, "You're next!"

"Well, I'm thankful for this wacky, weird, wild bunch, because you make me feel like family."

Torry smirked. "Ditto."

"Oh, no, you don't," Mark grumbled. "You're not getting away with that!"

"Okay, all right." One eye narrowed, he drummed his fingers on the table. "There are good ships, and wood ships and ships that sail the sea, but the best ships are friendships, and may they always be." He lifted his goblet and toasted those gathered. "I'm thankful to call each of you *friends*."

Ciara said, "I *love* that one, Torry!"

He chuckled. "So do I."

"Your turn, Dad…"

"Now, how am I supposed to follow a poem, of all things?"

Sam was glad he'd run his idea past Finn's father. Connor had come a long way in a short time, and Sam believed the changes—if they happened—would be good for him, too.

Connor cleared his throat and sat up straighter.

"Okay, here goes… We live in a great country—hardly perfect, but still one the best in the world. I'm in good health, there's a roof over my head and I can't remember the last time I went hungry. There's money in my bank account… A real good thing, because until recently, I didn't even have a bank account! I have the best job in the world, good friends and the most perfect, beautiful daughters a man ever had."

Bean spoke up next, followed by the rest of The Right Note staff, then The Meetinghouse band and employees.

That left Rowdy, Sam and Finn.

"Ladies first," Rowdy said.

Finn took a deep breath. "I'm thankful for good vision, so I can see all the people who've come to mean so much to me, and for the gift of hearing that lets me hear your beautiful voices. I'm grateful for time spent with friends and family—" she smiled at Ciara "—especially my sweet sister, whose big, gentle heart has taught me more about life and love—and *me*—than I could ever have learned on my own."

When she met his eyes, Sam thought his heart might beat hard enough to pop the buttons on his shirt. Under the table, where no one could see, he crossed the fingers of both hands. It had worked when he was a kid; maybe it would work now, and she'd say something like—

"And you, Sam, for…well, just for being you."

That was as close as he'd get to hearing she loved him. But he believed she did. It sparkled in her eyes and glowed from that little slanted smile. She hadn't said a word about the lawsuit, or that Misty had drained her bank account, leaving her no way to hire a lawyer to defend herself. Did she think no one knew how much trouble she was in, thanks to her mother? Oh, how he wanted to run to her side of the table and smother her with kisses, and promise that if he had anything to say about it, she'd never have to worry about money again.

All in good time…

"Guess that means it's my turn," he said on a gruff sigh, "so here goes. I'm thankful for everything that's already been said—and said very well. So I'll add that I'm thankful for a big, loving family, good friends, a fulfilling job and a future that's bound to be better, simply because all of you will be part of it."

He fixed a steady gaze on Finn. "I came to Nashville with high hopes, believing I had a fair to middlin' talent for stringing words together and putting tunes to them. But no matter how hard I worked at it, it seemed that was one dream that would never come true."

"Oh, good grief," Rowdy said. "I'm growing older by the minute, and you're talking about pipe dreams?"

He was kidding, and everyone knew it. When the good-natured laughter ended, the chef continued,

"I'm thankful that I had the good sense to squirrel away my money, so I could buy some stocks and make smart investments. As of January 1, I'm going to retire…"

He made a big show of clearing his throat and built the tension by taking a long, slow sip of water. "Okay, *semi*retire. I'm tired of getting up before dawn every day, picking through produce and pork chops and whatnot down at the market, then hotfooting it back here to cook for a bunch of strangers. Well, mostly strangers." He faced Finn. "Only one way that can happen, kiddo," he said, "and that's for you to sell me this place."

"Sell it? But, Rowdy! What would I do without the diner to—"

"Save it. Anybody with one functioning brain cell knows that Misty left you holding a bag of debt that'll take a lifetime to pay off. If you let me buy The Right Note, we'll both be happier. I can work part-time, and you can walk away from all those bills and the bad memories that caused them. You can start over."

"I—I need some time to wrap my mind around all of this."

"That's only fair," Sam said, "so while you're thinking, I'll finish my list." He got up and dragged his chair to Finn's side of the table and sat down beside her. "I'm thankful for my big clumsy leg, because if it hadn't knocked you off your feet, I never would have met the most beautiful, big-hearted woman on earth." He took her hands in his. "I know you aren't crazy about musicians—"

Every musician at the table complained at once:

"Hey, what's wrong with musicians?"

"We're beautiful souls!"

"Without us, the world would be...musicless," Mark said.

Finn's eyes grew big and round. "I never said I didn't like musicians."

"Yes, you did," Ciara put in. "You said they always put the next gig ahead of everything else because they're egotistical attention hogs."

Finn hid behind her hands while everyone else chuckled.

"Nice to know where we stand with *you*," Mark said, and the others agreed.

"As I was saying," Sam continued, taking her hands again, "I'm crazy about you, Finn Leary, and if being with you the rest of my life means—"

"I know what you're going to say," she interrupted. "But, please don't. Don't give up your dream for me. Go on the road. Make records. Be the guest star on talk shows."

"You can go with him if you want to," Rowdy said, "because I'm going to buy The Right Note." He leveled her with a serious stare. "Right?"

She shook her head. "Let's table that discussion for now, all right?"

"If you insist." He snickered, then whispered behind his hand, "She's gonna say yes. I feel it in my bones!"

"I'm hoping you'll join me on the Double M. At least for a while…"

She sat, blinking in wide-eyed, stunned silence. *Hurry up, idiot…tell her you love her. Say "marry me," right now, before you lose your nerve!*

"My folks have booked a world cruise," he said instead, "to celebrate their fiftieth anniversary. They leave on Valentine's Day and won't be back for six months. Somebody has to feed the ranch hands in Mom's absence. I know it's a lot to ask, but are you interested in the job?"

She shook her head. *Don't say no*, Sam thought. *Please don't say no…*

"If I said yes—and I'm *not* saying yes—what about Ciara?"

"Why, I'd go to the ranch, too, and help you with all your chores." Giggling, she added, "Who knows? Maybe I'll fall in love with a handsome cowboy like Sam and get married on the Double M!"

Her left brow rose. "And Connor?"

"The Double M foreman is retiring," Sam said, "*full-time* retiring. After we shuffle the duty assignments and hand out some promotions, there'll be an opening for a ranch hand."

"And you know I grew up on a ranch," Connor put in. "I'll be in my element."

"Yes, I remember. But what about your music?

You'd leave Nashville, now that you have a regular job playing with *these* guys?"

"In a heartbeat." He looked Mark and the Marks Brothers. "Sorry, guys," he said, shrugging.

Finn looked and sounded suspicious, but at least she hadn't shot down the idea. Yet.

"And *you*," she said, dark eyes blazing into his. "You expect me to believe you're giving up music *and* leaving the fire department?"

"What can I say? I got homesick for the Rockies," he admitted.

"And what about The Meetinghouse? You're leaving Torry and Mark in a lurch?"

"You know that old song," Mark said. "Got along without him before we met him…"

Torry snorted. "Anybody can plug in amps and go around tapping mics saying, 'Testing…testing?'"

"Hey," Sam said. "If it wasn't for me, you guys would trip or strangle yourselves on the cords."

"Oh, yeah. We shouldn't forget that." Torry leaned around Mark and said to Finn, "Trust us, we're okay without him. Spare us the rest of this lovesick fool's speech and just say yes, will ya?"

"Yeah," Torry agreed. "You have to say yes."

"I do?"

The comedian held up one hand. "No, no, no… save that for the wedding. Say yes now, so we'll all have a place to stay when we come visit you in Denver."

"Why would we go to Denver?" Mark asked.

"Why, to see us, of course!" Ciara rolled her eyes.

Finn's silence and furrowed brow worried Sam. He could almost see the wheels whirring in her pretty head, trying to think up a valid reason to stay in Nashville.

"What about the homeless shelter? It's barely off the ground. If Connor is in Denver, who will—"

"The mayor put his youngest boy in charge of it," Connor said. "The kid just earned a degree in...I forget what...but he already has a budget and a staff, all ready for when headquarters is renovated."

"Headquarters?" she asked.

"Oh." Rowdy chuckled. "Did I forget to mention? I donated another rental property. Your contractor? He's donating man-hours and materials."

Finn shook her head. "I can't believe all of this," she said, mostly to herself.

When she met his eyes, Sam's stomach lurched.

"And you seriously expect me to believe you'll be happy giving up the department and music to saddle up and run the Marshall spread?"

Y'gotta love her, he thought. And he meant it.

"I've done it before."

"Alone?"

"Yes'm."

She sighed. Had she finally thrown in the towel?

"You'll have a vested interest in the ranch, if..."

"If...?"

"Well, folks out there are old-fashioned."

She bit her lip, and he continued, "You'll have all the ladies in the beauty parlor's tongues wagging."

Now she frowned.

"You'll need a ring on your finger."

Her eyes widened and her lips formed a tiny O.

"My family hasn't been to Nashville in a couple of years. They can come out for the fund-raiser. If you'll say yes—"

"Yes to—"

"Date's set, performers signed, posters printed, media's on board," Torry said. "We're good to go."

"Good to go…"

Sam stuck a forefinger in his ear, wiggled it a few times. "Funny, but I never noticed before that there's an echo in here."

Finn was smiling—not much, but it beat that frown!—and he hoped it was because she'd remembered a similar conversation between them. He felt a little guilty, springing it on her this way, in front of everyone. But she'd shut him out, and he still wasn't sure why. He'd ask her forgiveness later… if she let him.

"What about the contract?"

"What about it?"

"You signed it, right?"

If he answered that, he'd blow the entire surprise.

"I don't need a record deal to write music. And I can do it anywhere."

"Songwriting. You mean to say you gave up on

your dream of performing, just like that, to write songs?"

Sam withdrew an envelope from his pocket and slid it to her.

"What's this? A Thanksgiving card?"

"Oh. Sorry. My mistake." He took it back and handed it to Ciara. "Happy birthday, kiddo."

"Thanks, Sam! I think I'll wait to open it—" grinning, she wiggled her eyebrows "—until we slice my cake. And stuff."

Sam extended another envelope.

"Well, don't just sit there," Rowdy said. "Open it!"

"Why do I get the feeling you've all seen what's inside?"

"They haven't," Sam assured her. "Everyone will be as surprised as you. I promise."

She got to her feet, then stood behind her chair.

"First, we need to get a few things straight."

Sam's heart sank. He should have known she'd resent being ganged up on this way. *Should have found another way to make her talk...to make her see how you feel.*

"I think I fell in love with you that first night—no, I'm sure of it—when that long leg of yours tripped me. I tried to deny it. Made excuses. Tried to convince myself it was something else I was feeling.

"The reason I avoided you last week? Because I couldn't bear the thought of you finding out that, as happy as I am that you earned a contract, I was terrified of what might happen if you went on the road."

Sam started to interrupt, but she held up a hand and silenced him.

"You can't just show up here with your gorgeous eyes and your sweet smile and your fancy speech and expect I'll turn to goo and fall into your lap!"

"Finn, I don't expect that. You've got my word."

Did she believe it? Not if that furrow on her brow was any indicator. *You blew it, idiot. So just shut up, and maybe you can leave here with some of your dignity intact.*

But wait…

"You…you love me?"

"Yes."

"Then, what's left to talk about? I love you, too!"

"There's this crazy deal to talk about, for starters, where I have to give up the business I've put *everything* into! Then this whole go-to-Colorado scheme! Honestly, Sam. Do you really expect me to drop everything and…and…and *marry* you?"

"At the risk of sounding like a heel, yeah. I want you to marry me. Nothing else is as important. Nothing."

She stared at the ceiling for a long, silent moment, then returned to her chair.

Ciara slid an arm across Finn's shoulders. "Aren't you curious about what's in the envelope?"

"Yeah, I guess." She rested her head on Ciara's. "A little."

Finn unsealed the flap and peeked inside, then upended the envelope and sent four squares of paper fluttering to the table. Her hands fluttered, too, as she arranged them in front of her plate.

"Look, Finn," Ciara said, leaning closer. "There's a word written on each square. It's a puzzle or something." She reached across the space between her and Finn and slid the squares round, moved them again. "I was right. It *is* a puzzle! And, Finn! Look what it says!"

Leaning forward, she read aloud, "I. Only. Want. You."

"Nothing puzzling about it," Finn said. She met his eyes and whispered, "It's what I want, too."

CHAPTER THIRTY-FIVE

Sam gave the Sunday paper a flap and folded it in half. "Will you look at this headline!"

Finn leaned closer. "New Prospects Opens Sixth Facility. Wow. Who would have predicted it would catch on so quickly, and go national!"

"Thanks to your dad."

Finn glanced across the lawn, where Connor and Ciara were playing croquet.

"He's come a long, long way."

Sam followed her gaze and nodded. "You can say that again."

"You know, he tried to straighten out a whole bunch of times. I sometimes wonder—if Mom had tried, too, could they have helped one another, maybe saved their marriage?"

"Wait. What did you just call her?"

Finn smiled to herself. "Ciara once asked me how I'd refer to her if I ever had kids." She shrugged. "Mom just seems right and proper, you know?"

He went back to reading the paper. "Well, I think that's great. Ciara will be happy about it, too."

She helped herself to the real estate section. "Take a look at *this* headline…"

"Market Prices Expected to Rise." Frowning, he met her eyes. "You aren't thinking of becoming an agent, I hope."

"No, and it makes me sad."

"Why? If it's something you want, go for it. I'll support you in anything you do."

"Sam…" Finn shoved the paper from his knees, let it fall to the porch floor and climbed into his lap. "You know it's Mother's Day, right?"

"Yeah, but don't worry, I left a message for my mom."

"You're a good son." She rested her head on his shoulder. "But I'm still a little sad."

"Aw, really? What's got you down in the dumps?"

"Well, I'm not sure I can compete with your planning and plotting skills."

"My…" He laughed, held her close and kissed her. "Sweetheart, what in the world are you talking about?"

"Think how much fun I could have had if only I'd figured out how to draw your attention to a headline."

"Headline…" He shook his head. "All I can say is, it's a good thing you're gorgeous, because…"

"Hand me the Arts and Entertainment section, will you?"

"Feel like catching a movie today, huh? What's playing?" He started to hand it to her but stopped when something caught his eye.

"Denver's Marshall Clan Still Growing," he read.

"Wait. That doesn't make a lick of sense. This is a picture of David Beckham and—"

Finn pressed a palm to each of his cheeks. "I did a pretty good job of making my own headline font, don't you think?"

"You... What?"

"I can't wait until your folks get back from California—it's so cute the way they've turned into globe-trotters, isn't it?—because I've already planned a huge welcome-home barbecue for the entire family. The ranch hands, the neighbors..."

"A barbecue..."

"So I can watch while you announce to everyone that you found out you were going to be a father... on Mother's Day."

Eyes wide, Sam said, "Finn...you're...you're pregnant?"

"Mmm-hmm."

"Man. Wow. Really?"

"Really."

"Aw, sweetheart." He hugged her tight.

He seemed happy, but then, he was such an easygoing, big-hearted guy. Would she know if he wasn't?

"Sam?"

"What...li'l mama?"

"It's been over a year now, Sam. You still don't regret walking away from your Nashville dreams?"

"Are you kiddin'?" His lips were touching hers when he said, "I. Only. Want. You. Remember?"

How many hours had she spent worrying that he'd regret that decision?

"Well, that isn't entirely true. I don't *just* want you."

The words chilled her to the core. *Not already,* she thought. *Not so soon!*

Sam pressed a palm to her stomach. "I want *this,* too."

* * * * *

LARGER-PRINT BOOKS!

GET 2 FREE
LARGER-PRINT NOVELS
PLUS 2 FREE
MYSTERY GIFTS

Love Inspired®
SUSPENSE
RIVETING INSPIRATIONAL ROMANCE

Larger-print novels are now available...

YES! Please send me 2 FREE LARGER-PRINT Love Inspired® Suspense novels and my 2 FREE mystery gifts (gifts are worth about $10). After receiving them, if I don't wish to receive any more books, I can return the shipping statement marked "cancel." If I don't cancel, I will receive 4 brand-new novels every month and be billed just $5.49 per book in the U.S. or $5.99 per book in Canada. That's a savings of at least 19% off the cover price. It's quite a bargain! Shipping and handling is just 50¢ per book in the U.S. and 75¢ per book in Canada.* I understand that accepting the 2 free books and gifts places me under no obligation to buy anything. I can always return a shipment and cancel at any time. Even if I never buy another book, the two free books and gifts are mine to keep forever.

110/310 IDN GH6P

Name	(PLEASE PRINT)	

Address		Apt. #

City	State/Prov.	Zip/Postal Code

Signature (if under 18, a parent or guardian must sign)

Mail to the **Reader Service:**
IN U.S.A.: P.O. Box 1867, Buffalo, NY 14240-1867
IN CANADA: P.O. Box 609, Fort Erie, Ontario L2A 5X3

**Are you a current subscriber to Love Inspired® Suspense books
and want to receive the larger-print edition?
Call 1-800-873-8635 or visit www.ReaderService.com.**

* Terms and prices subject to change without notice. Prices do not include applicable taxes. Sales tax applicable in N.Y. Canadian residents will be charged applicable taxes. Offer not valid in Quebec. This offer is limited to one order per household. Not valid for current subscribers to Love Inspired Suspense larger-print books. All orders subject to credit approval. Credit or debit balances in a customer's account(s) may be offset by any other outstanding balance owed by or to the customer. Please allow 4 to 6 weeks for delivery. Offer available while quantities last.

Your Privacy—The Reader Service is committed to protecting your privacy. Our Privacy Policy is available online at www.ReaderService.com or upon request from the Reader Service.

We make a portion of our mailing list available to reputable third parties that offer products we believe may interest you. If you prefer that we not exchange your name with third parties, or if you wish to clarify or modify your communication preferences, please visit us at www.ReaderService.com/consumerschoice or write to us at Reader Service Preference Service, P.O. Box 9062, Buffalo, NY 14240-9062. Include your complete name and address.

LISLP15

LARGER-PRINT BOOKS!
GET 2 FREE LARGER-PRINT NOVELS PLUS
2 FREE GIFTS!

ⓗ HARLEQUIN®

super romance®

More Story...More Romance

REQUEST YOUR FREE BOOKS!
2 FREE WHOLESOME ROMANCE NOVELS
IN LARGER PRINT
PLUS 2
FREE
MYSTERY GIFTS

✼✼✼✼✼✼✼✼✼✼✼✼✼✼✼✼✼✼✼✼✼✼✼✼

HEARTWARMING™
❦❦❦❦❦❦❦❦❦❦❦❦❦❦❦❦❦❦❦❦❦❦

Wholesome, tender romances

YES! Please send me 2 FREE Harlequin® Heartwarming Larger-Print novels and my 2 FREE mystery gifts (gifts worth about $10). After receiving them, if I don't wish to receive any more books, I can return the shipping statement marked "cancel." If I don't cancel, I will receive 4 brand-new larger-print novels every month and be billed just $5.24 per book in the U.S. or $5.99 per book in Canada. That's a savings of at least 19% off the cover price. It's quite a bargain! Shipping and handling is just 50¢ per book in the U.S. and 75¢ per book in Canada.* I understand that accepting the 2 free books and gifts places me under no obligation to buy anything. I can always return a shipment and cancel at any time. Even if I never buy another book, the two free books and gifts are mine to keep forever.

161/361 IDN GHX2

Name   (PLEASE PRINT)

Address   Apt. #

City   State/Prov.   Zip/Postal Code

Signature (if under 18, a parent or guardian must sign)

Mail to the **Reader Service:**
IN U.S.A.: P.O. Box 1867, Buffalo, NY 14240-1867
IN CANADA: P.O. Box 609, Fort Erie, Ontario L2A 5X3

* Terms and prices subject to change without notice. Prices do not include applicable taxes. Sales tax applicable in N.Y. Canadian residents will be charged applicable taxes. Offer not valid in Quebec. This offer is limited to one order per household. Not valid for current subscribers to Harlequin Heartwarming larger-print books. All orders subject to credit approval. Credit or debit balances in a customer's account(s) may be offset by any other outstanding balance owed by or to the customer. Please allow 4 to 6 weeks for delivery. Offer available while quantities last.

Your Privacy—The Reader Service is committed to protecting your privacy. Our Privacy Policy is available online at www.ReaderService.com or upon request from the Reader Service.

We make a portion of our mailing list available to reputable third parties that offer products we believe may interest you. If you prefer that we not exchange your name with third parties, or if you wish to clarify or modify your communication preferences, please visit us at www.ReaderService.com/consumerchoice or write to us at Reader Service Preference Service, P.O. Box 9062, Buffalo, NY 14240-9062. Include your complete name and address.

HWI5

LARGER-PRINT BOOKS!

GET 2 FREE LARGER-PRINT NOVELS PLUS
2 FREE GIFTS!

Ⓗ **HARLEQUIN**®

INTRIGUE

BREATHTAKING ROMANTIC SUSPENSE

YES! Please send me 2 FREE LARGER-PRINT Harlequin® Intrigue novels and my 2 FREE gifts (gifts are worth about $10). After receiving them, if I don't wish to receive any more books, I can return the shipping statement marked "cancel." If I don't cancel, I will receive 6 brand-new novels every month and be billed just $5.49 per book in the U.S. or $6.24 per book in Canada. That's a saving of at least 11% off the cover price! It's quite a bargain! Shipping and handling is just 50¢ per book in the U.S. and 75¢ per book in Canada.* I understand that accepting the 2 free books and gifts places me under no obligation to buy anything. I can always return a shipment and cancel at any time. Even if I never buy another book, the two free books and gifts are mine to keep forever.

199/399 HDN GHWN

Name	(PLEASE PRINT)

Address	Apt. #

City	State/Prov.	Zip/Postal Code

Signature (if under 18, a parent or guardian must sign)

Mail to the **Reader Service**:
IN U.S.A.: P.O. Box 1867, Buffalo, NY 14240-1867
IN CANADA: P.O. Box 609, Fort Erie, Ontario L2A 5X3

**Are you a subscriber to Harlequin® Intrigue books
and want to receive the larger-print edition?
Call 1-800-873-8635 today or visit www.ReaderService.com.**

* Terms and prices subject to change without notice. Prices do not include applicable taxes. Sales tax applicable in N.Y. Canadian residents will be charged applicable taxes. Offer not valid in Quebec. This offer is limited to one order per household. Not valid for current subscribers to Harlequin Intrigue Larger-Print books. All orders subject to credit approval. Credit or debit balances in a customer's account(s) may be offset by any other outstanding balance owed by or to the customer. Please allow 4 to 6 weeks for delivery. Offer available while quantities last.

Your Privacy—The Reader Service is committed to protecting your privacy. Our Privacy Policy is available online at www.ReaderService.com or upon request from the Reader Service.

We make a portion of our mailing list available to reputable third parties that offer products we believe may interest you. If you prefer that we not exchange your name with third parties, or if you wish to clarify or modify your communication preferences, please visit us at www.ReaderService.com/consumerchoice or write to us at Reader Service Preference Service, P.O. Box 9062, Buffalo, NY 14240-9062. Include your complete name and address.